MEET YOUR MAKER

RAVES for *Meet Your Maker*

A swirling mix of suspense and intrigue with high-octane thrills makes Meet Your Maker *an absolute gem for crime thriller lovers. Christine Noyes weaves a fast-paced plot with curveballs to keep you enthralled. Bradley is a gifted protagonist, and his investigative skills keep you invested every step of the way. The care and love between Bradley and his friends feel genuine and create a palpable emotional resonance with readers. It is a thoroughly entertaining read from start to finish.*

—Pikasho Deka

Meet Your Maker *by Christine Noyes is a compelling mystery with a colorful ensemble of characters, remarkably authentic writing, and a flawless investigation. Noyes is notably ingenious in the construction of the plot and her ability to evoke emotions in the reader throughout the entire story. This immersive crime novel takes readers into the heart of a challenging homicide investigation and culminates in a perfectly intense and thrilling ending.*

—Emma Megan

This is a magnificent piece of work! If you love a gripping mystery sleuth thriller entwined with a heart pounding tale of crime, guilt, love, loathing, money, death threats, and movie production, then Meet Your Maker *by Christine Noyes is just what you should be looking for. The spellbinding plot twists and thrills kept me on edge. It only gets better with the robust touch of humor in the narration. Agent Bradley is that intelligent, selfless, caring, ambitious, type of character you can't help but like.*

—Keith Mbuya

more on next page

Meet Your Maker *is a crime genre winner! The entire investigation is described in full—the clues, the disappointments, and the emotions of those involved. I felt as though I was part of the case. The final pages were fascinating and impossible to stop reading. The ending brought tears to my eyes and put a smile on my face.*

—Trudi LoPreto

Having the lead protagonist be wheelchair-bound is a bold move. In a genre priding itself on characters at their physical peak, Christine Noyes offers a superb and unique perspective on crime and action without compromising the excitement and suspense factors. Noyes proves determination, resourcefulness, and sheer grit make a true hero. I would not hesitate to recommend Meet Your Maker *for its sharp writing style, intelligent dialogue, and realistic, sensitive portrayal of humans pushed to their limits.*

—K.C. Finn

CHRISTINE NOYES

a Bradley Whitman novel

MEET YOUR MAKER

Haley's

Athol, Massachusetts

Haley's
488 South Main Street
Athol, MA 01331
marcia2gagliardi@gmail.com • 978.249.9400

Copy edited by Richard Bruno.

Cover designed by Christine Noyes with Pixabay images of Boston skyline and limousine and PNGing.com image of flames created by Lydia Simmons.

Library of Congress Cataloging-in-Publication Data
Names: Noyes, Christine, 1961- author.
Title: Meet your maker / Christine Noyes.
Description: Athol, Massachusetts : Haley's, [2023] | Series: A Bradley
Whitman Novel | Summary: "On the eve of his thirtieth birthday,
    wheelchair-bound FBI analyst Bradley Whitman's life blows up when a bomb
    causes the limousine his boss and six of his closest friends are
    traveling in to burst into flames. While his friends battle for their
    lives, Bradley battles his guilt and struggles to focus on capturing the
    perpetrator. When two of the city's iconic and heavily populated
    landmarks become the next targets, the stage is set for an explosive
    finish"-- Provided by publisher.
Identifiers: LCCN 2023003429 (print) | LCCN 2023003430 (ebook) | ISBN
    9781948380706 (trade paperback) | ISBN 9781948380713 (kindle edition)
Subjects: LCGFT: Thrillers (Fiction) | Novels.
Classification: LCC PS3614.O9745 M44 2023 (print) | LCC PS3614.O9745
    (ebook) | DDC 813/.6--dc23/eng/20230130
LC record available at https://lccn.loc.gov/2023003429
LC ebook record available at https://lccn.loc.gov/2023003430

To all those who have touched my life in big ways and in small.
And for Al, forever in my heart.

CONTENTS

ACTION

Grazing a parking meter and barely missing the woman who pushed a double-wide stroller, the black Dodge Charger careened around the corner and skipped over the curb as it made its way from Salem Street past the Old North Church and onto Charter. The driver slammed the brakes, forcing the car into a rubber-grinding spin that spewed clouds of noxious fumes into the street. The menacing vehicle stopped, facing the wrong way on the one-way street, and sat idling. A Massachusetts Armored Transportation truck headed toward the car and picked up speed with no intention of slowing down. The vehicles played a game of chicken, and neither looked like it would give in. A collision became imminent.

"Cut!" a voice yelled over a bullhorn. "Okay, we got it. Let's re-set for the crash scene."

The driver of the Dodge unfastened himself from the safety harness, removed his helmet, and walked through hordes of cameras, crew, and equipment toward the man holding the bullhorn. He sat in a chair that read Director.

"Is it ready?" the director asked.

"All set," the driver replied.

"Ready on the set."

Cate watched in fascination. She had never before been on a movie set. Filming of movies in Boston had inconvenienced her before, but she had never seen the action as she did now with her sister Sheila. As a producer of the film, Sheila's husband, David, invited Cate and her husband, Derek, to watch the filming. But to Cate's frustration, Derek could not get away from work.

"I'm sorry, Sheila. Derek is wrapping up a big case. He's worked ten straight days. I thought, it being Sunday, he may have been able to join us, but you know how my life is. I didn't just marry Derek. I married the Federal Bureau of Investigation."

"Well, Cate, David is over there working, too. I married him and the Hollywood movie industry." They both half-heartedly laughed.

"At least I get to see you. I've missed you so much," Cate smiled. "Let's go get ourselves a glass of wine and catch up. I want to hear all about the twins. There's a great place a couple blocks from here, right on the harbor."

"Perfect. I'll tell David."

Cate watched her sister as she found David in the crowd of movie personnel. Sheila hadn't aged a bit, she thought. Her tall, thin but firm figure showed evidence of daily workouts, and her silky, smooth skin shimmered in the sunlight. She wore her beautiful blonde hair shorter these days, but Cate thought she looked more lovely today than in their younger years. *Motherhood agreed with her,* Cate thought. A stitch of sorrow pinched her heart.

Although Cate was not a fan of working out, she took care of herself in other ways. She cooked mostly healthy foods for herself and Derek and could rarely be found lounging. Not as toned as her sister, Cate—in her mid forties—wore the same size clothing as when in her twenties. The occasional gray strand wove through her shoulder-length brunette hair, but it never stayed gray for long.

"Onward," Sheila said as she wrapped her arm around Cate's. "Sisters afternoon awaits. Let's go spend all the money that our menfolk are making," Sheila laughed. They hadn't gone more than a block and a half before they heard the unmistakable sound of metal crashing metal and a perfectly timed pyrotechnic explosion: Hollywood magic.

Their drinks in hand, Sheila filled Cate in on her two boys. "They're seventeen, and they think they own the world. Max has his whole life mapped out. We just don't know if it will play out on the East Coast or West Coast. He's applied to both Stanford and MIT."

"What does he want to do? I mean, what does he want to major in?" Cate asked.

"I was afraid you were going to ask me that. He wants to major in geophysics."

"Huh?" Cate said.

"That's exactly what I said," Sheila laughed. "Okay, let me see if I can get this right. It has something to do with the physics of the earth and . . . its environment in space."

"Wow." Cates eyes opened wide. "How about Alex? What's his plan?"

"Alex's plan is a bit more grounded, literally. He's decided to take a year off before he goes to college and backpack across the country, maybe even go to Europe. They are both adventurers in their own way."

"And you two are okay with Alex backpacking?"

"Yeah. We think it will be good for him. He's a wonderful writer, you know. And what a great experience it will be. I'm a little jealous."

"Well, I'm happy for all of you," Cate smiled, but Sheila could see the sadness behind Cate's praise.

Sheila placed her hand on Cate's. "They miss you and Derek, of course."

"Well, I'm rooting for Max to come to MIT," Cate said with a smile that did not quite reach her melancholy eyes. Until recently Cate had not regretted her and Derek's choice not to have children in their earlier years. When they finally decided they wanted to start a family, it proved more difficult than expected. After two miscarriages and her well into her forties, Cate and Derek found it too painful to try again.

Sheila wished to lighten the mood. "So, does Bradley have any idea that David and I are in town?"

"I don't think so. Derek has gotten much better at misleading people since we met. I taught him that," Cate laughed as she lifted her goblet to tap against Sheila's. "I can't believe it's been eighteen years since we all met on that cruise. I can't wait to see everybody at Bradley's party tonight. They're all coming, right?"

"As far as I know, yes. Holly and John are going to pick Mike up and meet us at our house at five-thirty. Bradley thinks his parents are just taking him out to dinner at the Envoy for his birthday. He doesn't know that Lynn and Doug made reservations for all of us. First, we'll have drinks on the rooftop lounge at six-thirty, then dinner at eight o'clock."

"What about Bradley's new lady friend, Laney? Am I going to get to meet her tonight?"

"She's hardly new. They've been together for well over a year. Yes, she's going to surprise him there. She made some excuse about having to supervise the hospital emergency room tonight to throw him off track. You are going to love her, Sheila. They are so good together. I've never seen Bradley this happy."

"I've never known Bradley not to be happy," Sheila replied.

Sometimes Cate forgot how little of her life she shared with Sheila. The distance between their living quarters lent to a distance in communication, and that felt unsettling. She thought it best not to mention Bradley's battle with feeling inadequate. Besides, Cate hoped that was all in the past. Instead, she replied, "We all have our moments. Oh, and you're going to get to meet Zayt and Shea."

Sheila's expression indicated a lack of recollection.

"They are Bradley's REACH business partners and my co-workers. I told you about them when I started volunteering there. Zayt is a former Navy Seal, and Shea used to be a real estate agent. Now Shea manages the housing portion of the business."

"You'll have to fill me in. I think the details get lost somewhere in Middle America during transmission from Massachusetts to California. Sometimes my attention span is that of a six-year-old," Sheila giggled.

Mildly annoyed that her sister paid little attention to something so important to her, Cate explained the Revere Enhancement and Community Housing program to Sheila.

"It was Zayt's idea. As a former homeless veteran himself, he knew firsthand the plights of the homeless. With Bradley and Shea's help, Zayt locked into a lease agreement with the City of Revere for the old sandpit behind Bradley's house, raised the funds, and built a community of tiny homes complete with a community center and kitchen. It has been an enormous success. I manage the kitchen and community center, Shea does the housing, and Zayt is security and enforcement. By enforcement, I mean no drugs or alcohol. Of course, sometimes that rule must be bent in order to help in the long run."

"Cate, I had no idea how big this project was. I pictured you volunteering at one of those homeless shelters somewhere in the middle of Boston. I would love to see the community. Maybe there's something David and I could do while we're here."

"Great. I can't wait to show you around."

"How are Holly and John? And their daughter . . . ?"

"Grace. Her name is Grace, Sheila. Holly says everything is going really well. She is so excited David bought the movie rights to her client's novel. I asked her if she were going to come to Boston for any of the filming, and she said she would only come here to see you and David. For a bigtime publisher, she's not much of a city girl."

"That's sweet. I'm so happy for her. Hey, I still need to get a gift for Bradley. Did you come up with any fantastic ideas?"

"He's impossible to buy for unless it's something for his kitchen. Or his dog," Cate laughed.

"Okay, so let's go find either a Williams-Sonoma store or a Petco."

At four o'clock, Derek emerged from his private office and headed into the bullpen, the shared open-office space of his FBI agents. Cate had told Derek to make sure Bradley left for home early enough to get ready for dinner. On the far side of the room, Bradley sat huddled at his desk with Agent Mara Thompkins as they sifted through endless financial statements.

"I thought you said your parents were taking you out to dinner tonight," Derek yelled across the near empty office.

Bradley momentarily looked up from his computer screen with a sour expression and then sank back into his screen.

"Yeah, well, I think I'm going to call and cancel. We're mired down in this mess," Bradley said.

Derek's six-foot frame froze.

"Ah, you can't do that," he said, his eyes wide and his face troubled.

"Huh?" Bradley looked up again. "Why not? It's just dinner. They'll get over it. I'll go visit them this weekend or something."

He hunkered back down.

Derek knew he couldn't spoil the surprise or Cate would never let him hear the end of it.

"You know, you can be one selfish son-of-a-bitch, Bradley Whitman."

This time, Bradley's royal blue eyes held Derek's gaze. "What are you talking about?"

"Your parents have been looking forward to this for weeks. What the hell is the matter with you? Lynn will be crushed if you cancel. And Doug will be pissed off at me."

"It's only dinner," Bradley stated emphatically.

"It's your parents," Derek countered equally emphatically. "Besides, I'm leaving in a half hour. I want both of you out of here before I go. It's Sunday, for chrissake." Derek moved his pointed finger between Mara and Bradley. "Pack it up."

Wondering if either one of them would listen to him, Derek walked back to his office.

"He's right, you know," Mara said. "Your parents would be totally disappointed if you cancel on them. Especially your mother."

Bradley liked Mara. The youngest agent in the bureau, she had excellent organizational skills, and he found her unwavering in her determination to be the best at her job. They had on occasion worked closely together and knew each other's inclinations.

"It really sucks that all my co-workers know my parents and always take their side."

"It's of your own doing. If you hadn't gotten yourself shot and stabbed a while back, I wouldn't even know you had parents," Mara chuckled. "I might have thought you were hatched."

"Alright, alright. Let's wrap this up and go home. Derek seems like he's in a lousy mood, and I don't want to escalate it."

Twenty minutes later Bradley backed his electric wheelchair away from his desk. The athletic build of his upper body contrasted greatly with his atrophied legs. He worked hard to keep the functional part of his body in excellent shape. And although he would soon turn thirty, with his thick brown hair and good-natured grin, he retained a boyish appearance.

He took the elevator down eight flights to the main lobby of Chelsea FBI headquarters, and out the front door to his custom Chevy truck. The driver and rear passenger doors had been replaced by a one-piece panel. Bradley used his key fob to unlock the wide door and initiate its opening. The panel automatically pulled straight out, stopped, beeped, and lowered a wheelchair platform. Bradley expertly backed onto the lift and rode the mechanism up to floorboard height. The apparatus beeped again before the platform slid Bradley into place behind the steering wheel.

The vehicle safety system would not allow the truck to start if Bradley did not strap in properly, so he hitched his seatbelt before starting the engine.

Bradley loved his truck. His truck meant freedom. He thought back to his younger days when someone, usually his mother, had to drive him around in a specially equipped van. He hated that. But his mother never complained. *Derek is right,* he thought. *My parents would be hurt if I canceled our birthday dinner celebration. How the hell did I become a thirty-year-old man?*

"John, we're picking my father up at four-thirty. Have you even started to get ready yet?" Holly yelled from the bedroom.

She put the finishing touches on her new outfit, the one she had bought specifically for this night. Earlier that day, she had her hair styled, her nails done, and, once home, spent a great deal of time on her makeup. She hadn't pampered herself like this since her wedding day and she enjoyed every minute of it.

On the cruise where they met eighteen years before, it was Cate and Sheila who taught her about coddling herself. Holly had been shy and anxiety-ridden at the age of twenty-four and she had never learned how to wear makeup properly or do her nails. Her mother had died when she was just a child, and she felt much too timid to ask anyone for help. Although she and her father were very close, Mike knew nothing of makeup, women's clothing accessories, or nail polish. But on the cruise ship where they met, Cate and Sheila took Holly under their wings and taught her everything she needed to know about fashion and making an entrance. And the last is what she intended to do tonight. Not because she wanted the attention, but to show Cate and Sheila how much they had helped her and how much she appreciated what they had done.

"Do I need to wear a tie for this thing?" John yelled back.

"If you do, you'll be the only one."

"Got it. No tie," John said as he strolled into the bedroom. "Wow! You look . . . wow!"

Holly smiled and playfully turned in a circle to showcase her new dress. She wore a deep-purple-lace, high-waist asymmetrical design, the skirt lower in back than front with a cami top. Her mother's pearls hung on her slender neck. Her opened-toed lilac shoes boasted a four-inch heel, and a white lace wrap lay waiting on the bed beside her. Her once golden brown hair had slightly darkened, and she wore it shoulder length, curled beneath her chin.

Holly felt intoxicated, and all it had taken was a dress and a little indulgence.

"Thank you, honey. You look . . . casual," she laughed.

"Five minutes."

Five minutes, Holly thought. *I've been at this all day.* She laughed at herself.

Holly didn't care about appearances. She never had. Her priorities lay in honesty, sincerity, and loyalty. Her father taught her those values a long time ago. The two of them shared a wonderful relationship. Holly grew from a young, self-conscious child to a woman of confidence. She could have worked for any large publishing firm in the country but chose to open her own small publishing company in the college town of Amherst in west-central Massachusetts, where she met John. She knew almost from the minute they met she would spend the rest of her life with him.

They met when she was a guest lecturer at the University of Massachusetts. Her boss was scheduled to speak but sent Holly in her place. The Introduction to Professional Writing students she spoke to seemed receptive to her talk. After class, a handsome man, somewhat older than the students who surrounded him, stayed behind waiting for his chance to converse with Holly. Because he was the only one in the room who audibly laughed when she addressed them, she suspected he would drill her on several controversial statements she had made that went against typical publishing standards. She stood ready to take his shots.

"Hello. My name is John."

"Hi. I'm Holly."

"That was an interesting take on the current state of big-house publishing. Who is it you work for again?" he asked.

Holly laughed. "Parrot Publishing. And yes, I meant what I said. The future of publishing won't take place in the castle but in the barn. Metaphorically speaking, of course. I couldn't help but notice your reaction. I didn't intend for it to be funny. Unfortunately, I think the idea got lost on the rest of the group, anyway."

"I'm sorry if I offended you," John said, "but it was unexpected. I teach a society and literature course, and I've been saying the same thing for years. Not quite as eloquently as you, though."

"Well, thank you. I hope my boss is as receptive. Better yet, I hope she never hears a word of what I said."

Holly giggled.

"Can I buy you a cup of coffee?" John asked.

And that was it. The tall, handsome professor had won her heart by laughing at her lecture. They married two years later, and Grace arrived two years after that.

"Okay, I'm ready, how do I look?" John twirled around to mock Holly's showcasing.

Holly laughed and took his hands in hers. "Perfect," she said as she reached up to kiss him.

"How much time do we have?" John softly teased.

"Not enough," she giggled.

The chauffeur pulled up in front of Cate and Derek's Medford home at 5:25 p.m. Sheila and David hadn't rung the doorbell when Derek opened the door. The movie production company had hired a limousine service for the duration of filming in Boston, so David had suggested they take advantage of it and all drive to the restaurant together.

"Right on time. You are nothing like your sister, Sheila," Derek pronounced. He and Sheila laughed.

"I heard that," Cate yelled from the kitchen.

"David, how did the filming go today? Sorry I missed it," Derek said.

"Surprisingly well. We only had twenty-seven death threats for shutting down Salem and Charter Streets. Bostonians are quite civil. First they tell you how they are going to hurt you before they actually try to do it," David snickered.

"Yes. We are still Puritans at heart. If we are going to break the rule of piety, we must be forthright about our intentions," Derek chuckled.

"Good to know," David laughed and shook Derek's hand. "It's good to see you. I hear you've been pretty busy."

"Just the usual. Things should be calming down soon."

"That's what he always says. Then, boom. A bigger case comes up, and we start all over again," Cate quipped as she walked into the living room.

The doorbell rang.

Derek threw up his hand. "Thank God for the doorbell!" he exclaimed as he opened the door to Holly, John, and Mike.

"Oh, Holly, you look gorgeous," Sheila screeched.

"You do. You look amazing. Damn. I might have to go change," Cate declared.

"Oh, please. You two always look stunning. It took me all day to look like this," Holly laughed. They hugged as the men shook hands, and exchanged banter all the way to the limousine.

"The plan is for us to be there before Bradley, Lynn, and Doug arrive. They'll meet us on the rooftop lounge, and we can all yell 'Surprise,'" Cate said as she stepped into the car. "Mike, sit back here between Sheila and me so we can catch up."

"You girls are as beautiful as ever," Mike said.

The two women giggled.

"I think you are the only person in the world who still thinks of us as girls, Mike!" Sheila pointed out.

"I can't help it. You haven't changed a bit in all these years. Except for getting more beautiful."

"Derek? Are you hearing this? This is the way you talk to a woman," Cate said.

"Okay. I'll try it out on Mara tomorrow, but I'm not sure how it will go over," Derek joked.

The limo exploded with laughter as the chauffeur pulled away from the curb. Eight minutes later, just before crossing the channel on Seaport Boulevard, they waited for the traffic light to turn green. They were less than two minutes away and right on schedule.

"Bradley is going to be so surprised to see all of you, Cate smiled. "I can't believe we . . . "

They felt the heat first, then heard the ear-shattering blast. The back end of the limousine violently jumped into the air, then came down hard, bouncing multiple times. Cate's head hit the roof as the explosion threw her out of her seat. She hurtled forward, and her blood-soaked crown contacted the dividing wall separating driver from passengers.

Mike and Sheila's bodies collided, both then thrust to the scorching floor. Mike sprawled on top of Sheila as the odor of her singeing flesh instantly permeated the scene.

Holly and John, who had been seated on the passenger side of the U-shaped sitting area shot into the air and forcefully struck their heads while broken glass from the windows behind them pierced their skin like pellets fired from a shotgun.

The blast propelled David and Derek, who had sat opposite Holly and John, out the side windows and into the street, where they landed almost eight feet away from the smoldering limousine.

The driver's head cracked the front windshield. He lay motionless across the front of the car. All lost consciousness as flames shot from the back end of the vehicle.

Bradley, Lynn, and Doug arrived at the Envoy Hotel a little after 6:40 p.m. The plan intended for the others to have already arrived and be waiting for them on the rooftop bar.

"Why don't we just go into the dining room?" Bradley asked as he moved his wheelchair toward the outdoor sitting area.

"Because it's a beautiful night and I don't want to rush it. I want to make this night last," Lynn smiled as they exited the elevator.

"Well, this is strange," Bradley said as he noticed the patrons lined up by the edge of the lounge, looking over the wall toward downtown Boston.

Doug and Lynn scanned the backs of the crowd, looking for the rest of their party. They spotted Zayt and Shea.

"Hey, what's he doing here?" Bradley rhetorically asked when he spotted Zayt. Then he saw Shea. He turned to his parents and asked, "What's going on?"

Uncertainty filled their faces. "I don't know," Doug said as he walked toward Zayt.

When Zayt noticed Doug, he broke away from the crowd and met him. "There's been some kind of explosion on the street just before the bridge. It's hard to tell from here what's going on, but traffic is backed up for miles. Ambulances and firetrucks have been arriving for at least twenty minutes. Whatever happened, it can't be good."

"Are the rest of the gang here yet?" Doug asked.

By then, Bradley, Lynn, and Shea had joined Zayt and Doug.

"The rest of what gang?" Bradley asked, confused.

"Honey, this is supposed to be a surprise, but I guess it's not going to happen the way we wanted. Sheila and David are in town, and so are Holly, John, and Mike. They are all coming with Derek and Cate to celebrate your birthday. But they must be stuck in the traffic," Lynn said.

"How did you three get here?" Zayt asked.

"We came in the other way, through the Ted Williams tunnel," Bradley replied.

"Doug, call Derek and find out if they can still get here," Lynn said.

Doug brought up Derek's number on his cell phone. It rang five times before his voicemail activated. "Hey, Derek," Doug told the voicemail. "We know you are probably stuck in traffic from the accident. Give us a call when you get this message." He hung up.

"I got his voicemail," Doug told the others.

"I'll try Cate. Derek doesn't answer his phone when he drives," Bradley said.

"Hi, this is Cate. Leave me a happy message," her recording sounded.

"Huh. Cate's went to voicemail, too." Bradley's eyebrows furrowed. "I'll try Sheila. Dad, you try Holly."

When neither answered, Bradley and Doug shared a concerned gaze.

"Laney. Try Laney," Doug urged.

"She's working. She won't know where they are," Bradley said.

"No, she's coming here. She wanted to surprise you," Lynn said.

Bradley called Laney's number and got the same result, voicemail. He left her a message to call him right away.

"Something's wrong," Bradley said. Excusing himself through onlookers, he made his way to the edge of the roof and rolled up to the railing. He saw three ambulances, lights and sirens blaring, leave the scene. He counted another six ambulances, maybe more. He couldn't be sure because buildings obstructed his view. He made his way to the other end of the roof for a better vantage point. The others followed. They watched a hectic scene. Black smoke billowed from the explosion. The position of the emergency vehicles suggested that the incident took place in the street, but Bradley could not get a clear look. They saw three more ambulances race away from the scene, then two more left moments after.

"We have to go," Bradley said.

"Go where, son? We don't know anything. Let's give it a little time. Derek will call when he can."

Bradley's phone rang. The caller ID identified Laney as the caller.

"Laney, where are you? Are you alright?" Bradley frantically asked.

"Yes, I'm fine. I'm on Seaport Boulevard. There's been an accident."

"I know. We are watching from the roof of the Envoy. It looks pretty bad."

"It is," Laney said quietly, then added, "Bradley, it's your friends. They were in the car."

Bradley's heart began to pound. "No. Oh, God, no. Which ones?"

Laney hesitated before she spoke. "All of them."

Fear filled Bradley's eyes as he choked on his next words. "Where . . . where are they taking them?"

"Mass General. I'm getting a ride with one of the police officers. My car is still stuck at the scene. I called ahead and informed the emergency room personnel so they can hit the ground running."

Laney tried to reassure him.

"We'll meet you there. Laney?"

"Yes?"

"I love you."

Laney could hear the emotion in Bradley's voice, and she ached for him. "I love you, too. Bradley, please, be careful driving. Please."

"I will, I promise."

"They're taking them to Mass General. Let's go," Bradley said, repeating what Laney had told him. He pushed hard on his chairs throttle. The others hurried to keep up with him.

"We've got Shea's car, we'll follow you," Zayt said as they rushed through the restaurant dining room to the elevator.

Bradley thought about taking Congress Street across the channel but chose to take Summer Street instead to avoid most of the re-routed traffic. Shea and Zayt followed. It proved to be a good decision. With the traffic tie-up behind them, Bradley then took the most direct route to the hospital. He parked the truck in a space designated for the handicapped next to the emergency room entrance as Shea found a spot nearby, and they all rushed inside.

Prospective patients and family members filled the waiting room while medical personnel scurried about. Bradley searched for Laney but did not see her. He went to the front desk and asked for her.

"Yes, she is here. But she is extremely busy right now," the woman replied.

"I know. Could you just let her know that Bradley is here? Please?" The woman shot him an annoyed glare but rose from her chair.

Bradley's cohort stood near the desk after looking for open seats in the waiting room and finding none. Doug seized one of the abandoned hospital wheelchairs so Lynn could sit. He worried about her. She looked pale and tired. She assured him she felt fine, but he knew the stress had gotten to her. They spoke little other than openly to wonder what the hell had happened.

Ten minutes later, Laney appeared. She wore a white gauze bandage taped to the left side of her head.

Bradley's eyes fixed on the bandage, and worry overtook his face.

"What happened to you? Are you alright?" He reached for her hand.

"I'm fine. It's just a bump."

"How?" Bradley asked.

"I'll tell you in a minute. First, you should know that your friends are all alive and getting the best care we can provide. I'll give you the details as I get them, but right now that's all I know."

"What the hell happened?" Doug asked.

Laney took a deep breath, then began. "I was two cars behind the limousine when the explosion happened. The blast made me bang my head on my car window—just a bump, that's all," she nodded to Bradley.

"When I realized what happened," she continued, "I ran to help the people in the limousine. We all did, everyone who saw it. There were flames coming out of the back of the car, so we determined we needed to get the people out in case the flames reached the gas tank. We pulled five people from the back and the driver out of the front seat. They were all unconscious."

Horrified, Lynn said, "But there should have been seven of them, plus the driver."

"There were. Two of them had been thrown from the vehicle," Laney explained.

"Oh, my God," Lynn cried.

Lynn started to shake. Tears streamed down her face. Doug knelt down to console her, but she couldn't stop shaking. Doug had seen it before when Bradley lay in the same emergency room a year and a half before.

"I've got to get back in there. I'll keep you informed on their condition," Laney said before leaving.

Two police officers entered the emergency room waiting area followed by a Boston Police Department detective. Bradley had seen the detective before when a case the FBI worked intersected with the detectives. Bradley tried to recall his name.

The detective walked straight to the front desk.

"I'm Detective Johnson of the Boston Police Department. I need to speak to the doctor in charge as soon as possible," he said to the same woman Bradley had spoken with. She responded in an equally unpleasant way.

"Excuse me, Detective Johnson," Bradley called as he moved to meet him. "I'm Agent Bradley Whitman, Federal Bureau of Investigation. I believe we've met before."

"Yes, Agent Whitman, I remember."

"Are you here investigating the limousine incident on Seaport Boulevard?" Bradley asked.

"I am. Does it have something to do with one of your cases, agent?"

"No, detective. Supervisory Special Agent Derek Richards and his wife were in the limousine along with some friends. I think it would be wise if you contact Executive Assistant Director Davis and let him know what happened."

The detective moved down the hallway so they could speak privately. Bradley followed.

"How do you know this, agent?"

"Because they were on their way to meet us at the Envoy Hotel, and my girlfriend, Doctor Weaver, saw it happen. She was on the scene."

"I'd like to talk to her. Is she here?"

Bradley pointed to the emergency room activity. "Yes, but she's busy right now."

"Right. I'll call Director Davis," Johnson said.

"Wait. Detective, do you know what happened? Have you been to the scene?" Bradley asked.

"I just came from there." He paused. "It looks like it was an improvised explosive device with a light charge. We don't know if it was on a timer or what. They're still examining the vehicle."

"It was in the car?" Bradley's eyes narrowed.

"Or under it. We really don't know yet," the detective said.

Bradley struggled to understand why anyone would target any of the people in the vehicle, except maybe Derek. It could be blowback from a case. *But how would anyone know he would be in that limousine?*

Bradley handed his card to Detective Johnson and asked him to keep him posted on the investigation.

"If Director Davis says it's alright, I'll keep you in the loop," Johnson said.

Great, Bradley thought. Bradley was not one of Director Davis's favorite agents, especially after the Joshua debacle eighteen months before that resulted in Bradley getting suspended for six months.

"Let me know if there is anything I can do to help, detective. Anything at all," Bradley stated.

"What did he say?" Doug asked when Bradley returned.

"It was a low charge IED, and they think it was either in the limousine or attached to it somehow."

Zayt flinched when Bradley used the term. He had lost many friends to IED explosions while serving three tours in Afghanistan. One of the reasons Zayt came to Boston was to find one of his Navy Seal brothers, a victim of one of those blasts, but thus far, Zayt hadn't found him. Shea noticed Zayt's reaction and took his arm.

"Why? Why would anyone . . . ?" Doug paused. "Do you think they targeted Derek? Someone from one of his cases?"

"I don't know, Dad. Maybe. I've got to make a call."

Bradley rolled outside to get out of earshot of the others. He didn't want to upset his mother any more than she already was.

He dialed the home number of Nick Gaston, a fellow agent whom Bradley had worked with on many cases.

"Yeah? What do you want, Bradley? It's Sunday night for chrissake," said Nick.

"Turn on the local news, Nick. Right now."

Bradley stared at the waiting room TV set broadcasting the explosion aftermath.

"Jesus, it looks like a war zone. What's the story?" Nick asked.

"Derek and Cate were in that limousine, Nick. With some other friends." Bradley couldn't bring himself to mention they were on their way to surprise him for his birthday when it happened.

"Holy fuck. Are they alright? I mean, Jesus!"

"I'm at Mass General now. All I know is that they are alive. I need you to jump on this and get all the information you can. Detective Johnson of the BPD is lead on the investigation, but I think it will be our case before too long. The working theory is a light load IED placed either in, on, or under the vehicle. Call Mara and Jim. Get on it."

"Got it. I'll call you later. Keep me posted on their condition."

Nick headed the unit including Mara Thompkins and Jim Jansen. They worked well together, and Bradley trusted them to be thorough and tenacious. He also knew that if Executive Assistant Director Davis would not allow Detective Johnson to communicate with him, he would steer the detective to Nick Gaston.

When Bradley reentered the waiting room, he saw a police officer talking with Lynn, Doug, Shea, and Zayt.

"What's going on?" Bradley asked nervously.

"He needs their names. Some of their identification was destroyed in the explosion. They need to contact their families," Doug said.

"Oh my God! The twins . . . and Grace!" Lynn's tears escalated. Doug wrapped her in his arms and held tight.

"Officer, we can only tell you who we think were in the car. We don't know for sure. We only know who was supposed to be," Bradley explained.

"Understood. But anything you can tell us will be of help," the officer said.

Bradley pulled him aside, away from Lynn and Doug. Zayt went with Bradley. He could see a pattern emerging, Bradley taking people aside or moving away to make a phone call, and he wanted to make sure Bradley didn't plan to go rogue and take matters into his own hands as he sometimes did. Zayt had once made a promise to Derek that he would help control Bradley's fierce urge to protect everyone around him even if he put himself in danger. Director Davis and Derek had warned Bradley several times, the most recent resulting in a six-month suspension after he set himself up as a target to trap a murderer. Zayt knew Bradley worked hard to resist his tendency but thought it important to give him a subtle reminder. He stood behind Bradley's wheelchair and placed his hand on Bradley's shoulder.

Bradley listed the names of his friends for the officer. "Derek Richards and his wife Cate. Derek is the supervisory special agent of the FBI, Chelsea headquarters." The officer raised his eyebrows at the mention of Derek's status. "Holly and John Davidson from Amherst. John is a professor at UMASS Amherst, and Holly owns Davidson's Publishing. Holly's father Mike Hayes, an engineer from Worcester. Then there's David and Sheila Carson from Hollywood Hills, California. David is producing the movie being filmed in Boston this week. Sheila and Cate are sisters. My guess is David and Sheila hired the limousine."

"Was this a planned event?" the officer asked.

"Apparently it was," Bradley answered.

"It's been planned for about a month," Zayt interjected.

Bradley looked back at Zayt and asked, "Really?"

Zayt nodded.

"Who knew about the limousine?" the police officer questioned.

Bradley and Zayt stared at each other.

"We don't know," Bradley finally replied. He saw Laney coming down the hall. "Excuse me, officer." He wheeled away with Zayt alongside. They met up with Laney as she reached Doug, Lynn, and Shea.

She took a deep breath before beginning. "Holly and John are both conscious and have suffered similar injuries. Both have concussions and many lacerations due to flying glass, some of which embedded in their skin. They are complaining of neck and back pain, but the x-rays show no indication of permanent damage. We still have many tests to do, but they are both resting comfortably with the assistance of pain medication.

"Mike and Sheila must have fallen to the floor before the glass shattered because they escaped the lacerations," Laney continued, "but Mike suffered a broken wrist and leg, a concussion, and burns on his hands. He is experiencing some abdominal pain, which may indicate internal bleeding. He is going in for tests right now. Sheila . . ."

She had to stop and regain her poise. Bradley reached for her hand and held it. "Sheila fell on the floor first," Laney continued after a moment. "Mike landed on top of her. The temperature of the floor of the vehicle became extremely hot. Sheila suffered burns on the front of her body and the left side of her face."

Lynn let out a gasp, and Doug held her close. Bradley did everything he could to keep from falling apart.

"Go on," Bradley managed as he squeezed Laney's hand.

"Sheila also suffered a concussion and possible damage to her left eye. They are dressing her burns and, once they finish with her tests, she will be heavily sedated."

Laney cleared her throat before going on. "Derek and David were thrown from the vehicle into the street. Each has suffered multiple bone fractures and breaks, deep contusions on the skull, and disc fractures. Both have been in and out of consciousness. But that is not all bad. Sometimes the body knows when to shut itself down in times of trauma. Their vital signs are erratic, and they are being very closely monitored."

"Cate. What about Cate?" Bradley's voice cracked when he asked.

"Cate is in a coma. She was thrown from one end of the car to the other, hitting her head multiple times. The swelling in her brain is severe, and we may need to go in and relieve the pressure if it doesn't happen on its own. We need to wait and see." She paused and sighed. "She also has a broken neck."

"Oh no, no, no, no . . .," Bradley muttered. Tears dotted his cheeks. He buried his head in his hands and sobbed.

"There's one more thing. The chauffeur is dead. The steering wheel crushed his sternum, and the impact of the windshield with his head most likely killed him instantly."

"Jesus," Bradley moaned.

Doug still held Lynn, who sat motionless, stunned.

Zayt turned and saw fear and pain in Shea's eyes. He knew she thought back to her time in the hospital after being beaten almost to death. Zayt went to her, whispered into her ear, then held her close to him as he had done many times in the past.

Laney knelt in front of Bradley and lifted his head so she could look into his terrified eyes. As a trauma doctor, she had been in that position many times. But she couldn't come up with magic consoling words for Bradley. She could only love him. He buried his head into her chest and wept.

The sound of multiple sirens prompted Bradley to gather himself and focus on the activity taking place outside the glass entrance to the emergency room parking lot. Several Boston Police Department vehicles screeched to a halt just outside the doors. All eyes turned to watch as the unmistakable thwapping of spinning helicopter blades grew close. Across the parking lot, a large dark blue helicopter landed on the helipad. It was not the Life Flight chopper Bradley expected to see.

Moments later, a group of five men in business suits exited the machine and marched through the glass doors, FBI Assistant Executive Director Paul Davis in the lead. He spotted Bradley and approached.

"Agent Whitman, what's the word? How is he?" he asked.

"Director Davis, this is Doctor Weaver. She was just filling us in." Bradley looked to Laney with pleading eyes, hoping she would take control of the conversation. He wasn't sure he could handle his emotions.

Laney stood and held out her hand. Her demeanor changed instantly as she morphed back into her professional role.

"Director Davis, I'm Laney Weaver. Let's move to the hallway away from the crowd, shall we?" she suggested.

Nick Gaston, Mara Thompkins, and Jim Jansen approached the caution-taped area on Seaport Boulevard. Nick flashed his badge to an officer on the edge of the crime scene and asked to speak with the person in charge.

"I'm Sergeant Grey. Detective Johnson's in charge of the investigation. He's at the hospital. What can I do for you?"

"Agent Nick Gaston, Federal Bureau of Investigation. We'd like to take a look at the scene, Sergeant."

"Our demolitions team is working the scene at the moment. I can't let anyone disturb the area."

"Sergeant, this is Agent Jim Jansen. He is an FBI explosives expert. I would appreciate it if you would allow him to assist your people."

"I . . ."

"Our boss was in that limousine, Sergeant. I'm not about to take *no* for an answer," Nick asserted. Nick nodded to Agent Jansen. Jim ducked under the yellow tape and worked his way to the mangled limousine.

Sergeant Grey made no move to stop him. "How is he?"

"Alive," Nick answered. "What have you got so far?"

"It looks like it was a pipe bomb fastened on the underside of the vehicle on the passenger side, either in the tailpipe or beside it. The bomber used black powder as an accelerant. Our guy says the damage could have easily been a lot worse."

"It was bad enough," Nick shot back.

"Our officers have been interviewing the witnesses. They all say the same thing. The limo was stopped at the signal light, first in line. Without warning, the back end of the vehicle shot into the air, about eight feet some say, then crashed back to the street. Two male passengers were thrown out onto the road."

"Any suspicious bystanders?"

"None that any noticed."

"I'm going to want to see the report of those interviews, Sergeant."

"You'll need to speak with Detective Johnson, Agent."

"I will."

Sergeant Grey excused himself.

"Mara, get in there and take pictures of the limousine. I want the license plate, company name, manufacturer, everything you can see. Get the damn VIN number if you can. Snap pictures of the surrounding area, too."

"They may not let me in," Mara said.

"Don't ask," Nick replied.

Nick called Bradley. "Hey, how is he?"

"No change. He's been in and out of consciousness. Director

Davis is here talking with the doctor now. The chauffeur is dead. What have you found?"

"I've got Jim working the limo now. BPD said it was a small black powder pipe bomb at the rear of the vehicle."

Bradley paused. "This is a homicide now, Nick, and attempted murder of a federal officer. I'm going to ask the director when he expects to take the case from the Boston Police Department. Call everyone in. I want them ready to go as soon as we get the word."

"I'm on it."

Bradley had no sooner hung up with Nick than Director Davis beckoned Bradley into the hallway. Laney had returned to the ER.

"Agent Whitman, what have we got?" the director asked.

"It was a small black powder pipe bomb placed on the underside of the rear of the limousine. Agent Jansen is examining the vehicle now." Bradley waited for that information to sink in before he continued. "Sir, will we be taking the case?"

"Yes." The director turned and spoke to one of the suited men. "Get me the chief of the Boston Police Department on the phone." He turned to another of his assistants. "Who is second to Agent Richards in Chelsea?"

The man leaned in to whisper his reply. Bradley watched as the director nodded his head and then glanced at Bradley.

"Get Agent Gaston on the phone," Davis said.

"Chief Hanson on the line," the first man said as he handed Davis a cell phone.

The director moved further down the hall, away from his subordinates to speak privately, and for a moment, heatedly to the BPD chief of police. With the call finished, he returned to the group. The second suit handed him a different cell phone.

"Agent Gaston, Sir," the man said.

"Agent Gaston, this is Executive Assistant Director Davis. As of now, you are temporarily in charge of the Chelsea office. The bombing case is ours. Take the lead and don't disappoint me. I want updates every two hours."

Bradley could hear Nick speaking on the other end of the phone, but he could not make out what he said.

"Whatever it takes." Davis flashed a sideways glance at Bradley as he responded to Nick. Then he hung up the phone.

"I understand you have other friends who were in the car," the director said.

"Yes, sir."

"I hope they all recover fully, Agent Whitman. I will pray for them." Director Davis put his hand on Bradley's shoulder.

"Thank you, sir."

"Now, go get this bastard."

Director Davis and his entourage exited through the glass doors and into the waiting helicopter.

The sting kept Bradley motionless for several minutes. Although anticipated, being passed over in the chain of command hurt more than he expected. *I only have myself to blame,* he thought. But it didn't lessen his disappointment. And it wasn't the time to think about that.

Bradley rejoined his parents, Zayt, and Shea.

"Well?" Doug asked impatiently.

"We just took the case away from the Boston Police Department. It's now officially an FBI investigation. Davis put Nick in charge of the office and the investigation. I'm going to head over. . ."

"Whoa, whoa, whoa! What?" Zayt asked, incredulous. "He put Nick in charge?"

"Yeah. I'm going to head . . ."

"But you have seniority over Nick and everyone else in that office," Doug said, as Zayt vigorously nodded his head.

"Yeah, Dad, but I have also recently come off a six-month suspension. It makes sense he would put Nick in charge. Besides, it doesn't matter who it is. We're all going to work together, just like we always do."

"Derek would want you," Doug replied. "You know it, and I know it."

Bradley sighed. "Look. It's alright. I just want to go do my job. I have to go to headquarters. Here are the keys to the house." Bradley handed his keys to his dad. "Are you staying here for a while?"

"Yes," Lynn quickly said. "We can't leave." She shot a panicked look at Doug.

"We'll be here at least for a while," Doug said, patting Lynn's hand.

"We'll stay too," Zayt said. Shea nodded in agreement.

"I'll call you later," Bradley told them as he moved to the exit. Once outside, he called Nick.

"Where are you?" Nick asked.

"Just leaving the hospital. I'm heading to the office."

"I'll meet you there. And Bradley, Davis was wrong to . . ."

"Hey! It's okay, Nick."

Mara read from her notebook. "The movie production company hired the limousine through Back Bay Limousine

Service. The movie people have three limos at their disposal for the entire week, one stretch limo and two luxury bus limos. The rental agreement, signed last month by the production's transportation coordinator, allowed for 24/7 use. The deceased chauffeur's name was Henry Case, a father of four with three grandchildren," she added somberly.

"Talk to the transportation coordinator and find out how far in advance the producer needed to reserve the limo for tonight. Also, find out who from the production company knew where the producer was going," said Nick.

Bradley barked loudly, "His name is David. David Carson. His wife's name is Sheila."

Bradley's manner jolted Nick and Mara.

"I'm sorry," Bradley lowered his head. I didn't mean to. . . I'm sorry. Go on."

Nick and Mara exchanged a glance before Nick continued. "Ask if David needed to provide a list of names or identification of anyone he would be picking up. We need to find out who, if anyone, knew about their evening plans. Bradley, did Derek tell you they would be arriving together in the limousine?"

Bradley sighed deeply. "No. They were coming to surprise me for my birthday. I didn't know anything about it. But I can ask my parents. Apparently, they planned the dinner a month ago."

"It's your birthday?" Mara frowned.

"Tomorrow."

Somehow it didn't seem right to wish him a happy birthday, so neither Nick nor Mara did.

Bradley got Doug on the phone and asked him if they knew about the limousine.

"All we knew is that they would drive in together. We assumed they would come in Derek's Suburban. Cate never mentioned a limousine," Doug explained.

"Has Laney been out to update you again?"

"Not yet. I'll call you when she does."

"Thanks, Dad. Give Mom a hug for me, alright?"

"I will."

Bradley put his phone down, placed his elbows on the arms of his chair, and clasped his hands to rest his forehead on them. He sat silent as Nick and Mara stared. A moment later he snapped his head up.

"They didn't know about the limousine. Cate definitely would have mentioned the limousine if that were the plan."

"Well, you can't know that for sure," Nick said.

"Yes, yes I can. I know Cate. If that had been planned, she would have absolutely told my mother. So, let's think about what this means."

"We have eight possible targets, one very high profile. We also need to consider the possibility this was a random act. Unlikely, but possible," Nick said.

Bradley said, "Mara, see if you can find the transportation coordinator. I'll call the limousine company and find out where the car was stored until use."

Nick added, "I'll start combing through the information the Boston Police Department gathered. Bradley, we need to put a timeline together for our victims, look for abnormalities. Are you up to it?"

"I'm good, Nick."

"Alright, the rest of the team are on their way. Use them. I want this asshole in the interrogation room before the sun sets tomorrow!" Nick pounded the desk.

By the time Laney made it back out to the waiting room, the backlog of patients had dwindled, and Lynn, Doug, Shea, and Zayt had claimed some chairs. The television recapped the story of the explosion, but no details came with it. Her eyes droopy and body slumped, Laney flopped into the empty chair next to Lynn.

"Sweetheart, are you alright? You look exhausted." Lynn put her hand on Laney's arm.

Laney patted Lynn's hand. "I'll be fine. I'm going to head upstairs shortly to take a nap. I wanted to give you one last update before I do. Where's Bradley?"

"He's at the office. The FBI has taken over the case. I told him we would call when you gave us some news," Doug answered. "Let me get him on the phone now. That way, he can hear it straight from you."

Bradley answered his phone on the first ring. "Bradley, I'm going to put you on speaker. Laney just came out to give us an update."

"Okay." Bradley sounded nervous.

"Holly and John are both doing well," Laney reported. "We've moved them into a room together. The tests showed no permanent damage to their necks or spines. They are banged up and covered in bandages for their lacerations, but they are going to be fine. Mike has also been moved to a room. The abdominal pain he had earlier was due to deep bruises, not internal damage. We've set his broken bones and attended to the burns. The three were able to see each other for a short time before settling in.

"Sheila's burns are the worst of her injuries," Laney continued, "but they will heal. The ophthalmologist is optimistic about reversing any sustained damage to her eye. We will keep Sheila sedated for tonight and evaluate whether to continue sedation tomorrow. Let me just stop here and say, this is all great news."

"Yes, it is. Very good news," Lynn said with a half smile.

"David, Derek, and Cate have been moved to the intensive care unit."

Shea began to tremor. Zayt put his arm around her and whispered in her ear. She nodded and concentrated on her breathing.

Laney continued. "In addition to the skull fracture, David suffered a broken clavicle and a fractured ankle. The brain swelling is slowly reducing, so we've realigned his collar bone as best we can, but we will need to operate once the swelling is at a minimum. The disc fractures most likely will heal themselves as long as he gives them time to. His vitals have stabilized, and he has been able to maintain consciousness.

"Derek is also conscious," Laney said. Bradley noticed that she sounded almost annoyed by the fact. "He has a broken hip and fractured discs. The discs in his back should heal if he follows doctor's instructions and takes things slow. His vital statistics were stabilizing, but his blood pressure has shot way up and remains high. We may need to sedate him to give him a chance to heal. He is being difficult, which is normally a good sign for recovery but in this case could create lasting damage to his back.

"And Cate. . ." Laney let out a sigh. "Cate remains in a coma. She is on a ventilator to help her breathe. We've put her in a brace to stabilize her neck and back, but we won't know if any nerve damage has occurred until she wakes. And there's no way of knowing when that will be."

"Have you told Derek?" Bradley's voice shook.

"No. We've told him that she is resting comfortably. I don't think he believes it."

"Two things, Laney." Bradley cleared his throat. "There are two things we need to do to calm Derek down. We have to tell him about Cate and the others, and I need to talk to him about what happened. He won't rest until we do."

"But he's not. . ."

"I know what you're going to say. He's not ready. He's not strong enough. But he will not sleep, he will not stop trying to see her, and he will hound all of you and risk hurting himself until those two things happen. I'm coming over there now, Laney. I can talk to him."

"Okay. I'll meet you in the ICU."

"No. You go home, get some sleep. Just leave word with someone that it's alright for me to speak with him. You sound exhausted, and they're going to need you at your best."

"But I. . ."

"Really. Go home."

"I can just g—. . ."

"Now who's being difficult?"

"Alright, but I'm sleeping here at the hospital."

Bradley had forgotten he was on speakerphone and that Laney sat in the waiting room with his parents. They could hear the entire conversation, but he didn't care.

"I love you."

"I love you, too," she replied.

"Nick, I've got to go back to the hospital. Derek is conscious and uncooperative."

"I'll bet he is. That's good to hear," Nick smiled.

"Except now I have to tell him his wife is in a coma and could possibly be paralyzed." Nick stopped smiling.

"Fuck," Nick muttered.

"Before I go, I found out the limousine spent most of today parked on Charter Street. That's one of the streets the city blocked from traffic so the production company could film some sort of car chase scene. The limo company said they spoke to the driver mid-afternoon, and he hadn't moved since he brought the movie bigwigs, his word not mine, to the filming location. Every pedestrian in Boston had access to the car. I've got Morrison's team working on the others' timelines. It's getting late, though. We may not be able to do much more tonight. Have you heard from Jim yet?"

"I talked to him an hour ago. He should be here shortly. Call me after you talk to Derek," Nick said as he repeatedly made tight fists with his hands.

"Of course. Relax, Nick. Don't get yourself all wound up. It won't help anyone, especially Derek."

Nick let his hands fall to his sides. "Right. We got this."

Bradley made his way out the building and back to the hospital. He assumed his parents were still in the emergency room waiting area, so he parked in the same spot as before. He found his mother sound asleep on his dad's shoulder and Shea quietly snoring and sprawled across three chairs with her head on Zayt's leg. Doug and Zayt watched the television to a local network showing a rerun of *The Big Bang Theory*.

"Hey," Bradley spoke softly.

Even though he barely spoke above a whisper, Lynn's eyes shot open and she lifted her head.

"Sorry, I didn't mean to wake you, Mom. I'm going to go talk to Derek. Then I might check in on Holly, John, and Mike. Then we'll go home."

"Tell them we love them," Lynn said.

Bradley smiled at his mother before heading to the elevator. Familiar with the hospital and some of its employees, Bradley quickly made his way to the intensive care unit and passed the nurses' desk, where he got the thumbs up from the desk nurse.

"Room 14," she pointed.

"Thank you, Miranda."

She smiled.

Well before he rolled up to the open door, Bradley heard Derek whose heavily bandaged head swayed side to side as two nurses tried to re-insert his IV line. He squirmed and shouted something about *his dead body*.

"That's not the kind of statement you want to be throwing around in an ICU ward, Boss!"

The nurses turned at the sound of Bradley's voice, and Derek looked relieved to see him.

"It's about goddamn time. Where the hell have you been?" Derek spat.

"I'm not going to say a word until you let these nice people do their job. Then we'll have the conversation that I know you want to have."

"I don't want conversation. I want out of here. Now!"

"If you stand up now, it may be the last time you do!"

Bradley spoke harshly and adamantly.

Once the words sank in, Derek stopped resisting and allowed the nurses to insert the IV back into his arm. The nurses smiled at Bradley as they left the room.

"They won't tell me anything. Where's Cate? Is she alright?" Derek pleaded.

Bradley moved to Derek's side and spoke softly and calmly. "Cate is here in the ICU. She suffered trauma to her head which has caused severe swelling in her brain. She's in a coma."

Derek brought his hands to his face as if covering it might somehow lessen the blow of what Bradley told him.

"The doctors say if the swelling doesn't reduce on its own, they will need to go in and relieve the pressure," Bradley continued. "They are watching her very closely."

"Jesus fucking Christ," Derek sobbed.

"Laney told me that a coma is not always a bad thing. It's Cate's body's way of helping her to heal without pain."

Derek nodded, unable to speak.

"There's one more thing, Derek. Cate's neck is broken. They won't know if there is any nerve damage until she wakes up."

Derek removed his hands from his ashen face and stared blankly at Bradley. Tears streamed down his cheeks. "I have to see her. I have to be with her, Bradley."

"You will. Just not tonight, Derek. You have a couple of fractured discs in your back and a broken hip. If you move now, you could end up in a chair like this for the rest of your life." Bradley lightly slapped his hand on his armrest. "And Cate is going to need you, healthy and strong, no matter what happens. Think about that."

Derek squeezed his eyes shut and wiped them with the palms of his hands. He took a couple of deep breaths. "Alright. Okay."

Bradley intuited Derek's internal conversation with himself. Derek often did so when a situation became intense.

"Okay," Derek said. "What about the others?"

Bradley relayed the general condition of the others. He didn't think it best to go into detail but didn't sugarcoat their situations, either. "You, Cate, and David are the only ones left in the ICU."

Derek nodded. Then Derek narrowed his eyes and rubbed his forehead as if trying to recall something. "Wait. What about the driver? How is he?"

Bradley looked down at his feet. He hadn't decided how much to tell Derek. Too little would keep him uneasy, too much might anger him enough to do something reckless.

"The driver is dead. His head cracked the windshield. He died at the scene."

Derek sighed. "What the hell happened, Bradley? One minute we were talking and laughing, the next. . . I don't even know."

This is where this conversation gets tricky, Bradley thought. *Once Derek realizes it wasn't an accident, he will become outraged. If I don't tell him, he will be infuriated.*

"We're still putting the pieces together. It's only been a few hours, still too early to know exactly what happened."

Derek's ashen face turned ruddy, and his cold eyes shot darts into Bradley's. A large vein on his neck began to throb.

"Goddamn it, Bradley. Don't give me the media line. What the hell do you know and why don't you want to tell me?" Derek tried to lift himself up using his elbow, but Bradley rested his hand on Derek's shoulder to stop him.

"Alright. Jesus, Derek. But you've got to stay calm." Bradley gathered his thoughts. "I'll tell you what I know to this point. It was a small black-powder pipe bomb placed on the undercarriage of the limousine. Jansen was still at the scene when I came back here, so I don't have any more details."

"Jansen?" Derek went silent as he had yet another internal conversation. "It's our case? Why?"

"Director Davis took it from BPD. He came here, by the way. He came to the hospital."

Derek laid his head back, placed the palm of his right hand on his forehead, and squinted his eyes.

"Are you okay? Should I call the nurse?" Bradley asked.

"I'm fine." He quickly blinked his eyes. "Just a headache."

"It's not just a headache. It's a concussion. I should go." Bradley started to move his chair.

"Damn it, Bradley, don't you move," Derek shouted. "Ahhh!" He placed both hands over his face as a sharp pain shot through his head.

A nurse hurried through the open door and went directly to the monitors. She adjusted the flow of the IV drip. "You've got to rest now, Mr. Richards. Your blood pressure is at a dangerous level." She looked at Bradley. "I'm sorry, sir, but you need to go now. Doctor Weaver's orders."

"I'm going. I'll come by in the morning, Derek, after our first briefing. Then I'll fill you in. Just try to get some sleep. Think about what I said. Cate is going to need you."

Bradley could see the effects of the IV adjustment by the time he left the room. Whatever they put in the bag calmed Derek down almost instantly. He asked the nurse, Miranda, where he could find Holly and John. She directed him to the fourth floor, Room 452.

He slowly rolled up to the room. The door lay open, so he could peek inside. Holly lay in the bed closest to the door, John lay sleeping in the bed by the windows. Holly held a magazine. Bradley lightly knocked on the open door.

Her smile melted his heart. Even with the bandages and visible bruises, he saw the beautiful, good-hearted friend he loved dearly.

"Bradley," she whispered as she put the magazine down. Bradley glanced over to John and gave Holly a questioning glance.

"It's alright. Come over here. Give me a hug."

Holly painfully scooched to the edge of the bed and reached her arms out.

Bradley pulled his chair as close as he could get and, careful not to squeeze too hard, leaned into her hug. A tear fell from his eye.

"I didn't think you would be awake. I just wanted to see you. I can only stay a minute. I promised the nurse I wouldn't stay long. How are you feeling?"

"Sore—and a bit of a headache. I probably shouldn't try to read, but I couldn't sleep. How are the rest? I know my Dad is alright, I got to see him, but they won't give us any information about the others."

Bradley did not wish to worry Holly, so he lied. "Everyone is going to be fine, some quicker than others, but I will fill you in tomorrow. I just had to see you."

"God, I love you, Bradley. I love you so much."

She reached for another hug.

"I love you too, Holly," he said as he returned the hug. "Get some rest. I'll be back tomorrow." He turned to leave.

"Laney is amazing," Holly said.

Bradley turned back and smiled. "She is, isn't she? Goodnight."

When he left the room, he couldn't hold back emotion any longer. He waited until he turned the corner before he let his tears flow. The day's events played in his head like a movie reel. He tried to dismiss the idea that he almost lost every one of his oldest and dearest friends. Then he thought about Cate and the prospect of her never walking again. It would be too much to bear. Bradley allowed himself a few more moments of tears before he called Nick.

"How is he?" Nick asked.

"Angry. The nurse had to sedate him to keep him calm. We need to make headway quick or he's going to explode. Shit! Sorry, that was a bad reference. You got anything?"

"A little. Jim has a good idea how the bomb was constructed. I'll fill you in tomorrow. Go home," Nick said.

"Yeah." Bradley had little strength left. "I'll see you in the morning."

Bradley steered his wheelchair to the elevators and back down to the emergency room.

"How's Derek?" Doug asked.

"Just as you would expect. He's sad, angry, confused, and in pain. The nurse had to adjust his IV dose to get him to calm down."

"Did you see Holly, John, and Mike?" Lynn asked.

"Just Holly, and only for a minute. She's doing alright, just a little trouble sleeping. I'm coming back in the morning. I wasn't quite truthful about the others' conditions, and I don't want her to find out from someone else. What time is it?"

"Almost ten," Doug said as he checked his watch.

Bradley called his favorite pizza place and ordered enough food for all of them.

"Let's pick up this food and go home. You two are staying with me tonight, right?" Bradley asked his parents.

"If it's no trouble," Lynn said.

"Of course not."

"Bradley, why did this happen to them?" Lynn asked.

"I don't know, Mom. But I intend to find out," Bradley said with an angry edge to his voice.

LONG SHOT

Rusty woke first, stretched his four legs, and craned his neck to check on Bradley. Since the night Bradley got shot, Rusty had taken to sleeping in bed with him. They had only been acquainted for two weeks by then but had formed a quick and solid bond. Rusty, a male black Doberman Pinscher with rust-colored markings, saved Bradley's life when they met. Bradley liked to tell people that Rusty saved his life more than once. They were best friends.

They woke at the same time every morning—five. Their routine usually involved Rusty making a morning visit to residents of the sandpit behind the house while Bradley did his morning workout. However, that morning, Bradley did not wish to disturb his parents who slept on the sofa bed near the fireplace on the other side of the room.

Bradley's home did not have walls to separate rooms other than the one bathroom near his bed. He purchased the metal structure, a former laundry service building in the largely abandoned industrial area of Revere, Massachusetts, and turned it into a comfortable and efficient home for himself. His backyard, all of twenty feet, dropped to a steep ledge leading into the sandpit where Zayt's idea of a community of tiny homes had come to fruition.

Bradley expertly shifted himself from bed into his wheelchair and opened the back sliding glass doors to let Rusty out. Instead of beginning his workout, he went to take a shower.

As he toweled himself off, he smelled coffee brewing. He knew then that his mother had awakened and dug out the very old percolator coffee pot that had belonged to his grandmother, the kind you brew on the stovetop.

"You know I have a coffee maker right there on the counter, right?" Bradley smiled as he made his way to the kitchen. "I'm sorry I woke you."

"Nonsense. I get up at five o'clock every morning," she joked, then leaned in and kissed him on the forehead.

"Well, I don't," Doug muttered while still lying on the sleep sofa.

"How did you sleep?" Bradley asked his mother.

Her eyes shifted from morning haze to somber. "I couldn't stop thinking about what it must have been like for them. And what they will need to overcome."

"I know, Mom. But they won't be alone. They have us, and they have each other."

"What about their families, Bradley? I would think they will begin to arrive today. Have you given any thought about how we can help?"

Bradley paused. "No, I hadn't."

"I have. I'm going to call around and see if we can book a block of rooms at one of the hotels close to the hospital. How many do you think we might need?"

"Cate and Sheila's parents will come in from California. Derek's parents, probably Holly's grandparents, but I don't know anything about David's family."

"I'll book four rooms, to be safe. Your father and I can use one if the others don't need it."

"No, you two should stay here. They're going to need to eat. You can do your magic in my kitchen, and we can pack up food for them, maybe have them here for dinner," Bradley said.

"Alright. I'll have your father bring me grocery shopping this morning. When are you going to the hospital?"

"After our morning briefing. I'm going to head to the office soon. I know it's early, but I want to get started."

"Then I'm going to make you some breakfast. And Bradley?"

"Yeah?"

"Happy birthday, honey."

Rusty returned, and Bradley gave him his morning meal, canned beef with gravy mixed with cooked rice. Under normal circumstances, Bradley would bring Rusty to work with him, but since he would visit the hospital and, even with Rusty trained as a service and therapy dog, Bradley thought it a good idea to leave the dog at home.

He left his parents eating pancakes at the kitchen table. When he pulled into the Chelsea FBI headquarters parking lot at 6:30, he noticed Nick's SUV covered in dew. He showed his badge to the overnight security guard and took the elevator to the eighth floor. Nick sat at his desk.

Hearing the ding of the elevator, Nick looked up with tired eyes and focused on Bradley.

"What the hell are you doing here?" Nick asked.

"I could ask the same of you. Didn't you go home?"

"No, I slept on Derek's couch for a couple hours."

"Tell me about the bomb."

"Jim said it was a basic design, black powder encased in a steel pipe and placed in the exhaust system. But here's the interesting part. It didn't have a detonator. The suspect relied on the buildup of heat to ignite the bomb. Highly inefficient. There would be no way of knowing when or if the bomb would explode. What kind of bomber does that?"

"Either an inexperienced one or an indiscriminate one." Bradley wrinkled his forehead at the thought..

"What? What are you thinking?" Nick asked.

"You told me the police officer at the scene, Sergeant Grey, said something that bothered you. He said the explosives guy mentioned that the blast could have been a lot worse."

"Yeah, Jim said the same thing. The suspect used a large grain powder, categorized as a double-F granulation, which is typically used in .50-caliber muzzleloaders. A finer grain would have ignited easier. So, our unknown subject either knows little about how to make an effective pipe bomb or didn't care about how much damage he—or she—created."

"Alright, so we do a database search for recent bombings where the unsub used FFg black powder," Bradley suggested, referring to the unknown subject..

"Who uses muzzleloaders? Hunters, Revolutionary and Civil War reenactors, and the New England Patriots Endzone Militia. Jim said he can determine what brand the powder is. Then I'll have him check every store in the state that sells it. It's a long shot but worth a try."

"Was there anything unusual about the pipe itself?"

"Not that he mentioned. He said it could have been bought anywhere. He did say that it was new. It still had a shine on it. They'll be checking the fragments for prints today."

The elevator dinged. Both Bradley and Nick stopped and watched the doors open. Mara stepped out, holding a cardboard carrier with four cups of coffee.

"Good morning," Bradley smiled.

"Good morning," Mara replied.

"Mornin'," Nick said.

Mara handed Bradley and Nick each a large cup of hot coffee. "Where's Jim?" she asked.

"He was here until 2 a.m. I sent him home," Nick said. "Thank you for the coffee," he smiled.

"You're welcome. Where do I start?"

"Run a database search for recent bombings using FF grain black powder," Bradley began. "Then we'll need a list of every Massachusetts hunting license issued for muzzleloader season for the past—let's start with five years. Black powder tends to pick up moisture easily, which makes it ineffective over time. Anything over five years old would be a gamble, but the buyer would probably have had a muzzleloader license."

"Okay."

Bradley continued. "Nick, I think we need to delve into the possibility of a revenge attack. It could be a direct link to any of our previous or current cases."

"Yeah, I'll get Taylor's unit on that."

"Do you have the report from Morrison's team on the timeline of our vict . . ." Bradley caught himself. A feeling of guilt engulfed him as he realized he had momentarily thought of his best friends as victims instead of some of the most important people in his life. ". . . the timeline of everyone's day?" he rephrased.

"Just a partial. The late hour and the fact that it was a Sunday prevented them from getting much done. I'm sure he'll have a full report for me today, as best he can."

"Derek was here all day, from eight-thirty in the morning until approximately four-thirty. Then he must have gone straight home to get ready for . . . dinner."

Had it not been his birthday, his friends would not be in the hospital. Bradley had thought about it all night. He felt responsible.

Nick could tell Bradley was distracted. But he also knew that a distracted Bradley was better than any other FBI analyst at their best.

"Why don't you start putting together the unknown subjects profile. I'll feed you information as it comes in. The morning briefing is at 9 a.m. You can present a preliminary profile of the unsub then," Nick said.

"I'm on it," Bradley replied.

The office filled quickly. Agents from the white-collar crime unit based on the third floor came upstairs to help, as did agents from the cybercrime, counterintelligence, violent crime, and organized crime units. Nick had his hands full coordinating the activity. He sent agents to speak with members of the movie production company, University of Massachusetts college campus in Amherst, Back Bay Limousine service, Davidson's Publishing office, Mike's engineering firm, and the Envoy Hotel.

Nick had agents scouring traffic cameras, canvasing the area on and around Charter Street where the limousine sat during the day, and, in hopes of finding a suspect or witness, collecting camera video from nearby businesses.

Bradley suggested Nick send agents to speak with the Massachusetts Bay Transportation Authority, MBTA, and to speak with bus drivers who worked on Sunday. He had agents calling all taxi, Uber, and Lyft drivers in the area. Nick funneled information to Bradley as quickly as it came in.

At nine o'clock, the few agents who remained in the building met in the briefing room. Among them were Nick, Bradley, Mara, Jim, Tony Morrison, and Kyle Taylor.

Bradley sat beside Nick, who stood at the front of the room. "The media has the story. They know Agent Richards is one of the victims. And they know that an incendiary device was involved. As always, we have no comment on an ongoing investigation. If I get wind of anyone discussing details of this case outside of this building, I will take quick action to end their law enforcement career. Make sure your teams know this. Now, Bradley has a preliminary profile on our unsub."

"Our unknown subject is most likely an older male between the ages of forty and fifty-five. He is someone who would have black powder readily available for some sort of black powder activity like hunting or possibly reenactment activities. He may be socially awkward, a loner, and believes he has been wronged in some way that makes sense to him.

"The pipe bomb was crude and unimaginative," Bradley continued. "The good news is it didn't cause as much damage as it could have. The bad news is anyone could have made it. The unsub either didn't intend to kill anyone, or he lacked the knowledge and easily attainable research to do so. My best guess to this point is we are looking for a male social misfit, forty to fifty years old, likely pissed off at someone who rode in the limousine or the company they work for, which includes the limousine company, and wanted them to know it."

Tony Morrison spoke. "How do we know it is an older man? Most of the bombers I've been involved with are under forty years old."

Bradley explained, "That's true, Tony, but this man used FFg black powder, the preferred powder for larger caliber black powder rifles. The average age of muzzleloader hunters has increased dramatically in the last four decades. New and younger hunters tend toward bow hunting while those over forty are more likely to use a rifle, shotgun, or muzzleloader. And as far as reenactors go, the same is true. The average age has increased and continues to do so. Look, you all know how this works. This profile is surely going to evolve with the information we continue to receive. It's just a likely place to start."

"Any more questions on the profile?" Nick asked. "None? Alright. Where are we at with the timelines, Tony?"

"Nothing out of the ordinary so far. David and Sheila Carson are staying at the Park Plaza Hotel. The limousine picked them and others up from the hotel at 8 a.m. and brought them to the filming site at the intersection of Salem and Charter streets. Mrs. Carson left with her sister, Cate, at approximately one o'clock. They had drinks at the Battery Wharf Hotel on the harbor then shopped at Williams-Sonoma before heading back to the filming site. We know Derek spent the day here after dropping his wife at the filming site. I'm still waiting for information about the other three."

"Nick, I'm going to the hospital as soon as this briefing is over. I will speak with Holly and find out about their activities yesterday," Bradley said.

"Good. We've got a lot of camera footage coming in, and we'll need eyes on all of it. As our people start coming back, put them to work on it. I want to be able to tell Derek and the director that we have leads.

"Let's go," Nick continued. He turned to Bradley. "Bradley?"

"Yeah, Nick?"

"Tell Derek . . . tell him . . . tell him we got this." Nick looked down at his feet.

"I will."

Bradley made his way to his truck, but before he started it, he called Laney.

"Good morning," she answered.

"Good morning to you. Did you get any sleep?" he asked.

"I did. More than I should have. How about you?"

"Yes. How's Cate? Any change?"

"No. But Derek is a little calmer. But that might be because they upped his dose of pain medication last night."

"I'm on my way over. I'm just leaving now. I think it's important for me to keep Derek informed to some extent. He'll be a bear if we don't," Bradley said.

"I know. You two are so much alike."

"We're brothers, Laney. Probably closer than blood brothers. Will I see you when I get there?"

"I'll find you. I've got to make my rounds," she said.

Bradley felt that warm feeling inside, the one that always made him feel balanced. While driving to the hospital, he turned the radio on to catch the news.

. . . weather for today. Early this morning, a homeless, wheelchair-bound veteran was attacked in the City of Revere. According to Sergeant Donovan Doyle of the Revere Police Department, at approximately five o'clock this morning the man was severely beaten while sleeping on West Main Street. The department is asking for the public's help to identify his attacker or attackers.

The victims of yesterday evening's limousine bombing on Seaport Boulevard have been identified. Among the victims were FBI Supervisory Special Agent Derek Richards and his wife, Catherine. Massachusetts General Hospital has declined to disclose their condition. Moments ago, Chelsea FBI headquarters issued this statement: *We at the Chelsea headquarters and the entire Federal Bureau of Investigation extend our deepest sympathy to the family of Henry Case, the chauffeur who died in yesterday's brutal bombing. Our prayers are with the victims and their families at this time.* When asked if the FBI has any suspects, acting Supervisory Special Agent Nick Gaston said that the bureau would not comment on an ongoing investigation. In other local news, the city of . . .

Bradley switched the radio off.

Zayt woke at 5am and went for his morning run along the outer edge of the sandpit. As he came up on the access road for the third time, he saw a familiar vehicle head toward him. He stopped as the silver Sebring approached.

"Good morning, Zayt," Doug said.

"Good morning, Zayt," Lynn shouted from the passenger seat.

"Good morning. Is everything alright? Did something happen?" Zayt asked.

"No, everything is fine. We, ah, we came to help. Lynn said Cate usually helps with breakfast and lunch, so we figured you could use some extra hands," Doug said.

Zayt marveled at their thoughtfulness. He squatted at the driver's door so he could look them both in the eye. "We definitely can use your help. I think I saw Shea walking over to the kitchen a few minutes ago. Why don't you drive right over. I'm going to get cleaned up, and I'll meet you there," he looked down to the ground. "And thank you."

The small, functional kitchen fed anywhere from 150 to 250 people per meal. They served breakfast and lunch and usually supplied bagged food later in the day for anyone needing nourishment. The residents helped with preparation, serving, and cleanup. Cate had been instrumental in setting up the food line as she had spent many years as a restaurant manager.

Lynn and Doug entered the kitchen through the back door and saw Shea fretting over a large box.

"Good morning, Shea," Lynn said.

Shea lit up like a firefly. "Good morning. Are you looking for Zayt?" she asked.

"No, we're here to help you with breakfast," Lynn said.

"Oh, thank God. I haven't even figured out how to turn the grill on yet," she laughed. "I'm not good in kitchens."

"Well, I love them. So, if you'll allow me to take over, I would be grateful."

"Absolutely."

Shea breathed a sigh of relief. "You just tell me what to do. I can follow instructions, and I know where most things are."

"What's on the menu for today?" Lynn asked.

"It's right here."

Shea showed them the weekly menu taped on the wall. "We have a repeating menu to keep things as easy as possible," she said. "Monday breakfast is pancakes, sausage, oatmeal, and fresh fruit. We also have cereal every day. Today's lunch is tomato soup with ham and cheese sandwiches and a bag of potato chips."

"Okay, Doug. Fire up the grill. We have pancakes to make," Lynn smiled.

Several residents wandered in and began setting the tables with silverware, napkins, syrup, butter, sugar, and creamers.

One resident made a large pot of coffee in the big urn, and another filled the juice dispensers. Two other helpers entered the kitchen and washed and dried the dirty pots, pans, and dishes as they received them. Everyone had a job to do and did it silently and capably. Lynn and Doug were impressed with how efficient their routine had become.

Doug flipped pancakes and cooked sausage while Lynn, Shea, and Rosie, one of the residents, served. When the line seemed to dwindle, Shea suggested Doug stop mixing more pancakes and cook only the remaining batter. When the last person went through the line, six pancakes and four pieces of sausage remained.

"How in the world did you do that, Shea? I am totally impressed with you," Lynn said.

Shea beamed. "I don't know. I guess I've gotten a feel for it. Cate is so good at estimating the food amounts. I must have picked it up from her."

Shea felt a twinge of sadness, and it showed.

Lynn hugged her and whispered, "She's going to be just fine. I know it in my heart."

Cleanup went as well as setup, and before Lynn knew it, an entirely different crew of residents stepped in to start preparing lunch.

Zayt came into the kitchen. "The residents can take it from here. Rosie has done the lunch meal before. Breakfast is always the hardest. We can't thank you enough for your help."

Shea added, "I don't know what I would have done if you hadn't shown up. Thank you so much."

She displayed her gratitude by hugging each of them.

"Tomorrow is scrambled eggs, bacon, and toast? We'll be here. Right, Doug?" Lynn asked.

"Bright and early. I haven't felt this useful since I left the Marine Corps."

"We are just a phone call away if you need anything," Lynn said as they left.

Not long after Lynn and Doug had gone, Sergeant Doyle of the Revere Police Department found Zayt in the kitchen. Zayt and Doyle had become acquainted more than a year before during a homicide investigation involving a homeless woman.

"Sergeant Doyle, hello," Zayt said, surprised.

"Hey, Zayt, do you have a minute?"

Doyle seemed disturbed.

"Of course. Let's get a cup of coffee and sit down," Zayt replied.

"First, I wanted to know if you could tell me how Agent Richards and his wife are doing."

"They're both in the ICU. Derek has a nasty skull fracture and broken hip, and Cate is in a coma."

"Dear God." Doyle hesitated before he spoke again. "Have you seen the morning news?"

"No, I haven't."

"A homeless man got badly beaten this morning. He's a veteran in a wheelchair. Two kids kicked the shit out of him for fun," Doyle said angrily. "I'm trying to convince him to come see you, at least to get some food, but I'm not having much luck. I hoped maybe you could convince him."

"Sure, I can try. Where is he?" Zayt asked.

"The ambulance brought him to Mass General, but I don't think he's going to be there long. If you can get away now, I can drive you over."

"Christ, I feel like I live in that place," Zayt said. "Let's go."

As he drove to the hospital, Doyle filled Zayt in on what he knew about the assault victim.

"His name is Eddy. It took me twenty minutes to yank that information out of him. He's a real loner. I had to threaten to arrest him to get him to go to the hospital. He didn't like that idea. That's when he told me his name. Eddy Pantela, originally from somewhere on the South Shore. He wouldn't give me an address."

Zayt's head shot around. "Are you sure? Pantela? P-A-N-T-E-L-A? Eddy Pantela?"

"Yeah, that's what he said. Pantela. What's wrong?"

"Pantsman," Zayt said under his breath.

"What?"

"Eddy Pantsman Pantela. I've been looking for him for two and a half years. That's why I came to Boston," Zayt said with a sense of urgency. "Hurry up. He's not going to stick around long. Use the siren."

Doyle turned on his siren and increased his speed. "How do you know this guy?"

"We served together for almost three full tours. He taught me everything I needed to know to survive. Pantsman got to Afghanistan two months before me, and he was scheduled to leave before me. But a month before he was supposed to go home, an IED blew up his vehicle. He was the only survivor. He spent over a year in the hospital. He lost a leg and a couple fingers, and he was burned real bad, but that wasn't the worst of it. He couldn't handle the guilt."

"What guilt?"

"Of surviving. When he got home, he couldn't deal with it. When his wife, Debbie, told me he left home, I set out to find him. That was a year and a half ago."

"Why do you call him Pantsman?"

Zayt smiled. "Because anytime anyone needed something, Eddy had it in one of his combat fatigues pockets."

The cruiser hadn't completely stopped before Zayt bolted out the door and into the emergency room. He looked in the waiting area. Eddy wasn't there. He looked down the hallways. Eddy wasn't there. He went to the front desk.

Doyle caught up with him. He flashed his badge to the receptionist and said, "I'm looking for Eddy Pantela. They brought him in by ambulance a little while ago."

The receptionist checked her records. "He's being taken care of, detective. You can't see him just yet."

"Well, thank you for the promotion, ma'am, but I need to see him as soon as possible. He is a flight risk," Doyle said.

The receptionist gave him a sideways glance, "You know he's in a wheelchair, right, officer?"

"It's Sergeant Donovan Doyle, ma'am. Yes, I know he is in a wheelchair. But he is surprisingly slippery," Doyle said with a bit of a sarcastic note.

Zayt couldn't help but chuckle through the interaction. "Excuse me. Is there any other way out of here?"

"Not without coming through this lobby."

"Thank you, ma'am. I appreciate your help," Zayt smiled.

The woman smiled at Zayt and sneered at Doyle.

"Why do people always think I am the bad guy?" Doyle asked.

Zayt grinned and took a seat in the waiting room.

Doyle sat next to him. "What's your plan?"

"I don't have one. I wasn't sure I would ever find him."

"I don't think it's going to be too easy to get him off the street. He seems like he's pissed off at the world. I've seen it before. It usually doesn't end well."

Doyle stared at the buffed linoleum floor.

"Yeah, I know." Zayt looked at Doyle with soft, caring eyes. "You're a good man, Doyle. Really. Thank you for bringing me here."

Doyle slapped his hand on Zayt's knee. "Good luck. I'm going to get out of here. I don't want to set him off again. Seems I have that effect on people." He smiled. "Call me if you need a lift home."

"Thanks, Donovan."

As he waited for his old friend, a reel of his Afghanistan days played through Zayt's mind; the same reel he often recalled. The one that always ended with an explosion.

From the examination area, Zayt recognized Eddy's voice adamantly refusing someone's help. Zayt's stomach clenched. He had been looking for Eddy for a long time, but he never formed a plan for what to say if he found him.

Eddy rolled his chair into the reception area, heading toward the exit.

He looks old, Zayt thought. A white gauze bandage covered his right ear. He had a split lip and labored with each turn of the wheel. Zayt could see pain shooting from his eyes. He stepped in front of the chair.

"Hey, Pantsman."

Eddy stopped spinning and focused on the man standing in front of him.

Zayt saw the glimmer of recognition, then an involuntary twitch of the mouth as if it wanted to smile but would be scolded if it did.

Eddy's eyes drew close together as he scrutinized Zayt's appearance. Zayt wore light brown fatigues bloused over his boots and a deep brown t-shirt. His tan canvas jacket had seen better days.

"You know they make clothes in other colors than brown, dude," Eddy said, straight-faced and void of emotion.

Zayt grinned, "How you been, Eddy?"

"Livin' the dream, man." He slapped the stump of his right leg.

"It's good to see you, dude."

"Yeah, Zayt, let's do it again in another three years or so, whaddaya say?" Eddy began to roll his chair around Zayt toward the exit.

Zayt reached for the handgrip on the chair and stopped him. With a harsh edge in his voice, Zayt asked, "What? No time for a brother?"

"We're not brothers, dude."

"We'll always be brothers, Pantsman."

Eddy looked over his shoulder and shot Zayt an angry glare. "My brothers are dead."

"Not all of them, Eddy. Some of us needed to live to make their lives worth something."

"And some of us should have died with them."

Zayt turned Eddy's chair to face him. He locked eyes with him, his soft and caring, Eddy's angry and darting. "Dude, why are you pissed off at me? I haven't seen you in three years, man."

Zayt could see the question threw Eddy off guard. Eddy turned his head away as he ran his hand through his greasy, tangled hair. "I . . . what?"

"What did I do to piss you off?" Zayt asked in a pleading tone.

"I'm not . . . I'm not pissed at . . . you," Eddy stuttered.

Zayt sighed in relief. "Jesus, Pantsman, you could have fooled me."

"Look, Zayt. I gotta . . . go." He started to move again.

Zayt stepped in front of him once more and smiled.

"Come on, dude. I missed you, man. Let's get a cup of coffee or something. I'm fucking hungry." Zayt reached into the side pocket of his fatigues and pulled out a candy wrapper covering a partially eaten Chocolate Nougat Chewy bar. He unwrapped it and took a bite.

Eddy's memories instantly transported him back to Afghanistan opening a care package sent by his wife. He saw himself pull two Chocolate Nougat Chewy bars out of the Fourth-of-July-themed package and hand them to Zayt. He smiled before he remembered not to.

"Chocolate fucking Nougat Chewy," Eddy said, his head shaking.

"I'm hungry." Zayt defended his action.

"Worst candy bar in the world, dude."

Zayt laughed. "Better than that ramen shit you used to eat. Might as well have eaten a box of salt tablets." Zayt carefully refrained from mentioning Eddy's wife, who sometime sent Eddy pre-packaged noodles, one of his favorite foods.

"Dude, you always did have bad taste," Eddy said.

Zayt walked through the glass doors into the parking lot. Eddy followed.

"Let's get a dog," Zayt said as he walked toward the hot dog vendor on Fruit Street.

Eddy looked down at his broken body. "I gotta go, Zayt."

"A fucking hot dog, dude. He's right there."

Zayt kept walking. He didn't want to give Eddy a chance to turn away, and to Zayt's relief, he didn't.

"Two with the works," Zayt told the vendor, "and two coffees."

Zayt handed the cardboard carrier of food and drink to Eddy and pushed his chair next to a bench on the sidewalk. He took one hot dog and a coffee from the carrier and sat on the bench.

"So, what happened? Why the bandages?"

Zayt chomped half the hot dog in one bite.

"No big deal. Just a couple local kids," Eddy murmured as he lowered his head. "What are you doing here, Zayt?"

"Just having an early lunch, dude."

"No, man. I mean what are you doing in Boston? Why aren't you back home in Philly?"

"Oh. I've been looking for someone," Zayt said as he chewed the remainder of his hot dog. He lifted his eyes and gazed at Eddy.

Eddy took a small bite of the hot dog, as if he didn't trust it. "Oh, yeah? Who?"

"You, Eddy. You."

BIRD'S EYE VIEW

Derek hadn't slept, and he looked terrible. His bloodshot eyes would not focus, and his left hand trembled. He had the appearance of a man going through withdrawal. But Derek never abused drugs nor alcohol. Bradley knew the withdrawal Derek experienced was due to being separated from Cate. Only one thing in the world meant more to Derek than his job, and she lay in a coma just rooms away. And Derek felt helpless, so he punished himself.

Bradley understood that helpless feeling. He had almost let it kill him once . . . more than once if he were honest with himself. He had put himself in harm's way to save others, which often steered the danger toward himself. Derek had helped Bradley deal with his flawed tendency. He intended to do the same for Derek.

"Derek!" Bradley snapped, grabbing Derek's attention. Bradley reached for Derek's shaking hand.

"Yeah?" Derek said softly. It took all the energy he had to turn his head to face Bradley.

Quietly, Bradley said, "Listen to me, Derek. If you don't sleep, you won't be able to help Cate. If you don't sleep, you won't be able to help Cate. Say it. If I don't sleep, I won't be able to help Cate."

"If I . . . don't . . . help Cate." He struggled with the words. Derek's eyelids drew shut. Bradley continued to hold his hand while repeating the phrase over and over until he was sure Derek slept. Then he slid his hand away.

Bradley turned to leave and saw Laney in the doorway. She wore a gentle smile. "You are still the most disarming human being I know, Bradley Whitman," she said as he moved into the hallway.

"And you are a sight for sore eyes." He reached for her to kiss him.

Laney quietly closed the door to Derek's room. She hoped, with him finally sleeping, to minimize any disturbance.

"Laney, I'd like to see Cate," Bradley said.

"Of course."

Laney led Bradley to Cate's room, only two doors further down the hall from Derek's.

"I'll give you a couple minutes," Laney said as she walked away.

Cate wore a brace on her upper body, and her head was heavily bandaged, but to Bradley, she looked like an angel as she lay sleeping. He sat next to her and held her hand.

"Hey, Cate. It's me, Bradley. I know you are usually the one to take care of everyone, and you're probably worried. But I've got this, at least until you come back. I'll take care of Derek and the rest of them. You concentrate on getting better and coming back to us. You're one of the strongest people I know, Cate." A tear streamed down Bradley's cheek. "I won't let you down, I promise. I love you. And Derek really loves you. Take the time you need, but then come back to us, Cate."

Bradley lifted Cate's hand and kissed it. Then he turned and wheeled away.

Laney rejoined Bradley in the hallway. He wiped his face. "Sometimes I just don't understand this world, Laney."

"I know what you mean," she replied and leaned down for another kiss.

"Oh, Doug, really? Cookies? Donuts? Potato chips? This is what you want to feed the families?" asked Lynn.

"Well, we need something good to go with the artichokes, apples, and spinach you're buying. We want to keep their spirits up, not their waistlines down, for chrissake."

"For your information, I planned to make an artichoke dip, one of your favorites. The apples are to make individual apple tarts, and the spinach . . . well, that's just for spinach."

"Why don't we make a big pan of macaroni and cheese? That's the best comfort food in the world," Doug suggested.

"Wonderful idea. And we'll get turkey for sandwiches and vegetables for salad."

Doug grew serious. "Lynn, what do you think we should do about Bradley's birthday?"

"I think it's best if we wait and celebrate the way we planned, all together," she replied.

Doug nodded, "Does that mean no cake and ice cream?"

Bradley assumed it was Holly's grandparents gathered in her and John's hospital room. Not wanting to intrude, he trundled to the other end of the hallway instead to Mike's room. Mike lay in the bed on the far side of the room.

Bradley lightly knocked on the open door, and both Mike and his roommate looked up. Mike smiled.

"Bradley, come on in. This is Paul," he introduced his roommate.

Bradley nodded to Paul.

"Jeez, it's good to see you, Bradley. Oh, happy birthday," Mike said.

"Yeah, well, let's just forget about that, shall we? How are you feeling, Mike?"

"I'm good. Someone upstairs was watching out for us, Bradley. It's a hell of a thing. I saw on the news they said it was a bomb. What the hell happened?"

Mike, his hands wrapped in bandages, also sported a cast on his leg and wrist. A small bandage sat on top of his head.

"We're still trying to figure it out, Mike. We know what and how. We just don't know why."

"Everyone is okay, though, right? The nurses said everyone's okay." Mike noticed a sadness in Bradley that scared him. "Bradley?"

"Derek, Cate, and David are in the ICU. Sheila is in her own room. They are monitoring all of them very closely. Sheila has burns on the front of her body and the left side of her face. They've kept her sedated and will reevaluate her today. Both Derek and David were thrown from the vehicle. They're going to need surgery to repair broken bones, Derek's hip and David's clavicle. They've also got some fractured discs and deep contusions on their head."

Mike's mouth dropped open. He tried to speak, but nothing came out. Then, his voice raspy and unsure, "What about Cate, Bradley?"

"Cate is in a coma," he answered. Bradley decided it wasn't the time to mention Cate's broken neck. He may have already said too much. Mike looked shaken. "I'm sorry, Mike. I shouldn't have sprung that on you."

"No, Bradley. Of course, I want to know the truth. But do me a favor?"

"Anything."

"Let me tell Holly."

"Of course. Mike, I need to talk to all three of you about your activities yesterday. We are creating timelines for everyone involved. I hoped to do that now."

"Okay. Well, let's start with me, and then I'll go talk to Holly."

Mike told Bradley about the uneventful Sunday before the explosion, and Bradley took notes on the pad he kept inside his chair seat pocket.

Then Mike pressed the button to call a nurse or orderly to help him into his wheelchair and push him to Holly and John's room. When Mike saw his parents there, Bradley sensed surprise.

"Mom, Dad, when did you get here?" Mike asked.

"Oh, sweetheart," Mike's mother went to him and hugged and kissed him. She didn't seem to want to let go.

"Mike," Mike's father said, bending down to hug his son. "Thank God you are all okay."

Holly saw Bradley at the door. "Bradley, come in. I want you to meet my grandparents," she smiled. "Grandma and Grandpa, this is Bradley, the one I've been telling you about all these years."

"Oh, my goodness, it's nice to finally meet you. Holly has been talking about you forever," said Holly's grandmother.

"It's nice to meet you," Bradley replied.

"Yvonne. Call me Yvonne. And this is my husband, Sam."

"It's very nice to meet you both," Bradley said.

"Mom and Dad," Mike said. "I need to talk to Holly and John for a moment. Would you mind talking to Bradley out in the hallway, please?"

His parents looked confused but did as Mike asked. They followed Bradley into the hall.

"I hope everything is alright," Yvonne said.

"Everything is fine," Bradley assured her. "Mike just wants to give them an update on the others' condition."

"Oh, I'm sorry. I hadn't thought. How are they?"

"We're hoping for the best. I'll let Mike fill you in. In the meantime, I wanted to let you know that my mother has held some rooms open at the Wyndham across the street if you need a hotel room, assuming you plan on staying. I'm sure she worked out a good deal. She usually does," Bradley chuckled.

Yvonne teared up, and Sam smiled. "That is so kind of her and you. We are so grateful my son and granddaughter have such lovely friends. We did plan on staying overnight but hadn't gotten around to doing anything about it. That would be wonderful."

"Okay, I'll get the information from her. I think she is probably planning dinner for all the family members tonight. Can I put her in touch with you directly?"

"Of course. Mike has my number. You can get it from him. I don't have a clue what it is or how to look it up in my cell phone," Yvonne giggled while Sam shook his head.

"My mom's name is Lynn," Bradley said. "I'll have her call you soon."

When they reentered the room, Holly's eyes were moist. Her mood had shifted. John sat in a chair next to her and held her hand. Mike suggested he and his parents go to his room to visit so Bradley could talk with Holly and John. Bradley made sure to get Yvonne's contact information before they left.

"Are you alright, Holly?" Bradley asked.

Sadness spread across her sweet face. "We've been sitting here laughing and smiling, and the whole time our friends have been in such pain. They should have told us." Her expression turned to one of displeasure. "You should have told me last night, Bradley."

"I'm sorry. I just couldn't, Holly. I'm sorry."

Bradley sunk his head into his chest.

"Honey, you can't blame him," John told her. "Think about what he went through last night."

Holly sat silent, contemplating John's words. "You're right. I can't imagine. I'm sorry, Bradley. I didn't mean to . . . it's just I feel so . . . horrible."

"I know, and I'm sorry I need to ask you to do this, but . . . "

Holly interrupted him. "It's alright. Dad told us you need to know where we were yesterday. You go first, John. I need to think."

"I was home all day. I did some yard work in the morning, but other than that I had a nice relaxing day until—well, you know," John said.

"Did anyone stop by or anything unusual happen?" Bradley asked.

"No, nothing. I was alone most of the day," he replied.

Bradley turned to Holly.

"I spent an hour or so in the morning answering emails, I finished reading a manuscript. Then I went to my hair and nail appointment at eleven in the morning. I left there around twelve-thirty and then stopped at a local boutique and did some shopping. Then I drove home. I think I got home a little before two o'clock. We left to pick up my father at 3:30 and arrived at Cate and Derek's in Medford at 5:29. I know that because it surprised me that we were exactly on time."

"Did you notice anything or anyone unusual during the day?" Bradley asked.

"No, except for the limousine parked at their house."

"You didn't know you would be going to the restaurant in the limousine?" Bradley asked.

"No. That was a nice surprise," Holly smiled without thinking. Then her expression morphed into one of unease. "Derek didn't know either. He had his keys in his hand when we got there, but Sheila said they had the limousine for the whole evening, and we could all go in that."

"What about when you arrived at the house? You said the limousine was already there. Did you see anyone nearby? Maybe walking a dog or jogging?"

Both Holly and John thought about it and shook their heads to indicate they hadn't seen anyone near the car.

"How long were you in the house before getting into the limo?"

"Only a few minutes. In fact, we never closed the front door," Holly said, and John nodded.

"Do you have any idea how long David and Sheila had been there before you showed up?"

"No. But they were all standing by the front door when we rang the bell. I assumed Sheila and David had recently arrived."

Bradley released a deep sigh.

"I'm sorry if that doesn't help, Bradley." Holly sounded dejected.

"But it does help, Holly. Really. The more information we have, the quicker we can find out what happened. It's just as good to eliminate possibilities as it is to find them."

"The doctor said we can probably go home tomorrow, all three of us. Now I don't think I want to."

Holly glanced at John.

"There's nothing you can do here, Holly. You all need to go home and heal. And it's not like you are that far away, right? A two-hour drive."

"Right," she half-smiled.

Bradley said goodbye and promised to see them again before they were discharged. He texted Yvonne's contact information to his mother so she could call her. He wondered if any other family members had arrived to look in on the injured, so he decided to swing by the ICU before he went back to headquarters.

He found Laney speaking with Derek's parents and another couple. He could tell by their similar features the two were Cate and Sheila's parents. Bradley knew Derek's parents, Ron and Marci Richards, but he had only ever met Mr. and Mrs. Wayland briefly at Cate and Derek's wedding. Not wanting to interrupt, he stopped his chair twenty feet from them. When Marci Richards saw him, she motioned for him to join them.

Tears streamed down her tired face, and she embraced Bradley with a fierce hug. She didn't speak a word. Laney continued to discuss their childrens' and David's condition.

"David is in surgery to repair his clavicle. His head wounds are healing, and the swelling of his brain is diminishing. Derek is finally sleeping, so we can't disturb him. He had a hard night. If we can keep him calm, we may be able to operate on his hip tomorrow. We have begun to wean Sheila off sedatives. You should be able to see both her and David later today. There has been no change in Cate's condition but as long as her vitals remain stable, we can be hopeful she will wake soon."

"Mr. and Mrs. Wayland, my name is Bradley Whitman." Bradley held out his hand to shake.

"Bradley, of course. I remember you. The girls talk about you all the time. It's nice to see you again. Call me Janet. And this is Bill," Cate and Sheila's mother said.

"What can you tell us about the accident?" Bill asked Bradley.

"This was no goddamn accident, Bill," Ron Richards said. "It was a bomb. A pipe bomb, the news said." Ron showed great anger and emotion. "What's the Bureau doing about it, Bradley?"

"Everything we can, Ron. We've got every department on the streets today working this case. This is our priority."

"Well, Derek will be glad to hear you have taken control of the investigation. You know he has the utmost confidence in you, and so do we," Ron said.

"Actually, Ron, Agent Nick Gaston is lead on the investigation. I can have him contact you if you would like to talk to him," Bradley said, correcting the misunderstanding.

"What?" Ron asked. He was about to continue but Bradley's phone rang.

"Yeah?" Bradley answered. "On my way." He hung up. "I've got to go. Marci, call my mother to talk about arrangements for your stay. I'll get back to all of you as soon as I know something."

Bradley glanced at Laney. "Would you have them call me when he wakes up?"

Laney smiled and nodded. Bradley shot down the hallway.

The eighth floor of the Chelsea FBI headquarters swarmed with activity. Conversations clashed and became entangled. Bradley likened the noise to the worst song of the worst heavy metal band he ever heard. He could not think straight.

He found Nick in the chaos and drew him down the hall toward Derek's office. Hazel Hadley, Derek's longtime secretary, sat at her desk with headphones slipped over her ears. When she saw Nick and Bradley approach, she removed them.

"Hazel. How are you holding up?" Bradley asked.

"I'll be alright, Agent Whitman. How are Agent Richards and his wife?" she asked sincerely.

"Fighting," Bradley said. "Hazel, we need to use Derek's office for a private conversation, alright?"

"Of course."

Bradley led Nick inside the corner office with a view of the Charles River in the distance.

"Nick, it's a madhouse out there," Bradley stated.

"I know. Everyone came back at once. I need help organizing all this information. That's why I called you. That's your thing, Bradley. I need you here," Nick said.

"Alright. Let me have Mara to help," Bradley replied. "In the meantime, you need to spread these people out. They're getting in each other's way. Move everyone who's reviewing video into the conference room. Those researching previous case files can take their laptops into the briefing room. All other fact gathering can be done downstairs. Just make sure they bring all the information to me and Mara."

"Excellent idea. I'll start moving everyone around right now."

"And Nick, you should use Derek's office. You need to show that you are in command."

"Ah, I don't know about that, Bradley."

"I do. Derek would tell you the same thing. I'll let Hazel know you're moving in here now. When is the last time you talked to Director Davis?"

"He called a few hours ago. I didn't have much to tell him," Nick admitted.

"Call him now. Tell him we have all but eliminated the idea that the bomber knew Derek and his wife would be in the limousine, and it's unlikely the bomb was placed on the limousine at Agent Richards's house."

"Are you sure about that?" Nick asked.

"Pretty sure. But the point is, you need to keep him in the loop completely, or he will get in our way. We don't need him bringing anyone in from outside this office. Make sure you call him multiple times a day." Bradley opened Derek's office door. "Hazel, could you please get Director Davis on the phone for Nick."

"Okay."

Nick rounded Derek's desk and sat in his chair.

Hazel's voice came over the intercom to announce, "Director Davis' office on line two."

Nick took a deep breath, picked up the phone, and pressed the number two on Derek's phone.

"This is Agent Nick Gaston calling for Director Davis, please." After a slight pause, he said, "Yes, I'll hold."

Bradley left the room and stopped at Hazel's desk. "Agent Gaston will temporarily be moving into Derek's office. Please remind him to call Director Davis every few hours to give him an update."

When Nick returned to the chaos of the eighth floor, he got everyone's attention and began assigning work areas to specific groups as he and Bradley had discussed. The volume in the room steadily decreased, allowing Bradley and Mara to concentrate as they dug deep into the piles of information already collected.

"Thank God. The noise was driving me crazy. I didn't know Nick had it in him," Mara said.

"Nick is a man of many surprises," Bradley noted. He wondered if Mara had any idea that Nick had feelings for her. Bradley had discovered that a year and a half before when Nick showed signs of jealousy at Mara's friendship with Bradley's friend, Zayt. But, as far as Bradley knew, Nick had yet to make a move toward more than a working relationship with Mara.

"Apparently, he is. Where do you want to start?" Mara asked.

"Piles. We need to put all of these reports in piles. You tell me the subject of the report, I'll put it in a pile. Then we analyze the piles and decide where to go from there."

"Go back to fuckin' Philly, Zayt," Eddy yelled. "Who asked you to come look for me? Was it my wife? Did Debbie send you?"

"Nobody asked me to look for you, Eddy. I heard you moved out of your house. Christ, Eddy, you didn't even give it a chance. How could you do that to her? You love her!" Since Eddy had brought Debbie into the conversation, Zayt tried to use her.

"None of this is your business. Just leave me the fuck alone."

Something in Zayt snapped. The tension he felt inside needed an escape, and Eddy had opened the door.

"Look, you son-of-a-bitch, I have seven friends in that hospital right there who got blown up last night." Zayt stood and pointed to the hospital. In a short time, he and Eddy had attracted the attention of everyone within earshot.

"They are fighting to stay alive because that's what we do." Zayt's voice cracked as he continued. "We fight to live. Not one of them would think of giving up on their family or friends. We mourn our dead, but we fight to live, because that is what they would want us to do."

Zayt portrayed resentment as his volume rose with each point he tried to make. "It doesn't matter if it's a damn Humvee or a fucking limousine, the bomb doesn't care. It just wants to kill. My friends won't go easily, you can bet on that. Just like your unit fought to stay alive. It's an insult to every one of them that you are wasting what so many suffered to give you. You're letting the bomb win. How do you think your crew would feel about that?"

Zayt breathed heavily and angrily, towering over Eddy who sat in his wheelchair, mouth open and eyes filling. Zayt couldn't remember the last time he lost control of his emotions like that. He flopped down on the bench and hung his head in his hands.

"Jesus, I'm sorry, Eddy. I'm so fucking sorry. I don't know . . . "

Hands hanging by his side, Zayt stood, despondent and defeated. "I'll leave you alone. I won't bother you again." Zayt turned and walked away.

Zayt made it all the way to the corner before Eddy yelled, "Zayt, wait."

"Doug, what are you doing?" Lynn shouted from Bradley's kitchen.

Doug bent down to the cabinet below the unique bookcase hanging on Bradley's wall. Bradley's grandfather had been a master at turning discarded things into usable, one-of-a-kind items. He had taken the body of a piano and turned it into a beautiful bookcase that hung on Bradley's wall. Doug didn't appreciate his father's talents as much as Bradley did. And he didn't appreciate that Bradley, as a boy, had taken to collecting junk off the street and storing it in their garage for his own projects.

"I'm looking in the liquor cabinet to see what I need to buy. I think we will all be ready for a drink tonight," Doug said. "He doesn't have much here. His wine rack is almost empty, too."

The wine rack Doug referred to had a previous life as a library card catalogue cabinet altered by Bradley's grandfather. "What kind of wine goes best with honey-glazed ham and macaroni and cheese?"

"Riesling and Zinfandel. But get a mix to fill up Bradley's case for him. Laney likes Merlots. And make sure there is beer in the refrigerator, and we have everything we need for martinis."

"It would have been cheaper to hire a caterer," Doug mumbled.

"What?" Lynn hollered.

"Nothing," Doug hollered back. Under his breath, Doug said, "I know you heard me first time."

"Douglas Jackson Whitman, are you seriously complaining about money when our friends are in the hospital?" Lynn asked, perturbed.

"No, I'm seriously complaining about you pretending not to hear me when I know you hear every word spoken within a three-mile radius."

"Just what are you insinuating?"

All the while, Rusty lay on the floor, his head veering from one, then the other, and back again, like watching the volley of a ping pong match.

"Nothing, I'm sorry. I'll fill up Bradley's wine rack, refrigerator, and liquor cabinet. Is there anything else I should get?"

"Yes. We need an eight-foot folding table and some chairs, about eight of them. Maybe we could borrow them from the REACH community. I'm sure Zayt wouldn't mind. Tell him we will bring them back in the morning."

"I'm sorry I asked," Doug whispered.

Lynn said, "What?"

Doug shook his head and left through the front door.

The morning had turned to afternoon before Nick asked Bradley, Jim, and Mara to meet in Derek's office.

"Jim, tell us everything you found out about the bomb," Nick said.

After reviewing the construction of the bomb, Jim made some key observations.

"In my opinion, after looking at how the bomber made this device, where it was placed, and how they intended for it to detonate, this person did not discriminate. It didn't matter to him, or her, who was in the limousine at the time the bomb exploded.

"I also don't think they meant to kill anyone," Jim continued. "There just wasn't enough powder to ensure that outcome and there easily could have been. The bomb had to be small in diameter so it wouldn't completely block the exhaust. If it was too big, it would have caused the limousine to stall. But it was short in length. A longer pipe would have allowed for more powder. Also, there was no way of knowing when or if the bomb would explode.

"Let me explain," Jim went on. "Black powder can self ignite at a temperature of 450 degrees Celsius—that's 842 degrees Fahrenheit. The typical exhaust system of a car runs between 600- and 930-degrees Fahrenheit but can reach temperatures of 1,600 degrees if driven hard or for long periods. So the factors involved are too numerous to determine exactly where the device would explode. How far would the limo go, how fast, how much idling—all are factors that determine how hot the exhaust would get."

Jim took a deep breath and continued. "Then there is the adhesive. If you put a cylindrical pipe bomb into a cylindrical exhaust system and bounce it around, what are the odds it stays inside the pipe? Not very good. It would need an adhesive to ensure the pipe didn't end up on a downtown Boston neighborhood street. This means that whoever placed the bomb in the tailpipe would have to have used an inorganic based adhesive that could withstand temperatures of up to 650 degrees Celsius or 1,202 degrees Fahrenheit.

"Are you still with me?" Jim asked.

Bradley, Mara, and Nick shrugged their shoulders and nodded.

"Okay. I found fragments of the pipe caps with thread-like marks on the outside of the caps. That is unusual. I would fully expect the two endcaps of the bomb to have threads on the inside, but the outside is normally smooth. This tells me that the bomber went to great lengths in order to use the same ceramic thread-locker adhesive to help keep the bomb in place inside the tailpipe as he did to keep the caps on each end of the bomb.

"If the bomb maker just applied the thread-locker to the smooth outer side of the pipe," Jim continued, "it would not have stuck to the tailpipe as well. The perpetrator gave it some thought—so, a rudimentary device without a detonator, placed in a vehicle that may be driving for one mile or for twenty miles, seems like a shot in the dark. Why go through the trouble of threading the outside of the pipe? Why not take your chances with duct tape or something easier? Why put so much thought into that when the rest is so . . . unreliable?"

Bradley, Mara, and Nick just looked at each other with questioning expressions. Then they focused their attention back to Jim.

"He didn't want it to end up on a Boston neighborhood street. It shows some compassion. He didn't want to hurt innocent bystanders. That may also explain why the charge of the bomb was so small. He couldn't be sure it wouldn't detonate near a schoolyard or park. Anyway," Jim said, "those are my preliminary findings."

"Jesus," Bradley smiled, "they're damn good ones."

"How so? What does it tell you, Bradley?" Nick asked.

"It tells me we can stop looking at previous and current FBI cases. This has nothing to do with Derek. Nobody, not even Derek, knew he would ever set foot in that limousine. It narrows our target focus to just a few possibilities."

"Well? Which possibilities?" Nick sounded impatient as Bradley worked through his thoughts.

"The limousine company, the limousine driver, or the movie production company."

"I've got to call Director Davis," Nick said.

"Mara and I will start digging into the information we have on those three components," Bradley said.

Mara and Jim left the room. Bradley hung behind and shut the door.

"Nick, I wouldn't completely dismiss the Derek angle when you talk to the director. Just say the information is leading away from that or something like that. Just in case we're wrong. Also, I think we should keep everyone on course with their individual investigations, at least for now. That way we can be sure we covered every angle."

"I agree. At least until we have something more concrete to go on," Nick said. Then, as Bradley turned to leave, he said, "Thanks for keeping me grounded, Bradley." Bradley waved his hand in the air as he left the room.

Mara had already begun moving piles of paper. She put the reports concerning the limousine company, driver, and movie production company on Bradley's desk. The others, she put aside.

"Mara, why don't you take the limousine driver and the limousine company. Get Morrison to help you. I'll start with the production company."

Mara picked up the reports pertaining to Henry Case, the deceased limo driver, and brought them to her desk. She texted Tony Morrison that they had a new avenue to pursue.

Bradley perused the movie company reports to see who interviewed the people from the filming.

Agent Christine Woods usually worked the white-collar crime unit. Having nearly fourteen years of experience behind her, the thirty-four-year-old held an impressive record. Her colleagues knew her best for her investigation into and the subsequent conviction involving insider trading activities of a prominent Boston politician who previously sat on the board of directors of a pharmaceutical company. She was intuitive and tenacious.

Bradley found her reports impeccable. He welcomed her brevity while noting her comprehension of the information the investigation required. The papers revealed she had spoken to the film's director, multiple camera operators, the transportation coordinator, and the two drivers of the shuttle limousines. Based on her interviews, Bradley felt the beginnings of an itch, a typical feeling he got when he felt the need to know more particulars about certain statements.

Bradley looked up Agent Woods's extension in his directory and dialed.

"Agent Woods," she answered.

"Agent Woods, this is Agent Whitman from the eighth floor. I'd like to talk to you about your interaction with the movie company this morning. May I come down and see you?" Bradley said.

"Of course, Agent Whitman. I can make some time now if you'd like."

"Yes, thank you. I'll be right down." Bradley hung up the phone.

She stood by the elevator on the third floor. They had met before but only briefly and without much interaction. That's the way things were with Bradley. He performed most of his work at home. It was unusual for him to spend so much time in the office.

"Hello, Agent Whitman," she said as she held out her hand to shake.

Bradley shook her hand and said, "Bradley. Please call me Bradley."

"And I'm Christine," she replied.

He followed her to her tidy desk neatly topped with folders, magazines, and newspaper articles. Bradley got the impression she had put them aside when he called.

"Christine, there are a couple of points I would like your opinion on regarding your interviews from this morning. But first I want to thank you for your help. All of us on the eighth floor appreciate it."

"We're family. That's what we do, Bradley. How is Agent Richards? And his wife?"

"Last I knew Derek was finally resting, but his wife is still in a coma. We are hopeful, though."

He paused, then observed, "You said in your report that the two shuttle drivers didn't have much to say about Henry Case, the chauffeur, and you thought it may be an avenue to explore. What impression did you get from them?"

"They didn't like him. Neither one came right out and said it, but it certainly seemed implied."

"Did they give you any indication of why?"

"No. I tried to pursue the subject with each of them individually, but neither were interested in talking about him. It's almost as if the subject of Henry Case was taboo."

Bradley made a note on his pad. "Okay, thank you. We'll get on that. Excuse me for a moment."

Bradley texted the information to Mara. Then he asked, "Am I right that the travel coordinator told you that David Carson didn't ask to use the limousine for the evening until midday yesterday?"

"That's right. He said David assumed the limo had already been reserved for the evening and was surprised to find out it was available."

"Great. That helps. So, the director—I'm sorry, I can't remember his name," Bradley said.

"Cecil Rhymes," Christine chuckled. "How could he be anything other than a Hollywood director with a name like that?"

Bradley laughed. "True. But I'd bet he's no DeMille." Bradley referred to one of the most successful and prolific film directors and producers in movie history, Cecil B. DeMille.

"Who was born right here in Massachusetts, by the way," Christine added. She paused, then said, "Sorry, I don't know why I brought that fact up. It just came out."

"It's alright. I'm a fact geek from way back. Just ask anyone I went to school with," he smiled. "So, Cecil Rhymes mentioned something about the filming of this movie being . . . " Bradley looked at his notes, " . . . challenging. How did he mean that?"

"In different ways, really. First, he said the location shoots were in difficult areas, such as downtown Boston and New York City. He also said that, since they arrived in Boston, a lot of little things have gone wrong."

"Like what?"

"Some of their gear has gone missing. They had a small fire in the make-up trailer, and some drunk pulled a fire alarm at three o'clock in the morning at the Ritz-Carlton Hotel where all the top-billed actors and actresses are staying. Didn't you read about that in the paper?"

"No. When did all that happen?"

"Within the last week, since they started filming," Christine said with a slight grin.

"Who's the drunk who pulled the alarm? Is he with the production company?"

"Oh, they don't know who did it. They just have video of the back of a guy holding a bottle of whiskey. It shows him stumbling down the hotel hallway. Then he reaches out and pulls the alarm and stumbles away. A terrible thing to do, I know, but the video was all over the news, and it is hysterical to watch.

"The Boston Police Department put it out to the public to see if anyone could identify the guy," she continued. "No luck so far. Anyway, everyone had to evacuate the hotel while the fire department did their thing. It took almost two hours before the guests could go back to their rooms."

Bradley noted the smirk on Christine's face and gathered she was not a fan of Hollywood stars.

"I'd like to see that video," Bradley said, curious about the incident.

Christine brought YouTube up on her computer and typed the words, *Ritz-Carlton drunk alarm*. Up popped the video. It had more than five million views in only three days, giving it the distinction of going viral.

Bradley watched with interest. The man never showed his face, and the clothes he wore disguised his body type. He also wore a hat, a wide-brimmed fedora that covered his head completely. The only visible part of his body was the right hand, which held the bottle of whiskey for everyone to see.

Christine observed Bradley as he watched the video. He replayed it three times. "What is it?"

"I'm not sure, but I would like to talk to this guy," Bradley said, not smiling.

Mara and Tony dug into Henry Case's life. Born in East Boston, Henry spent stints as a young adult in juvenile hall with his best friend, Gino Calletti, for assault, breaking and entering, and possession of stolen property.

"He got married at the age of nineteen to a woman who must have been a good influence on him, because his police record stayed clean for six years," Mara said.

"Or," Tony noted, "maybe he just got better at his crimes."

"It says he had four kids by the time he was twenty-four. When was his next conviction?" Mara asked Tony.

"When he was twenty-four."

"What did he do for a living?"

"He drove a cab. Then he executed a home invasion on Beacon Hill. The woman he robbed recognized him as her cab driver even though he wore a disguise, and he went to Walpole State Prison to serve a twenty-year term. He got out six years ago."

"He needed a job, so he went to see his old friend Gino, who now owns Back Bay Limousine Service. Henry's record is clean since he's been out," Mara stated.

"In the fifth year of his incarceration, his wife divorced him. We need to talk to her and to Gino Calletti," Tony said.

Mara's phone buzzed. She looked and saw a text from Bradley. *Shuttle drivers did not like Henry Case, may have been afraid of him.*

Mara showed the text to Tony.

"Let's go see Gino," Tony said.

It took them twenty-five minutes to drive the five miles to Clarendon Street in the Back Bay. They made small talk the entire way, neither wanting to think about Derek and Cate lying in the hospital, until Tony parked the car.

"We need to be smart about this, Tony. We can't go in there with guns blazing. Derek is counting on us. We play sympathetic, lost-your-best-friend roles today. Agreed?" Mara asked.

"Agreed."

All activity stopped as the two federal officers walked through the door. Every eye in the spotless garage concentrated on them.

Mara smiled at the closest person to her, a man in a chauffeur suit and cap holding a cloth that he had been using to polish the outside of a limousine. She showed him her FBI identification badge and asked where she might find Gino Calletti.

The man gestured to a wooden stairway with a glassed-in room at the top. Gino stood at one of the windows.

"Thank you," Mara politely said.

Mara and Tony ascended the stairs. A large man wearing a black suit opened the door before they could knock.

"Come in," Gino said from behind his desk. "Please, have a seat."

"Thank you, Mr. Calletti. I'm Agent Thompkins, and this is Agent Morrison." She showed her badge. "We are from the Chelsea headquarters. We know this is a bad time for you, and we are very sorry for your loss. But we would like to ask you a couple of questions about Henry Case if you don't mind."

"Ask away, Agent Thompkins."

"Could you tell me how your business works regarding drivers? Do they have their own cars, or do they drive whatever you need them to?"

"Each driver takes care of their own ride. They keep 'em clean and gassed. Sometimes we gotta switch it up and sometimes we gotta use multiple drivers when the client wants 24/7 service, like these movie people. But we didn't need to use anyone else 'cuz Henry wanted to be on call for every shift. I guess he needed the money."

"Is there anyone you know of who would want to hurt Henry?"

Gino laughed. "Only a coupla dozen. But kill? Nah, I wouldn't go that far."

"We're not entirely sure the device was meant to kill, Mr. Calletti. It may have been meant to warn someone. Could you tell us about those couple of dozen people?"

A quick flash of surprise crossed Gino's face before he reined it in. "If one of 'em wanted to hurt Henry, they woulda taken a pipe to his kneecaps, not a sissy pipe bomb. Look, the guy was a prick to almost everyone he met except his kids and grandkids. He was doin' his best to stay outta trouble for 'em."

"Well, it was a sissy pipe bomb that killed him. One placed in your limousine," Tony said adamantly.

Mara shot Tony a quick glare.

"I'm just saying, if someone blew up *my* limousine with one of *my* oldest friends in it, I'd want to do everything I could to find that person," Tony explained in a more subdued tone.

Gino narrowed his eyes and pursed his lips. "Agent Morrison, is it? It's your job to find out who killed Henry, not mine. But 'cuz Henry and I go way back, I'll tell you this. Henry liked to gamble. Sometimes he got himself in deep. Have a nice day, agents."

"Thank you for your time, Mr. Calletti," Mara said as they left.

Once back in the car, Mara said, "Henry's gambling debt could have been the motive for sending Henry a message."

"Yeah. Or a message to Calletti? We both know there's something else going on there," Tony said.

"Alright, I'll take Henry, you take Calletti and his business. Let's get back to the office."

ESTABLISHING SHOT

Mara and Tony got back to the office at three-thirty. Mara noticed a difference in the way the throng of agents conducted business. Like a well-planned highway system, people stayed in their lane, conversed quietly at desks to exchange information, then yielded into the flow of traffic to their next destination.

Impressive, she thought. She began to see Nick as other than an arrogant agent who was good at his job, but also a leader. Mara felt a surprising stir at the thought.

Bradley brought her back to the present as he approached her and Tony near the elevator.

"How did it go?" Bradley asked.

"Interesting. You?" Mara asked.

"The same. Nick is waiting for us to fill him in."

Bradley led them down the hall to Derek's office.

Hazel hit the intercom and said, "Agents Whitman, Thompkins, and Morrison are here to see you, sir."

"Thank you. Send them in, Hazel."

Nick's voice came out of the speaker. Mara smiled.

Nick sat behind the desk, a messy pile of paper in front of him.

"Alright. What have we got?" Nick asked.

Bradley motioned for Mara to begin.

"It is feasible that the chauffeur, Henry Case, could have been the intended target. His criminal history is extensive. He got out of Walpole six years ago after a twenty-year home invasion conviction and went to work for his old friend Gino Calletti at Back Bay Limousine Services. According to Calletti, Henry has a gambling problem which sometimes gets him in deep with collectors. My next step is to find out who he owed money to and how badly they wanted it," Mara finished.

"That sounds like a good motive to me," Nick grinned.

"Yeah, well, I'm not sure this Calletti guy's information can be trusted," Tony said. "We walked into that place, and every lip shut as tight as a trunk hiding a dead body. He gave up the gambling thing too quickly. I don't trust him. I'm going to check with the organized crime unit of the Boston PD and see if they have anything on Calletti or his business. I think it warrants some digging."

"Okay. I agree," Nick said.

Bradley spoke next. "The movie production company has been experiencing difficulties since they got here a week ago. The disruptions have been small but unusual. First, some of their sound equipment went missing in broad daylight during filming. Also, they had a fire in the makeup trailer. The fire chief says it seems to have started in a duffel bag that was placed in the makeup storage closet.

"Although he can't say for sure," Bradley continued, "the accident may have occurred due to spontaneous combustion of rags covered with oil-based residue that were stuffed in the duffel bag. No one I spoke with had knowledge of where the duffel bag came from or how it got there. Then, a few days ago, the fire alarm at the Ritz-Carlton, where the stars of the movie are staying, was pulled during the night."

"I saw that on the news," Nick said. "The video is all over social media."

"It's hilarious," Tony said. "The guy's drunk out of his mind."

"Maybe," Bradley said. He received inquiring glances from the others. "I've got the lab guys enhancing the video now. Something seems off about it."

"Bradley, over five million people have watched that video. What could you see that millions of other people can't?" Nick asked.

"Maybe nothing," Bradley looked to Mara, who studied him hard. She trusted his instincts too much to dismiss his hunch.

"Okay. Three small instances that could be explained away," Tony scoffed.

"Four," Bradley stated. "Let's not forget the limousine service provided that car to the movie production company for its entire stay."

"Right. It's worth pursuing. It looks like you've each got some work to do. What do you think about ceasing the other avenues of investigation? We could use the manpower to move more quickly on these three theories," Nick said.

"I think it makes sense now," Bradley said. "Judging by the information we've got, I don't see how any of the others could have been the target."

They all agreed.

"Alright. I'll call them in, and we'll split up into three teams. Each one of you take lead of your team and report to me at every turn."

Mara's eyes shot open. "Wait. What?"

Nick looked at Mara. "What? Is there a problem?"

"You want me to lead a team?"

"Yes, Mara. You're already invested in Henry Case. Pick your team and get to it," Nick said insistently.

Mara blinked rapidly, then replied, "I'm on it," as she had heard Nick say so many times before.

Bradley unsuccessfully tried to hold back his grin.

"Everybody out of here. I have a mound of paperwork to go through."

Mara, Tony, and Bradley made their way down the hall. Behind them, they heard Nick holler. "Hazel, could you come in here? I need your help."

The three chuckled at the thought of Nick stuck behind a pile of paper.

"You built this place?" Eddy asked Zayt as the van equipped to transport the handicapped drove up to the REACH community of tiny houses.

"Not just me. We had a lot of help."

A wooden walkway had been built on top of the sand throughout the entire complex. What had originally been a sandpit housed fifty-four residents year-round with plans calling for adding twenty more units in the next two years. Zayt built his own place on the back edge of the pit where he used to live in his plywood and corrugated tin structure.

The van stopped there to let them out.

"Come on in. It's not much, but it's home," Zayt said.

The two-room dwelling had minimal furniture and no decorations. The living room also served as the kitchen and dining room and boasted a futon, a round table with two chairs, a small cooktop, a microwave, and an apartment-sized refrigerator. The bedroom held a double bed, a small dresser, and a closet. In between was a bathroom, a walk-in shower, and compostable toilet. All the tiny houses, including Zayt's cabin, were built for wheelchair accessibility, but Zayt's was the only one with a private bathroom and cooking area. The other residents shared facilities.

"I see your interior decorating hasn't changed," Eddy said.

"I don't need much."

"No, man. This is great. How do you pay for it?"

"I work here. I'm in charge of security and enforcement. I also help in the kitchen when they need me."

"You're a fucking cook?" Eddy asked.

"No way. I wash dishes or set tables. There are much better cooks here than me. Everyone who lives here works here. It's the rule. Housing and food are provided as long as people live within the rules and pull their weight."

"How many are vets?"

"It varies. The average would be around sixty percent, I'd say. We have people moving in and out all the time. Most times they move on to a real job and a new place to live. Sometimes we lose a few who go back to the streets. I take those personally. I don't like losing people."

"Yeah. I remember that about you." Eddy went quiet, jerking his head occasionally, his eyes searching for something that wasn't there. Then he said, "That's why you've been looking for me."

"I guess. I don't really know. Sometimes I just get shit in my head, and I don't stop until it's done. That's kind of how all this happened." Zayt spread his arms, palms up.

Zayt noticed Eddy's eyes droop and his head bob slightly.

"Dude, you look like you could use some rest." Zayt pulled the futon out so it lay flat and got a blanket from his bedroom closet. "I've got work to do. Relax. Mi casa es su casa." He didn't plan to say it. It just came out. "Mi casa es su casa" was what their SEAL buddies said to each other when they shared holes in the desert floor, rooftop sniper nests, or any of the uncomfortable places they had to be. Knowing it would be an uphill battle to get him to stay, Zayt left Eddy alone.

"He's awake," Bradley heard Laney say through his phone. "He's asking for you."

"Are you with him now?" Bradley asked Laney.

"I'm out in the hall."

"Could you hand the phone to him, please?"

"Alright."

Bradley could hear Laney walk into Derek's room and the beep of monitors.

"Bradley?" Derek asked.

"Yeah, Derek. It's me. How are you feeling?"

"Like I got hit by a bus. Where are you?"

"At the office."

"What's happening with the investigation?"

"Derek, I've got to put a few things in motion here, and then I'll come by to fill you in, I promise. I'll be there within the hour. I promise."

"Okay."

Bradley heard Laney speaking with Derek.

"Are you still there, Bradley?" Laney asked.

"Yes, I'm here. Leave the room, please, Laney."

"I'm out in the hall again."

"He doesn't sound right. What's going on?"

"He's showing signs similar to indicators of depression or intense guilt. When you see him, he may not come across as the confident man you know. Be prepared for that."

"Alright. How are you doing, Laney? Have you been home yet?"

"No, not yet. But I'm leaving very soon. I will probably be gone by the time you get here," Laney sighed.

"I'll wait for you to call me. I wouldn't want to wake you. I love you, Laney Weaver."

"I love you, Bradley Whitman. I'll call you later."

Surrounded by a team of four agents, Bradley brought them up to speed on the theory that the movie company had been the target of the bombing. He sent a team to follow up on stolen lighting equipment and talk to the lighting crew, one to determine the outcome of the makeup trailer fire and talk to employees from makeup and costume, one to talk to Ritz-Carlton personnel and security, and one to talk to actors and actresses. In each case, agents were to look for reasons someone might want to disrupt or prevent the film from going forward.

Bradley realized he knew nothing about the movie being filmed. Whether a drama, action, or comedy might be helpful to know. He didn't even know the name of it. What he did know was that the movie was based on a novel written by one of Holly's clients. He decided to talk to Holly again after seeing Derek. Besides, he had promised to see her before she checked out the next day and wasn't sure if he would have time in the morning.

Mara, self-conscious and surrounded by FBI agents with a lot more experience than she had, reviewed the theory that the limousine driver may have been the intended target.

Checking her notes multiple times to make sure she got the facts correct, she told her team about the pipe bomb. She discussed the gambling angle and how they should plunge into the underground gambling scene. Someone would need to look into Henry's past to see if anyone held a large enough grudge to warrant the action and finally the possibility that someone from the limousine company resented Henry enough to discredit or hurt him.

Once she finished, she saw nothing but eager faces awaiting a job. She passed out assignments and asked for reports as often as possible. Her group dispersed, and Mara felt a surge of satisfaction. She sat back in her chair and looked over at Bradley as he packed things up.

"Hey," she said.

"Hey," he grinned. "You looked like you were in your element over there. How did it feel?"

Mara smiled. "Powerful."

Bradley nodded. "'A power that can easily and unintentionally become bastardized.' A quote from a very wise man," Bradley said.

"It's good. Who said it?"

"The same man who's right now lying in a hospital bed and feels like he got hit by a bus. I'm not sure if I'll be back tonight. Call me if you need me."

"Goodnight, Bradley."

"Goodnight, Agent Thompkins."

When he was halfway to the hospital, Bradley's phone rang. The screen in his truck told him his father was calling. He used the handsfree button on his steering wheel to answer the call.

"Hey, Dad."

"Bradley, hi. Your mother wanted me to call and tell you that dinner is all set at your house tonight. Ron and Marci Richards are bringing Bill and Janet Wayland. And Yvonne and Sam will also be joining us. David's parents are still on their way. They won't get in until tomorrow morning. They were in Bora Bora when they got the call. We haven't heard if John has anyone here."

"Great. I'm on my way back to the hospital. I'll stop and see Holly and John to find out about his family. Don't wait for me to start. I've got things to take care of."

"Yes, I understand. But Bradley, it would be a boost to all of them if you could at least let them know the FBI is making progress. I assume you are?"

Bradley chuckled, understanding that his dad fished for information. "Yes, Dad. We are. But that's all I can say. I'll get home as soon as I can. Thanks, Dad. And thank Mom for me too."

Many times in his life, Bradley had taken his parents for granted. This was not one of them. He tried to recall if there were ever a time when either one of them disappointed him or wasn't thinking about him, and he couldn't. Even when he was a child with all the extra attention he required, his parents never complained nor showed signs of wanting a different sort of life. And even more recently, when they discovered Bradley's continuing difficulty in dealing with his own reality, they were there for him—not to judge or tell him how he should feel, but to understand how he did feel. Maybe, he realized, it had taken him thirty years to admit just how lucky he was.

Bradley noticed some activity happening in Cate's room a few doors beyond Derek's. He wanted to see what was happening, but Derek spotted him as he tried to sneak by the open door.

"Hey!" Derek yelled.

Rather than cause a problem, Bradley stopped and turned into Derek's room.

"Where the hell were you going?" Derek asked.

"Huh? Oh, I was just thinking and missed your room," Bradley lied. "You look a little better than you did this morning."

Derek's forehead scrunched as his eyes searched for a memory.

"What? Were you here this morning?" Derek asked.

"Yeah." Bradley turned his head slightly.

"I don't remember that. What did we talk about?" A disconcerted edge snuck into Derek's voice.

"Just that you needed to rest, Derek, that's all. I was only here for a few minutes." Bradley tried to calm him. "You were very tired."

"Cate still hasn't woken up, Bradley."

"She will, Derek. It hasn't been that long. I know it seems like it has, but it hasn't. She's going to wake up. And when she does, you'll be ready to take care of her. What's happening with your hip?"

"Tomorrow. They're going to operate tomorrow. I'm getting a titanium hip," Derek said with little emotion.

"Good. You'll be chasing Cate around the house in no time." Bradley tried to smile.

"Enough, Bradley. No more small talk. What the hell happened?" Derek asked.

"How much do you remember me telling you?"

Closing his eyes and squeezing them hard, Derek searched his memory. He put his hand up to his forehead as if trying to hold the memories in place.

"I remember you saying it was the FBI's case now and it has something to do with a bomb in the limo."

"Yeah, well actually it was a small pipe bomb in the tailpipe of the limousine. We don't think the bomber intended to kill anyone."

"What the fuck does it matter if he tried to kill anyone? My fucking wife is in a coma," Derek yelled.

Bradley heard the nurse run down the hall before she entered the room.

"I'll have to ask you to leave, sir," she said to Bradley.

"No, no," Derek said to the nurse. "I'm okay. I'm sorry. I'm fine. No more outbursts." He turned to Bradley, "I'm sorry. I didn't mean to . . . I'm sorry."

The nurse glared at Bradley, then left the room.

"She's not going to let me in here if you keep doing that, Derek."

"I know. I can do this. Go on."

"These are our working theories. The bomber was sending a message to someone. Our first thought was that it involved you and the FBI. But that's not the case, Derek. This incident had nothing to do with you. Nothing. This is not your fault. Do you understand what I'm saying?"

"How do you know?"

"Because we've investigated it. No one knew you would be in that limousine. No one could have guessed. And the car was in full view the whole time it was parked in front of your house. It's just not possible based on the evidence."

Bradley waited for the words to sink in. He knew Derek thought he was the cause of Cate being in a coma and the others getting hurt. He could see the heaviness in Derek's eyes. But as he let the facts settle in, Derek couldn't help but release the anxiety he'd been harnessing.

Derek put both hands over his face and wept. Bradley sat quietly with his head down. He waited for Derek's emotions to run their course.

Derek wiped his face and, with a tone more confident and determined, he said, "Go on."

"We've got three avenues we are pursuing. First, the chauffeur had a criminal background and possible current gambling debts. Second, the limousine company is owned by someone of questionable character who may be running an illegal business or businesses on the side. Lastly, the movie production company has experienced multiple incidents that could be considered suspicious. It's possible someone does not want the film to succeed."

"You've considered every other avenue?"

"We have. We covered our bases before we honed in on these three motives."

"Who have you got leading each unit?" Derek asked.

"Ah. Tony is leading the limousine company angle, Mara the chauffeur, and I'm on lead with the movie company investigation."

"What? Jesus, Bradley, you can't lead a unit and be supervisor. What the fuck is Nick doing?"

"Nick is the supervisor, Derek. Nick is in charge."

Derek's face dropped. Bradley could see his brain working. For the first time since the accident, Bradley felt that Derek thought clearly.

"Director Davis put Nick in charge," Derek said, eyeing Bradley.

"And rightfully so."

"No," Derek said as he slowly shook his head.

"He's doing well, Derek. We are all working together to find this bastard. And we will, I promise."

Derek went quiet. His mind raced. "Make sure Nick keeps Davis informed. If he doesn't, Davis will bring in someone from the outside."

"He's talking to Davis every three hours. I put Hazel on that."

Derek showed signs of a grin. "Good." Then his expression turned serious, and Derek said, "Jesus, Bradley, I just remembered something."

Bradley sat up straight. "What, Derek?"

"Happy birthday."

When Bradley left Derek's room, he looked to the right to see if there was still activity around Cate's door. There was not. He stopped at the nurse's desk to speak with Miranda.

"What was going on with Cate, Miranda? What was all the activity about?"

"Mrs. Richards's neurologist ordered an electroencephalogram to be performed on her."

"That tests brainwaves, right?"

"Yes."

"Well? What did they find?"

"I'm sorry, I don't know. You'll need to talk to the neurologist."

"Okay. Thank you, Miranda."

Bradley thought about calling Laney but didn't want to take the chance of waking her. Instead, he made his way to Holly and John's room.

Their visitors gone, Holly and John had snuggled side-by-side in Holly's hospital bed, Holly wrapped in John's arms. The television played, but neither of them seemed to be watching.

Hating to interrupt their sense of peace, Bradley knocked lightly on the door.

"Bradley!" Holly lit up when she saw him. "Come in."

"I swear you two could make a mop closet feel like a honeymoon suite," Bradley smiled. "I'm sorry to interrupt."

John lifted himself on his elbow, his hand holding his head. He peeked at Holly and smirked. "We didn't think to try the mop closet."

Holly giggled like a six-year-old girl holding cotton candy at a carnival. "John!" Holly said, pretending she felt mortified.

Then, "You are never an interruption, Bradley. Besides, I feel terrible about the way I treated you this morning. John is right. This whole thing has been horrible for you, too. I was just upset. I'm sorry."

"Holly, we've been friends for too long. You know you can always say whatever you feel. But I'm afraid this is not a strictly personal visit. I need to ask you some questions. Are you up to it?"

"Absolutely. I want to help any way I can."

Bradley rolled his chair next to Holly's bed. John moved to a chair on the other side while Holly used the electronic button to raise herself to a sitting position.

"How much do you know about the filming of this movie?" Bradley started.

"The filming? Not much. I know they shot most of it in Hollywood, but they have location shoots in New York and here in Boston. I don't know the schedule, but I could get it for you if that would help."

"No need. I think we may have that already. So you, as the publisher of the book, aren't involved in the movie production?"

"That's right."

"What about the author of the novel?"

"I know Micah has been on the set, but he doesn't have any say in the screenplay or how the movie is filmed."

"None? I would think the author of the story would be of great use to the director or producers."

Holly laughed. "Yes, you would think so, right? But that's not the way Hollywood usually works, Bradley. Once they buy the rights to a story, they can do whatever they want with it. Sure, the author can make money by selling the rights, but they give up any artistic input. The screenwriters and production staff take over. Now and then, they involve the author but not very often."

"But I've seen movies where they list the author as a consultant or one of the screenwriters."

"That doesn't happen very often, and it's usually only with big name authors, you know, regular best-selling types. I'll tell you what I know about the Hollywood process from my perspective. They find a story they think will make them money and fill the author's head with dreams of fame, fortune, and future deals. But once that contract is signed, they want nothing more to do with them. The author has no standing, and they are considered a nuisance. They usually get invited to watch the filming process and probably the movie debut but only from a seat behind the scenes."

"That's got to be very frustrating for an author."

"Very. The first time one of my authors got a movie contract, I was so excited. But I and the writer learned quickly that it's not all it's cracked up to be. Unless an author just wants to make money and doesn't care if their work gets commercialized, Hollywood is not the place for them."

"Tell me about this author, Micah. Tell me about how you came to publish his book and the relationship you have with him."

"Okay. His name is Micah Wistoff. He's in his early fifties and lives in Pelham, a small town next to our town of Amherst. He walked into my office about five years ago with his manuscript. I don't always take unsolicited manuscripts but sometimes I get a feeling and decide to take a chance."

Bradley interrupted. "What do you mean by unsolicited?"

"Manuscripts are usually sent to me by an agent not directly from the author. But, like I said, sometimes I make an exception."

Bradley nodded as he made notes. "And you liked it."

"Yes. His writing style is very honest and simple. But it suits the story line," Holly said.

"What is the book about?"

"It's a crime novel—a lot of action, very fast-paced. Fiction readers love that. That's why James Patterson has sold so many books. Not that Micah is a James Patterson, but his story is compelling and a good read."

"Is he upset about the way Hollywood is treating his novel?"

"No, I don't think so. We discussed it at length before he made the deal. I warned him. I think he is just happy for the money and recognition." Holly paused and smiled. "You know how they say every person has one good book in them?"

"Yeah."

"This is Micah's one book. He just got very, very lucky," Holly said.

"Lucky he found you," Bradley smiled.

A rosy flush crept across Holly's face. "He's an interesting story, really. He grew up in the Boston area, had a difficult childhood, and got himself in trouble. He ended up at Walpole state prison for ten years. I didn't ask why, and he didn't tell me."

"Is that when he wrote the novel?" Bradley asked.

"That's when he started it. He finished once he was released."

"What's the name of it?"

"*Meet Your Maker.*"

"It's catchy."

"I thought so, but apparently Hollywood has a different idea. They changed the movie title to *Maker's Mark*. They think it will sell better."

"*Meet Your Maker* sounds more ominous. *Maker's Mark* just makes me want to pour a drink," Bradley said.

"Maybe they hoped for easy advertising and endorsements," Holly chuckled. "You would make a great publisher, Bradley. You, with your love of reading."

"Maybe I would have gone that way if I didn't get into the FBI," Bradley grinned.

"Oh, please. That was a forgone conclusion. We all knew where you would end up."

"Yes, and here we are." Bradley grew somber. "John, my mother wanted me to ask if you have family in town or coming to town."

"Tell her I said thank you, but I told my father not to come. We'll be going home tomorrow, and the trip would be a lot for him. I didn't want to put him through that."

"Well, I've got to go. I'm not sure if I'll see you before you go home tomorrow, but I will stay in touch." Bradley hugged Holly and shook John's hand. "I'll leave you so you can check out that mop closet."

Bradley left them laughing.

❧

Zayt carried a paper bag and bottle of water through his front door. The futon no longer lay flat but sat ready to function as a couch. The blanket he had given Eddy rested neatly on the arm of the futon. Zayt's head sunk until he heard running water coming from his bathroom.

"Yo, Eddy. Don't put those clothes back on, man. They still smell like Ghazni, for chrissake."

"Yeah, well, it should smell sweet to you, bro. I saved your ass there," Eddy yelled from the bathroom.

"Yeah, well let's talk about Kandahar, dude," Zayt laughed. "Just throw my bathrobe on. I know where I can get you some clothes that will fit perfect. They might be a little academic, though."

Zayt picked up his cell phone and called Bradley. "Hey, how are Derek, Cate, and the rest of them?"

"Cate's still in a coma. Derek is getting better. At least we got him to calm down. Sheila and David made good progress today, and Holly, John, and Mike are going home tomorrow."

"Take the good news, dude. And Cate's going to come around. I can feel it. Where are you?"

"On my way home from the hospital. Mom and Dad have got the families at my house for dinner. Hey, why don't you come? I'm sure there's plenty of food," Bradley said.

"No, thanks. I can't. I've got a favor to ask, though," Zayt said.

"Sure, what do you need?"

An hour later Bradley and Rusty showed up at Zayt's door, Bradley with a suitcase filled with clean clothes.

"Rusty was dying to see you, man," Bradley said to Zayt. Bradley saw Eddy wearing Zayt's bathrobe and sitting by the futon.

"Hey, you should keep that robe," Bradley said to Eddy. "It makes Zayt look like a sumo wrestler." He wheeled over to Eddy and put the suitcase on the floor next to him. "I'm Bradley."

"Eddy," he replied.

"Zayt, Mom packed you up some food. I told you she would have too much. It's in the truck," Bradley grinned.

Zayt went out to the truck while Rusty examined Eddy.

"This is Rusty. If you stick around, you'll see him every day."

"Nah, I'm just visiting," Eddy said.

"Ah, too bad. Zayt could use the company," Bradley replied with a disappointed frown.

"What's that you're saying about me?" Zayt asked as he carried an armload of food containers into his house.

"Nothing." Bradley gave Eddy a warning glance as if to caution him not to mention what he had said. "Just asking Eddy about your sumo wrestling days," Bradley chuckled. "Sorry, but I've got to get back. All the families are waiting. I told them to eat without me, but they insisted on waiting. I'll talk to you tomorrow?"

"Yeah, dude. And don't worry. Cate is strong, she's going to pull through. Tell your folks I'll see them in the morning."

"You will? What for?"

"They didn't tell you?" Zayt laughed, raising Bradley's curiosity. "Go ask them."

"It was nice meeting you, Eddy," Bradley said as he turned to exit. "I hope we have a chance to hang out before you leave."

"Yeah," Eddy replied.

Bradley and Rusty left, and Zayt turned to Eddy. "You going somewhere, dude?"

"Yeah, man. At some point I'm going somewhere. But not in this thing," Eddy pointed to the bright red robe with white stars. He picked up the suitcase and brought it to the bedroom where he changed into jeans and a light blue Oxford shirt.

When Eddy came back out, he said, "Alright, who's the gimp with the dorky clothes."

"Hey! Use that word again and I'll throw you out on your ass," Zayt flared.

"Relax, man. I didn't mean to . . . that's just what we call each other . . . dude, I didn't mean to, you know, offend you or anything."

"Don't you think if you'd stop calling each other that then maybe some of you might start thinking of yourselves as human beings again?"

"Jesus, Zayt, alright. I'm just not used to being around people."

Zayt decided to let it go. He didn't want to push too much.

"His name is Bradley Whitman. He's an analyst with the FBI. He lives up there in the house at the top of that ledge." Zayt pointed in the direction of Bradley's home. "He also had seven friends blown up yesterday. One of his very best friends, a woman named Cate who volunteers here, is still in a coma. They don't know if she will wake up. And if she does wake up, they don't know if she will ever walk again."

"That's the bombing from last night?"

"Yeah. But he's been working the case all day, been to the hospital twice to see his friends, and now he's spending the night with the families of his friends to try to give them some peace of mind that their kids are going to be alright. And he still had time to pack up clothes for you and food for both of us. So, you can call him a dork, a geek, or a nerd, but don't ever call him a gimp."

"I'm sorry, dude. I wasn't thinking," Eddy hesitated before he asked. "What happened to him? Why's he in the chair?"

"He got a virus when he was six-years-old. A one-in-a-million chance. He's been in the chair ever since."

"Dude, that sucks."

"Yeah. But I'll tell you something, Eddy. He's come through a lot of shit." Zayt paused. "And they don't make them any better than Bradley Whitman."

When Bradley returned home, the eight-foot table held four table settings on either side and one on the end. Bradley knew where his mother expected him to sit because of the absence of a chair at the head of the table.

While Doug carved the ham, he asked how the investigation progressed.

"We're making progress, Dad, good progress," Bradley replied. "Things are moving quickly, but it's still early in the investigation."

"Bradley, that's what we heard on the news, almost word-for-word," Derek's father, Ron, said.

"I know, Ron. And you know Derek would be telling you the same thing. In fact, ask him tomorrow, and I'm sure that's what he'll tell you. This is too important to rush to judgement. We'll follow the evidence and the facts, and it will lead us to who did this, I promise. We've got the best team on the East Coast working on this."

"You're right, I know. It's just frustrating," Ron said.

"I think our focus should be on Cate, Derek, Sheila, and David. I do have good news," Bradley said.

"Oh, please tell us. We need some good news," Lynn sighed.

"Holly, John, and Mike are going home tomorrow."

"Oh, Bradley. We already knew that," Lynn said as she smiled at Yvonne and Sam.

"Yes, we convinced Mike to stay at Holly and John's house for a while. We'll stay there with them until they have recovered fully. It will be a full house but it will be wonderful to be together again," Yvonne said, smiling.

"Speaking of tomorrow," Bradley said, "Zayt said he'll see you in the morning. What's that all about?"

"We're helping them with breakfast again. It's scrambled egg day," Lynn said.

"Again?"

"Yes, honey. We helped with the pancakes this morning. It was so wonderful. Your father was a flapjack flipping phenom."

Doug's laugh drowned out the rest. "And your mother would have made a terrific restaurant manager. You should have seen her take charge."

"I don't doubt it for one minute," Bradley smiled.

After dinner, Bradley managed to get Bill and Janet Wayland aside. He hadn't had the chance to talk to Cate and Sheila's parents alone.

"Have you heard anything about the electroencephalogram results for Cate?" Bradley asked.

"No," Bill said. "They told us it could be two days before they had them. I don't understand why."

Janet agreed with Bill's assessment. "It seems to me if you have someone in a coma, you would make their case a priority." She began to sniffle.

"I'm sure they are. I don't understand how these things work," Bradley said. "I don't know her schedule, but I can ask Laney to get in touch with you tomorrow if you would like. Maybe she can give you some insight as to how the procedures work. Are you going to be at the hospital all day?"

"As long as they let us stay," Bill said.

"Cate is going to be just fine. I can feel it in my bones. And Sheila isn't going to let a few burns stop her. She is a force of nature, a force of the sun itself," Bradley smiled.

"Just promise us that you are going to catch this son of a bitch, Bradley," Bill scowled.

"You can bet on it, Bill."

CLOSE-UP

Bradley once again skipped his morning workout so as not to wake his parents. By the time he got out of the shower, shaved, and dressed, both were sitting at the kitchen table with a fresh cup of percolator brewed coffee. The clock read 5:25.

"What have I done to the two of you?" Bradley laughed.

"Not you, son. Not you. It's the prospect of being useful that gets us out of bed early today. We have breakfast to make for about 150 people, lunches to pack for eight people, and dinner to make for whomever may want it. You know, Lynn, we should open our own restaurant after all this is over," Doug laughed.

Bradley shook his head.

"Don't worry, Bradley. I'm sure your father will come back to earth soon," Lynn said.

"Hey, I think it's great that you're helping out at the REACH community. Really, I do. I wish I could watch you guys in action. But I've got to get to work. Oh, one more thing. Zayt has a visitor. His name is Eddy. If you have a chance, drop hints around Eddy that Zayt could use some long-term company. Tell him Zayt needs someone he can talk to, things like that."

Lynn had a worried look on her face. "Bradley, is Zayt alright?"

"Oh, sure he is, Mom. It's just that if Eddy thinks Zayt needs him to stay, he's more likely to stay," Bradley said.

"Does Zayt know about this?" Doug asked.

"Well, no. I haven't had a chance to talk to him. I just think it's worth a shot. You don't have to do it if you don't feel comfortable."

Lynn smiled. "Undercover work, Doug. Are you up to it?"

Bradley grinned and winked at his mother. "You two are something."

Bradley left for the office after saying goodbye to Rusty. The sun had yet to rise. He pulled into the parking lot and noticed Nick's vehicle sitting in the same spot as the day before. He reached the eighth floor and turned on the lights as he realized nobody else had arrived, meaning Nick had stayed all night again, probably in Derek's office. He would have to do something about that, but not at the moment. Nick probably still slept on the couch, and he didn't want to wake him.

He brewed a pot of coffee before he booted his computer. His first order of business was to see if he had received the enhanced video of the drunk man. He found nothing in his email. Next, he checked the background of Holly's author, Micah Wistoff.

As Holly stated, Micah Wistoff grew up in Roxbury. His first arrest at the age of twelve was for breaking and entering a neighborhood grocery store. A high school dropout, his record showed eleven additional arrests before the age of eighteen. His stints in juvenile hall ranged from one month to one year for offenses such as robbery, defacing public property, drug possession, destruction of public property, and breaking and entering. It would be another twelve years before a conviction for breaking and entering in the daytime warranted him a ten-year stay at the former Walpole State Prison, later known as MCI/Cedar Junction.

He served his full sentence in the company of his only cellmate, Vincent Vega, earned his general education diploma, and was released at the age of forty-one. According to his parole reports, Micah had then been a model citizen. He held a steady job at a local supermarket before selling the rights to his fiction novel, *Meet Your Maker*. He was fifty-one years old.

"How the hell does a guy like that write a best-selling novel and get a movie contract?" Bradley asked out loud.

"How the hell does a guy end up talking to himself at six o'clock in the morning?" Nick asked as he walked into the bullpen.

If Bradley could have jumped, he would have come right out of his chair.

"Jesus, Nick. Warn somebody, huh?" Bradley blasted.

"Is there coffee yet? What's got you so worked up, Bradley?"

"Yeah, the coffee's ready. Something about this author doesn't feel right. It's too much of a rags-to-riches story to be believable."

Nick got himself coffee and sat down next to Bradley.

"Run me through it," Nick said.

Bradley gave him the details of his talk with Holly and the history of Micah Wistoff.

"So, what are you thinking? Ghostwriter? Maybe he stole the book? What?"

"Well, yeah," Bradley said. "Could be either. Or maybe he did write it. Maybe he's a savant of some kind. I think I need to talk to this guy. But first, I need to get a copy of his book," Bradley looked at Nick. "You need a shave, man. You look like shit."

"Yeah, I got my kit in my desk. I'll go get washed up."

"Nick, there's no reason for you to be here all night. It's not healthy. You only live twenty minutes away. You're not going to help anyone if you're not at your best."

"I know, but the director is pushing. He's questioning why I suspended some of the other investigative avenues. I wanted to spend some time reviewing the details to make sure we made the right decision."

"And? What did you come up with?" Bradley asked.

"I can't find any reason or evidence that makes Derek the target of this blast. I think we're on the right track," Nick said.

"So, you lost sleep for something we already knew. Not helpful, but I get it. When you talk to the director this morning, tell him you've exhausted all the possibilities that Derek was the target. Be adamant but respectful. Do I need to tell you what those words mean?" Bradley grinned.

"Fuck you, Whitman. Go buy a book," Nick took his coffee back to Derek's office, thankful that he had Bradley to talk to and for the levity he provided.

Bradley decided the best way to manage his time was to go to the hospital, then the bookstore. He'd hoped David rose early, as he wanted to discuss problems surrounding filming of the movie.

Although nobody had ever known David to rise early in the morning, he was awake when Bradley arrived. He looked older, sitting up in his bed, his hair disheveled. His right arm hung in a sling, and his eyes glazed over a bit. He saw Bradley in his doorway and smirked a younger man's smile.

"Hey, Bradley. It's good to see you."

"Not as good as it is to see you, David. You had a hell of a ride."

David chuckled. "Yeah, you could say that. I'm still riding a little high, actually." The smirk appeared again.

"Do you mind if I ask you a couple of questions?"

"Fire away. No, no. No fire. Shoot." David's smirk drooped to a grimace.

"What can you tell me about all the mishaps you've had filming this movie?"

"Holy shit, Bradley, it's been a nightmare. Equipment stolen and vandalized, generators breaking down . . . and," he whispered, "fires. This film is fucking cursed."

"Is it only here in Boston that this is happening?" Bradley asked.

"No, it started back in Hollywood with the death threats."

Bradley's eyes squinted, questioning what he had heard.

"Did you say you got death threats in regard to this film?"

"Hell, yeah, a couple of them. No, three, I think. I don't remember."

"David, what kind of threat exactly?"

"Letters. They said that if we made this movie, people would die or something like that."

"Where are those letters, David?"

"My secretary has them, I think. They're probably in the threat file."

Bradley again, squinted in response to David's comment.

"You have a threat file?"

"Oh, yeah. We get threatened all the time."

With raised eyebrows, Bradley wondered whether he should believe anything David told him. David evidently felt the effects of the juice running through his intravenous line.

"Who threatens you?"

"Authors, directors, strangers, other studios, you name it."

"Did you show the threats to the California police?"

"Sure, we always do. But nothing ever happens."

"Have you ever had this many things go wrong on a movie shoot?"

"Um, let me think. Ah, no. Not as many as this. This one is the pits. It's going to make us a lot of money, though—as long as we get the chase scenes right and blow up enough stuff," David paused as a thought seemed to occur to him. "No more fires, I hope."

"Okay, David, thank you. I've got to go now. But I'll be back to see you."

"Sure, I'll see you later, Bradley."

Bradley didn't know what to think. *How much of what David said was real?* He decided to call David's secretary and talk to her when he got back to the office. Meanwhile, he wanted to check in on Sheila. He felt bad he hadn't seen her yet.

Sheila lay flat on her bed, a gauze bandage wrapped around her head and down the left side of her face. Her arms and hands, also wrapped in gauze, lay flat by her sides. Hidden by the bandage, an IV drip drained into her arm.

"Hey, sunshine," Bradley whispered.

Sheila's right eye opened slowly. It took a moment for her to focus, and a tiny smile spread across her face. Bradley knew it would be a short visit, as she was heavily drugged.

"Bradley," she said.

"How's my dance partner?" Bradley asked. They spoke often how Sheila was the first person that Bradley ever danced with. On the cruise ship, she showed him moves from his wheelchair he never knew he could do. He had replicated them a few times since he was twelve years old.

"I'm ready to go. Where's the dance floor?" Her voice sounded like a child's.

"I'm getting it ready for you, don't you worry." He smiled and placed his hand on her right cheek.

"I thought the room would be bigger," she said.

"It's big enough for us. Go to sleep. I'll be back later with our dance shoes." His eyes began to moisten, and he turned away so she wouldn't see them, not that she could.

"Alright." Her eye closed.

He sat with tears falling down his cheek.

As much as he wanted to stop in and see Derek, Bradley knew it to be a bad idea. Derek's surgery was scheduled for that morning, and he did not want to disrupt the process or distract Derek.

As he planned to leave, he rolled through the lobby of the hospital and spotted the gift shop. A thought occurred to him. He glanced through the glass window at the book display. Among the best sellers of Patterson, Rowling, and Steel sat *Meet Your Maker* by Micah Wistoff.

The gift shop would open in five minutes. Bradley rumbled across the quiet lobby to purchase a cup of coffee while he waited.

He couldn't shake the sight of Sheila. Although he didn't see the explosion, he had created an image in his head from details he later learned. He saw Sheila, head bloodied, pressed against the limousine floor, Mike sprawled on top of her. He saw flames tickling the back end of the passenger compartment, broken glass, and bodies. He squeezed his eyes tight to rid himself of the images. When he opened his eyes, he saw a woman maybe sixty-five years old and wearing a bright yellow pant suit unlock and enter the door to the gift shop.

Bradley entered the open door and went straight to the books. He lifted one of four copies of *Meet Your Maker* out of the rack and placed it on the counter.

"This is a very popular book these days," the woman said.

"Is it? I just found out about it."

"Yes, it's so exciting. They are filming the movie here in Boston. It's made a mess of traffic, but it's fun to think I could bump into a movie star."

"Well, I hope you do," Bradley grinned as he left the shop.

Tuesday morning commuters jammed the city streets. The five-mile drive back to the office that took him ten minutes to complete earlier took him thirty. By the time he wheeled off the elevator, it was nearly eight o'clock.

Seeing Kyle Taylor with a mound of papers on his desk, Bradley asked, "Hey, Taylor, what are you working on?"

"I'm packing up all the previous FBI cases. I guess we're done with them," Taylor answered.

"Yeah, we are. I need you to stop that for now and call Hollywood. Find out who David Carson's secretary is. He's one of the producers of the movie. Have her send us copies of threatening letters they received regarding this film, *Maker's Mark*. And check with their police division to see if they have any information on the sender."

"Got it," Taylor said.

Bradley opened his email program and found the lab had finally sent him the enhanced copy of the video of the drunk man. He watched it on his large monitor.

The video angle showed the man from above, making it difficult to determine his height but giving Bradley a clear view of the wide-brimmed fedora. From the black and white video, Bradley could see the wool felt hat had been cared for. Though seemingly wobbly, the man walked with even strides, something a drunk individual would have a difficult time doing.

Bradley surmised the person put on a show to make a statement. He honed in on the man's right hand, the one holding the bottle, and knew immediately the man had staged the entire scene. The unique rounded rectangle design of the empty bottle, smaller on the bottom and angling up to a larger dimension before it gathered at the base of its long neck, revealed the wax drippings. Bradley did not need colored video to know that the wax would be red, and the label, if one could decipher it backwards from behind and through the glass would read Maker's Mark Kentucky Straight Bourbon Whisky.

Bradley smiled.

"I've got something," an excited voice called. Bradley looked up to see one of the bureau's interns standing in the hallway holding a laptop. "I think we have him on video," he yelled.

Bradley rolled his chair over to the excited young man and asked him his name.

"Earl, sir. Earl Waters. I think we got him," he repeated.

"Okay, Earl. Let's go down the hall to see Agent Gaston. We'll take a look at what you've got."

Earl followed Bradley to Hazel's desk.

"Hazel, we need to see Agent Gaston, please. It may be important," Bradley said as he glanced at Earl, slightly sweaty and flushed.

Hazel picked up the phone and spoke with Nick.

"You can go right in, Agent Whitman." She smiled at the intern.

"What's up?" Nick asked.

"Not sure yet. Nick, this is Earl Waters. Earl has been going over some of the collected video. Earl, why don't you tell us where the video came from and what we're going to see," Bradley said.

Earl's excitement shifted to nervousness. He set his laptop on the desk. When he removed his hands, Bradley noticed the evidence of his sweaty palm on the cover of the computer.

"Well, sir, it's video from a small hat shop on Charter Street. The recorded time is 3:33 p.m. on the day of the explosion. The limousine is parked directly across the street from the store," Earl said.

"Okay, Earl, let's see what you got," Nick said.

They gathered around the laptop, and Earl tapped the play function.

The limousine sat unattended with no sign of the driver. A man, wearing a wide-brimmed fedora hat and carrying what looked like a laborer's lunchbox, came into view from behind the limo at left of the screen. He reached the back end of the limousine and knelt as if to tie his shoe.

The video clearly showed the man opening his lunchbox and retrieving a thermos. He then shifted slightly. His back faced the camera, but his right hand could be seen twisting the top off the thermos and setting the cap on the ground next to him. He seemed to pour something into his hand from the thermos, then he bent his head down to look under the vehicle. His left hand reached for something they could not see. He put the cap on his thermos, placed it into his lunchbox, stood up, and walked back the way he came.

"That's him," Nick said. "Get a copy of that video to the tech guys right away. Bradley, get everything you can from that video now—time stamp, location, everything. Earl, gather all the video we have from that area and approximate time. I want this guy's face on my desk before lunch. Go!" Nick buzzed Hazel. "Hazel, get me Director Davis."

"Follow me, Earl," Bradley said.

Earl had yet to blink his wide eyes shut. Bradley led Earl to his desk, where he copied the video from Earl's laptop to his desktop.

"Alright. This is what you need to do next." Bradley handed Earl a pad and pen. "Write this down. Go back in the conference room and get everyone's attention. Tell them we need all the video from Charter Street and the surrounding area captured between three and four o'clock that afternoon. Show them this video, but make sure they know the suspect could have changed his appearance. Maybe he took his hat or jacket off.

"I want all the relevant video scrutinized. If anyone finds anything that looks like our guy, bring it to me right away. I want all the video checked by three different people. Do you understand what I'm saying? Three times, even if they think there is nothing there. Are you getting this, Earl?"

Earl looked up from his pad and nodded. His unblinking eyes focused on Bradley.

"Earl, I know you are nervous, and this is a lot, but it's time to take charge. Can you do this?" Bradley asked.

Earl looked at his feet, then looked up at Bradley, blinked his eyes, and said, "Hell, yes, sir."

"Excellent. Get to it. I'm here if you need me."

Earl started to walk away.

"And Earl," Bradley said, "great job."

Earl stood tall, picked up his laptop, and strutted back to the conference room.

Bradley watched the video five more times. He wanted to make sure he hadn't jumped to conclusions. He felt sure the man in the Charter Street video was the same man who portrayed himself as a drunk.

He sent both videos to Nick before returning to see him. Hazel told him to go right in.

"They're the same guy, Nick," Bradley said as he entered the office.

"Who?"

"Pull up your email. I sent you the enhanced video of the drunk man in the hotel. Watch it."

Nick retrieved the video and brought it up on his screen. Bradley moved to Nick's side of the desk to watch the video with him.

"Look at his movement down the hallway. He makes even strides, even when he seemingly wobbles. And look at the hat, a wide-brimmed fedora, just like the one in the Charter Street video."

"Okay, maybe. It's thin, Bradley."

"Nick. Do you know what the name of the movie is that they are shooting?"

"Ah, yeah, I read it somewhere. Oh, yeah. *Maker's Mark*. I remember because of the bourbon," Nick said.

"Look at the bottle he's holding, Nick."

Nick zoomed in on the bottle, and Bradley saw the recognition on his face.

"Son of a bitch."

"It's the same guy. I'll bet a bottle of bourbon on it."

"Have we got a clean shot of his face?" Nick asked.

"Not yet, but we will. Also, well before they came to Boston, the production company got some threatening letters about making this movie. I've got Taylor on that now."

"Do you want me to pull Mara and Tony off the limo company?"

"No, not yet. It still could just be harassment or something. Let's cover all the bases," Bradley said. "What did Davis have to say?"

"Same as always. He said to keep him posted."

Bradley stopped at Taylor's desk.

"Anything from David's secretary?" he asked.

Chewing the half donut he had just shoved into his mouth, Kyle Taylor glanced sideways at Bradley. Kyle's mouth moved furiously until he finally swallowed, and a large round lump slid down his throat.

"It's barely past six in the morning in California. These movie people don't get to work until at least nine, which means noon our time."

"Well, Kyle, why don't you try the Hollywood Police Department. Don't you think someone will be working there?" Bradley asked with a slight sarcastic tone.

"Ah, yeah. I'll call them right away." Kyle put the second half of his donut on his desk and picked up the telephone.

When Bradley got back to his desk, he found the reports about the stolen equipment, fire in the makeup trailer, and employee interviews from the Ritz-Carlton waiting for him. He still waited for the report from the agent assigned to talk with actors and actresses performing in the movie.

He began with the Ritz. The information confirmed that no one had seen the seemingly drunk individual in the hotel, and he did not have any traits that stood out to any of the employees. The general manager reported no recent threats nor having any knowledge of unhappy guests who may have held a grudge. Although the hotel is locked in the evening with many of the guests coming and going, it could not be ruled out that someone could get into the hotel without a keycard.

Bradley next picked up the report on stolen lighting equipment. It stated that the area where the lighting equipment had been staged teemed with people including lighting technicians known as grips, some extras cast in the movie, and workers for the catering company set up nearby. The agent concluded that almost anyone could have stolen the ETL Hyper 31 LED Gaffer Light kit because the equipment sat packed in its rollaway case. The narrative concluded that someone dressed as a grip or with the look of a technician could have easily gone unnoticed.

The report on the fire in the makeup trailer proved more promising. The fire investigator found pieces of coffee filters with traces of white phosphorus near the origin of the fire. The agent's report explained that when white phosphorus is dissolved in carbon disulfide, applied to coffee filters, and allowed time for the carbon disulfide to dry to white powder, the filters will spontaneously combust. This time, the report said, the filters burst into flames and ignited the oil-covered rags in the duffel bag along with the coffee filters. That allowed the arsonist to place the duffel bag in the closet well before the carbon disulfide evaporated, flee the scene, and have an alibi for the time the fire erupted. In conclusion, the report stated, there was no doubt the fire that occurred in the makeup trailer resulted from arson.

Bradley made his way to the conference room. Some agents, some interns, seven people sat around the table absorbed in their laptops. Bradley caught Earl's eye and motioned for him to come into the hallway.

"Yes, Agent Whitman?" Earl said.

"Earl, do you know if any of the video-camera footage covers the area where the makeup trailer is positioned in Charter Street Park? That would be just opposite Unity Street."

"Let me get the master sheet."

Earl returned with a clipboard with multiple hand-drawn pages. The forms included a column for description of the street area of the video, home number or business location of the camera, a blank column, and a column containing three lines to record which three people had watched the video.

"Did you make these?" Bradley asked.

"Ah, yes. Is that okay?" Earl asked.

"Of course. It's very helpful. What's the blank column for?" Bradley asked.

"That's in case we find something unusual and we need to make notes, like the timestamp or anything.

Bradley smiled and nodded.

He scanned Earl's forms looking for street names close to Charter Street Park. He found that a video had been collected from a hair salon on Greenough Lane which ran alongside, and through parts of the park. He noted that two people had already watched the video.

"Earl, could you go back inside and ask these two people to come out here, please?" Bradley pointed to the two names on the form.

Charise Jones and Lucas Gonzalez followed Earl into the hallway.

"Do you both remember looking at this footage from the hair salon camera on Greenough Lane?" Bradley asked.

"Yes, I do," Charise replied.

"Yeah," Lucas said.

"Tell me. Can you see a mobile trailer in any of the video?"

"Yeah," Lucas said, "but only part of it."

Charise nodded in agreement.

"Thank you for your help," Bradley said. "I won't hold you up any longer."

The two went back into the conference room.

"Earl," Bradley said, "put a copy of that video on a thumb drive and bring it to me at my desk, please."

"Right away."

Bradley took another look in the agents' report about the fire in the makeup trailer. The arson occurred on Monday, six days before the pipe bomb exploded.

"Taylor," Bradley called. He saw the young agent look up from his computer with nervous eyes. Bradley motioned him over.

"Yes?"

"Anything from the police department yet on the threats?"

"I spoke to the sergeant on duty, and she didn't know anything about the letters. She said she would send someone to look through the evidence room and would email them to me as soon as they found them."

"Okay. While you're waiting, I want you to call the hair salon business on Greenough Lane and get a copy of their camera video from last Monday. Anything they have from 6 a.m. to 2 p.m.," Bradley said.

"What's the name of the business?" Kyle asked.

"I don't know. You'll have to look it up. It's at 12 Greenough Lane."

Taylor hurried back to his desk as Earl brought the thumb drive.

"Thanks, Earl. I'll have some new video coming in soon. I want you to go over it personally. I'll email it to you when I get it."

"Yes, sir, Agent Whitman."

"Earl. Call me Bradley."

"Yes, sir, Bradley," Earl smiled.

Lynn, Shea, and Rosie dished out scrambled eggs, bacon, and toast while Doug cooked up a fresh batch of eggs. Eddy laid the bread on the conveyer toaster, and Zayt used a basting brush to butter the toast as it came out the other end.

Doug paid special attention to Eddy most of the morning. Sometimes Zayt's friend seemed comfortable helping with the meal, while other times it appeared he wanted to bolt out the door and never look back. Doug understood the struggle. He and Zayt had talked about their time in the service. Though each had different experiences, one as a Marine in the Gulf War, one as a Navy SEAL in the war in Afghanistan, they shared similar occurrences. Doug appreciated having Zayt to talk with and he assumed Zayt felt the same. He hoped to give Eddy the same opportunity. But he could tell it would not be easy.

"How are those eggs coming, Doug? We're getting low here," Lynn said.

"Coming right up."

"We could use more toast, Zayt. Keep it coming. We have a big turnout this morning. The line is still out the door," Shea smiled.

"What do I do when I run out of bread?" Eddy asked.

"There's more out in the back room on the shelf next to the freezer by the back door," Zayt told Eddy.

"Uh-huh," Eddy said and left the kitchen.

Doug replaced Lynn's almost empty pan of scrambled eggs with a full pan and walked into the back room where he saw Eddy staring at the back door.

He hesitated, then said, "It's good to have you here, Eddy. I'm glad Zayt has someone he can talk to. We talk, but I'm so much older than he is, and the Gulf War was different than what you guys signed on for."

"You were in Iraq?" Eddy asked.

"Yeah, and Kuwait. Marine Corps."

"What do you mean about Zayt needing someone to talk to? He seems like he's got it together," Eddy said.

"Huh, well, we try to look like we've got it together, don't we? My wife, and my son . . . they don't know the dreams I have. But that's my fault because I don't tell them. I think a lot of us do the same thing, including Zayt."

Doug didn't lie. He didn't even stretch the truth.

"Well, I need more eggs," Doug continued as he opened the refrigerator door.

Eddy turned from the door and reached for three loaves of bread.

Bradley found a quiet spot in headquarters cafeteria where he could scan Micah Wistoff's book. He knew he wouldn't have time to read it in its entirety, but he had become good at speed scanning. The story is based on a career criminal who grew up in Dorchester, Massachusetts, and spent his youth in and out of juvenile hall. It could very easily have been a memoir, Bradley thought. But then the novel escalates into large-scale elaborate robberies, some extremely successful, some not. The main character spends his adult life either planning or performing his crimes.

Halfway through scanning the book, Bradley understood how Hollywood perceived the story as a money maker. The robberies included a successful armored car heist, a Federal Reserve heist, an unprecedented art theft, and a botched bank robbery. The main character, Denny Duke, masterminds the crew and chooses his accomplices by testing their abilities, making them perform smaller crimes specific to his needs. If they failed, they usually went to jail. If they succeeded, they ended up on Denny's crew.

Only the character of Denny would talk during a heist. For example, during a bank robbery, he bursts through the door and at gunpoint says, "If you don't want to meet your maker, then get on the floor now." During a robbery of an armored car, Denny says, "Get down now, or you're going to meet your maker." Hence, the name of the novel. Bradley could not understand why the producers chose to switch the title, but he began to realize that he didn't understand anything about Hollywood.

It's not a movie Bradley planned to see, but he had to admit some of the details he read were quite plausible and realistic, not like in some of the blockbuster movies Hollywood currently presented.

He left the cafeteria and returned to his desk. Afternoon had replaced morning, and Bradley realized he had not spoken or texted with Laney. He sent her a text asking her to call him when she found some free time.

When Kyle Taylor saw Bradley return to his desk, he jumped out of his chair and scurried to Bradley's side.

"I emailed you the video from the hair salon cameras and copies of threatening letters sent to the production company. And I talked to the producer's secretary, a Mrs. Diaz, but she couldn't tell me much. Only that the letters arrived about a month ago, she showed them to David Carson, and he told her to forward them to the police department."

"Thank you, Kyle." Bradley said, already opening his email.

Kyle didn't move. Bradley glanced at him sideways and said, "Is there something else?"

"Ah, no," he awkwardly replied. "I . . . just thought maybe you would have something else for me to do."

"I'll let you know, Kyle." A wondering wrinkle stretched across Bradley's forehead. *Did he really have nothing else to do?*

Bradley forwarded the newly acquired hair-salon video to Earl with a message to keep him informed on the progress.

The threatening letters had no abnormalities to distinguish them from any other letter reproduced by a computer inkjet printer letter. The plain white copy paper could have been purchased in any store that stocked copy paper. If they were going to make use of the letters, Bradley knew it would be through the text itself.

He forwarded the three files to the Federal Bureau of Investigations Forensic Science of Communication department. Each letter included an advertisement for the book, *Meet Your Maker*. The advertisement seemed to have been printed from the internet. The first letter received about one month prior to the Boston filming and already well into the studio filming, read simply, **make this movie and i put you in a johnny** without any punctuation or capitalization. The second letter about a week later, read (complete with original spelling), **make this movie and i bery you in my celar** and the third a week after that, **stop now or you wont live to regret it.**

Bradley didn't need a psycholinguistic analyst to tell him the author of the letters came from the Boston area or at least from New England and possessed little formal education. The use of the words johnny to describe hospital garb and cellar, although misspelled, instead of basement were dead giveaways. Besides, it wasn't until they filmed in Boston that problems arose. He hoped the analyst could tell him more about the person who wrote the threats.

Why this film? Bradley wondered. He decided he was ready to talk to the author of the book, Micah Wistoff. He knew from reports and from Holly that the author had attended the filming every day since the production crew arrived in Boston.

He found the schedule for the movie shoot in his files. That day, they filmed scenes on Paul Revere Mall where the famous bronze statue depicting Paul Revere on his horse sits atop a granite base with Old North Church steeple in the background. Bradley thought about driving to the location but realized the time-consuming logistics of getting through traffic and finding a parking spot. Instead, he had another idea.

"Hey, Taylor," Bradley called over the din of occupants of the eighth floor.

Taylor rushed to Bradley's side.

"Yes?"

"We've got to interview the author of this book." Bradley held up *Meet Your Maker*. "He should be on location of the movie shoot. They are filming on Paul Revere Mall today. Would you go pick him up and bring him in? His name is Micah Wistoff." Bradley showed Taylor the picture of the author from the back cover of the paperback.

Taylor smiled. "Yes, sir, Agent Whitman." And before Bradley could say another word, he had gone.

It had struck Bradley that if there were a chance that Micah Wistoff had a ghostwriter or stolen the story, it might be beneficial to question him in official FBI headquarters. Even the most honest of people found it intimidating to be interviewed in the building.

Bradley's phone rang. "Hey, Laney," Bradley answered.

"Derek is out of surgery, and everything went fine. He will be in the recovery room for the next couple of hours but then will be moved to a regular room. He won't be going back to the ICU."

"Well, I guess that's good news, but he's not going to be happy leaving the ICU while Cate is still there."

"It's best if we keep her where she is right now. Also, both Sheila and David have moved to the general medical floor. We were able to put them in a room together. They are both doing well."

"How about you, Laney? Are you doing well?" Bradley asked.

"I miss you."

"Me, too. I don't know when . . . this whole thing is just . . . I don't know," he paused. "I used to be able to form full sentences."

Laney chuckled. "I've got to go. I love you."

"That one I can still form. I love you, too."

Mara sat across the desk from Nick. *He's exhausted*, she thought.

"Anyway, the other drivers in the limousine shop did not like Henry Case," she told Nick. "Actually, they hated Henry Case. Apparently, when Henry got out of jail six years ago, Gino fired a guy and gave his job to Henry. The guy he fired was brother-in-law to one of the other drivers, Ace Molinaro. The brother-in-law couldn't find another job, so he left. And I mean, left. He left his wife and kids high and dry. Instead of blaming the brother-in-law or Gino, Ace blamed Henry."

"Could be motive," Nick shrugged.

"Could be, but I'm not sold on Ace as our guy. And I checked Henry's finances, if you can call them that. He had no savings, and his checking account is smaller than mine," Mara snickered.

"He favored a bookie who works out of a barber shop on Boylston Street near Fenway.

"I talked to the guys downstairs from organized crime," she continued, "and they've heard of this operation, but assured me it's not mob related. He's a heavy hitter by the name of Ray Dituleo. So, I contacted the state gaming enforcement division and talked to one of their investigators. He just got back to me. It seems Henry Case owed Ray Dituleo in excess of fifty-six thousand dollars."

Mara peered at Nick over the top of her readers.

"What do you think?" Nick asked.

"Me? What do *I* think?"

"Yes, Mara. What do *you* think?"

Nick smiled and shook his head.

Mara returned the smile. "I think it would be counterproductive to kill or maim someone who owes you that much money."

"I agree. Still, it's a lead we have to follow," Nick said.

"Nick, have you even been out of this building in the last two days?"

"What's that got to do with anything?"

"Nothing. But I haven't eaten lunch, and I'm guessing dinner isn't going to happen, so I'm going across the street to that lousy deli to get a bad sandwich. Why don't you come with me?"

"I don't think I should leave."

"Do you have your phone with you?" Mara asked.

"Yes."

"We will literally be across the street."

Nick paused. "Okay. But we make it quick, and you're buying."

He reached for his suit jacket.

"I didn't figure it any other way," Mara laughed.

Lynn and Doug arrived at the hospital just before noon and went straight to Holly and John's room where they knew they would see Yvonne and Sam.

"Holly, you look wonderful. You've got color back in your face, and your eyes are sparkling again. Thank God for that," Lynn said as she gave her a hug. "I don't mean to ignore you, John, but your wife is just stunning."

"I agree," John said with a wide grin.

"We've brought food for anyone who might be hungry. Roast beef sandwiches, potato salad, and chocolate fudge brownies."

Doug unpacked the large bag they brought.

"Where's your father, Holly?" Lynn asked.

"He went to visit Sheila and David. They moved them to this floor this morning. David's parents arrived a little while ago, so John and I came back here to give them space. I'm sure he'll be back shortly."

Outside the door, Mike stood on his crutches. Every part of him felt dark and heavy as if he were trapped in a black tar pit breathing noxious fumes. He felt sick. He finally willed himself to smile and tried to keep things light and upbeat, for Holly's sake. He maneuvered into the crowded room. "Who will be back?" he asked.

"Mike, it's good to see you up on your feet," Doug said. "Looks like we'll be back out on the golf course in no time."

"Maybe my broken wrist will improve my slice," Mike said weakly. "Is that real food?"

"It is," Yvonne said. "Lynn and Doug just brought it. Can I make you a plate, Michael?"

"Sure," Mike said as he claimed the chair in the far corner of the room.

Doug followed Mike to the corner and stood in front of his chair. "How are Sheila and David?" he asked.

"David is coming along," Mike replied. "His surgery went well yesterday, and they've got his arm immobilized to let the collarbone heal properly. I guess he's got some nuts and bolts inside to hold things in place."

Mike's face darkened, and his eyes went somewhere that Doug could not see.

"What is it, Mike?"

Still looking off in the distance, Mike whispered, "I heard some of the staff talking." His eyes became moist. "They said Sheila was so badly burned because she was pressed to the floor of the limousine."

Doug closed his eyes. He knew then what Mike had heard. Doug opened his eyes and crouched in front of Mike. "Mike, none of this was in your control. You know that."

The moisture ran down Mike's cheeks. He tried to nod but couldn't.

Doug reached into his pocket, retrieved a handkerchief, and handed it to Mike. "There's nothing any of you could have done differently. Do you hear me?"

Mike didn't respond. He only looked at the floor.

"What are you two whispering about over there?" Holly called.

Mike dabbed at his eyes with the handkerchief and tried to hand it back to Doug. Doug put up his hand.

"We're just trying to figure out if we brought enough food," Doug said. He stood in front of Mike, blocking him from the others, to give him another moment of privacy.

"Yeah, where is that sandwich, Mom?" Mike asked in his best nonchalant tone.

"Doug, I'm going to bring some sandwiches to David's parents. Are you coming?" Lynn asked.

Doug glanced back at Mike. "No, I'll wait here. I don't want to get in the way. Invite them to Bradley's tonight."

Lynn looked puzzled but didn't question Doug.

"I'll go with you, Lynn. I need to stretch my legs," Mike's father, Sam, said.

Yvonne handed Mike a plate and plastic fork, then returned to conversation with Holly and John.

"So, when are you getting out of here?" Doug asked Mike.

"They said we should be able to leave by two o'clock. Yvonne and Sam are going to drive us to Derek and Cate's so we can pick up John's car. Then we're supposed to go back to Holly and John's house in Amherst, but I don't know. I may have them drop me off in Worcester."

"Mike, your daughter is going to need you. And you are going to need her. Don't keep this from her. You two have always been open with one another. Talk this out with her. It's going to take all three of you working together to heal."

Mike looked over at Holly. She caught his eye and smiled. He faintly smiled back.

"I don't know if I can. How will I ever be able to look Sheila in the eye again."

"Sheila doesn't blame you. Nobody does. Because there is no one to blame but the person who did this to all of you. You've gone through worse. You raised an amazing daughter after losing your wife. But you did that together. And you will all get through this too, as long as you do it together."

"You're right, Doug. Thanks." Mike sat up straight from his slouched position. "You are a damned good friend, Doug."

"Right back at you . . . Michael."

Bradley's text tone beeped.

The guy just finished lunch. Will be there as soon as I can get through this traffic.

"Poor Taylor," Bradley murmured. He texted Taylor back and told him to bring Micah Wistoff directly to Interrogation Room A when they arrived.

Bradley sat checking his email when the elevator doors opened and Mara and Nick sauntered onto the floor laughing loudly at something only they were privy to. Bradley watched as Nick walked her over to her desk before he turned around and walked down the hall to his office.

A smile spread across Bradley's tired face. *It's about time*, he thought.

He knew it would be a little while before Taylor arrived with Micah Wistoff, so he made his way to Hazel and asked her to announce him to Nick.

She chuckled at Bradley's choice of words and did as he asked.

Nick sat, smiling, behind the desk.

"Oh, I'm sorry. I came in to see Nick. You know him, the guy with the scowl on his face and an insult on the tip of his tongue?" Bradley smirked. "Do you know where I might find him?"

Nick rolled his eyes, but he couldn't remove the boyish grin he displayed.

"What can I do for you Bradley?" Nick asked.

"I just wanted to bring you up to date on developments. Then maybe you can do the same for me?" Bradley smirked.

"Jesus, grow up, Whitman."

"Wow, there's a surprise reversal of roles for you. So, the fire in the makeup trailer was arson. Someone used the old magician's trick of white phosphorous and carbon disulfide to create spontaneous combustion."

"Okay, let's pretend I know what that means for the time being."

"I've got Earl and the others checking to see if we have anything on camera from the day of the fire."

"Good."

"Taylor is bringing the author in now. I want to make this guy uncomfortable so I'm going to bring him into the interrogation room. Can you make an appearance part way through the interview? Just stand in the corner and look important? Just for a few minutes. Don't say anything. Just look like the boss."

"I am the boss."

"Right, good. Get into character."

Nick chuckled and shook his head. "Now I know why Derek is losing his hair. It's all because of you."

"And finally, the threatening letters definitely came from this area. The guys downstairs have not confirmed that yet, but I'm sure of it. The author of these letters lives here."

"Mara doesn't think Henry was the target. I mean, he was sunk deep with a bookie, and nobody liked him, but I think she's right."

"What about Gino Calletti's limo company?" Bradley asked.

"Getting nowhere. Looks like a dead end."

"Well, what do you want to do, Nick?"

"I'm pulling Tony off the limo company and pairing him back up with Mara to see if they can find any evidence linking

Henry Case as our target. We'll give it a little more time. If they can't find anything, we go full bore on our drunk arsonist."

"Alright. That makes sense. Taylor should be back with this guy within the half hour."

On the way back to his desk, Bradley stopped to see Mara. She displayed a dreamy expression.

"Hey, Mara, how was lunch?" Bradley asked.

"Awful. If it weren't so convenient and I didn't get tired of our cafeteria food, I would never set foot in there again."

"Then why are you smiling?" Bradley grinned.

"Am I?" She seemed embarrassed.

Bradley went back to his desk.

"Thanks for your help this morning, Eddy. I don't know how we would have kept this going without you, Lynn, and Doug. I never realized how valuable Cate was around here."

Zayt's eyes looked around his cabin, then drifted to the floor.

"She's the one that's in a coma, right?" Eddy asked.

"Yeah."

"It's fucked up, isn't it?"

"What is?" Zayt asked.

"You spend your days in Afghanistan watching your friends get blown up, then you come home and . . . it's just fucked up. It's like, no matter where you go, you can't escape."

"Except here we know who the enemy is, Eddy. It's not the same. They are going to find this guy. Bradley will make sure of it."

"So, what then? They're still going to have to live with the fallout."

"And they will. We all will . . . together. Because that's what we do. We fight for each other. Remember?"

Zayt could see he was losing Eddy. He threw his head back and sighed in resignation. "Jesus, Eddy. What the fuck do I know? I'm just a guy from Philly who is doing the best he can in a fucked-up world."

"It seems to me you got your shit together, dude. Look at this place," Eddy spread his arms apart and swept his eyes around the room.

"No, not me. I was hiding out down here. I pulled away from the rest of the world like so many of us do. I lived in my own cardboard box. Then, one night, a beautiful soul of a woman was stabbed to death, right over there." Zayt pointed to the other side of the sandpit. "That's how I met Bradley."

Zayt told Eddy about writing a note and placing it on Rusty's dog collar to get help. He told how he and Bradley met, how they became friends, and how Bradley had to fight for his life from his wheelchair.

"If I hadn't met Bradley, I might still be living in a box." Zayt's gaze looked far away.

Eddy hung his head and softly said, "You're stronger than I am. I can't do it. I can't come out of my box, dude. I know you want me to, but I can't."

"Look, Eddy. I wanted to see you again. I spent every day since I got out wondering what happened to you, man. You're my best friend, Pantsman. I miss you, dude."

Eddy's eyes welled with tears. He pressed his palms to his eyes and sat with his head down. When he lifted it, he looked into Zayt's eyes and said, "Pantsman is dead. I gotta go."

Eddy pushed himself out the door.

Zayt knew it wouldn't do any good to go after him. He had made up his mind. But Zayt was not about to give up on him. He would have to find a way.

SUBTEXT

Taylor shepherded Micah into Interrogation Room A, got him a glass of water, and waited with him until Bradley came through the door.

"Thank you, Taylor," Bradley said as he made a motion with his eyes for Taylor to leave the room. He noticed a slight annoyance in Taylor's expression.

Bradley set the paperback book on the table in front of him.

"Mr. Wistoff, I am Agent Whitman. I'm sorry to pull you away from your lunch, but I need to ask you a few questions about your book, *Meet Your Maker*. I'm sure you are aware of the complications surrounding the shooting of this film," Bradley said.

"Yeah. Yeah, I am. This ain't gonna take long, is it? I'm not feeling too well."

Micah Wistoff sat slumped in the chair across from Bradley. A fair-skinned man, he had the look of an aged gangster from a black-and-white film. Not quite Jimmy Cagney—more like Paul Muni from the 1932 version of *Scarface*. His voice, however, did not fit with the gangster mold. Rather than a deep, methodical, threatening cadence, he spoke with a high-tone pitch that would shatter glass if loud enough.

"I guess that depends on you, Mr. Wistoff."

"How's that?"

"Well, I have some rather pointed questions about the process you went through while writing your novel."

"Huh?"

Bradley's doubt about the true author of the book increased with every second that passed.

"Well, for instance, when you developed the plot, did you have the entire story worked out in advance?"

"Um, what do you mean?"

"Okay, let's try this. Did you write from beginning to end? Or did you have a plot and work your way around it?"

"I . . . I just wrote the stories, that's it."

"And they are very well written, Mr. Wistoff. So, are you saying you had these separate stories and you strung them together to make a novel?"

"Yeah."

"That's very impressive. So, who helped you write the story, Mr. Wistoff?"

"Huh? Nobody. I did it myself."

He swallowed hard, a pained expression on his face.

"With all due respect, Mr. Wistoff, you use words in here like . . . irrepressible . . . and intractable. Can you tell me what either of those words mean?"

The door opened, and Nick stepped in. He stood in the corner with his arms folded and a blank but interested look. Micah Wistoff inspected Nick before turning back to Bradley.

"Hey, what's this about, anyway?"

"Mr. Wistoff, I'm not convinced that you wrote the book on your own."

"Yeah, well test me, then. Ask me anything about it."

Bradley flipped through the paperback and landed on the page describing the armored car theft.

"Alright, tell me about the armored car theft."

"Yeah, that was a good one. So, Denny Duke, he's the main character, blocks the street with his car so the armored car can't get by. Then he drives the car right into the front of the armored car hard enough for the airbags to blow, but not enough to hurt him 'cuz he wears a helmet, see?"

Micah stopped and put his hand on his stomach. Sweat formed on his upper lip. He continued, "Then he gets out of the car with his gun drawn and says to the driver, 'If you don't want to meet your maker, get out now!'

"See, I told you I wrote it." Micah tried to smile but winced instead.

Bradley caught Nick's wide-eyed expression out of the corner of his eye and glanced his way just as Nick hurried out of the room.

Bradley pushed on.

"That just means you know the stories, Micah. It doesn't mean you wrote the words. Tell me how you described Denny's urge to shoot the tires of the armored car or what you wrote about his reaction to changing his original plan."

"I don't remember the exact words. I wrote it a long time ago. Fuck, man. I don't feel too good."

"Fair enough." Bradley said. "But I just mentioned both words no more than two minutes ago."

Bradley saw Micah trying to concentrate, as if the words buzzed his head and he just needed to grab them.

"I don't remember." Micah began to squirm.

"Micah, listen. It's not a crime to use a ghostwriter to write a novel. Plagiarism isn't even a crime, although you would probably end up in civil court if that were the case."

Micah squinted his eyes and tilted his head.

"Stealing someone else's work, I mean. That's not technically a crime. You can get sued for it, but I wouldn't arrest you for it. Do you see what I'm saying? But fraud is a different story, no pun intended." Bradley chuckled at his turn of phrase.

"Huh?"

"Never mind. What is a crime is murder. That's all I care about. I'm here to solve a murder. So, I need to know everyone who was involved with writing this book. We've established you are the story guy. Now, who put it all together?"

Micah rocked back and forth. His hand rested on his stomach, and his face grew flush. "Ryan Danforth," he answered. "I gave him the stories, and he wrote the book."

Bradley thought the pressure had gotten to Micah, who looked extremely uncomfortable. "Good. And why isn't Ryan Danforth's name on the cover of the book with yours?"

"He didn't want it to be."

"Why not?"

"Jesus, I'm going to be sick. Where's the bathroom?" Micah jumped out of his seat.

"Across the hall to the right." Bradley barely got it out of his mouth before Micah hit the hallway.

Bradley entered the bathroom and found Micah lying on the floor, foam oozing from his mouth. Bradley opened the door and called for help. Then he reached for the phone from his chair pocket and dialed 911.

"This is Agent Bradley Whitman calling from the eighth floor of FBI headquarters at 201 Maple Street in Chelsea. I need an ambulance right away. A man is having some kind of seizure and is foaming from the mouth."

Kyle Taylor, Mara, and a couple of interns ran into the men's room while Bradley was on the phone.

To prevent him from choking, Kyle positioned Micah's body so he lay on his side.

"Mara, call downstairs and tell them an ambulance is on its way and they should send them here immediately. Tell them to hold the elevator for them," Bradley directed. "Where's Nick?"

"I saw him get in the elevator a few minutes ago. He seemed like he was in a hurry," Taylor said.

Bradley texted Nick to let him know what was happening.

"What happened?" Taylor asked.

"I don't know. He said he didn't feel good. I thought he was just nervous. Then he started to sweat and said he was going to get sick and ran out," Bradley said.

Micah stopped shaking and lay motionless on the floor, his eyes glazed and half open. Bradley cleared everyone from the room except Taylor.

"Stay with him, Taylor. I'll be right outside the door. I don't want to be in the way when the paramedics arrive. I'll leave the door open."

Bradley pushed the restroom door to lock it open and set himself just outside. He heard Taylor talk to Micah. "Stay with me . . . You're going to be alright . . . Just breathe."

Bradley saw Nick burst out from the stairwell door. Out of breath, he looked into the restroom at Micah.

"Is he breathing?" he asked Taylor.

"Barely."

"What the fuck happened?" He asked.

"I don't know," Bradley replied.

Paramedics from the fire department were first to arrive. Taylor backed out of the room to let them work on Micah.

They asked what had happened, and Bradley told them what he knew.

"Has he eaten or drunk anything lately?" one paramedic asked.

"I gave him water," Taylor said. "And he had just finished his lunch at the filming site when I picked him up."

"Get that water to the lab downstairs," Nick said, pointing through the glass walls of the interrogation room to the cup of water sitting on the table. One of the interns complied.

Bradley's phone rang. It was Laney. Bradley moved down the hall to answer it.

"Hey, Laney."

"I don't have time for details, but I thought you should know. The ER is filling up with people from the movie set. They all have the same symptoms. I think they've been poisoned. I'll call you later."

"He's been poisoned," Bradley yelled as he headed back to the restroom doorway. Paramedics were just rolling a gurney off the elevator. He continued, "I just got a call that people from the movie shoot are filling up the emergency room. One of the doctors says it looks like they've all been poisoned." He aimed his comments to the paramedics but spoke loudly enough for everyone to hear.

The paramedics hoisted Micah Wistoff onto the gurney. He wore an oxygen mask and had a blood pressure monitor hanging from his arm. They whisked him to the elevator. Then all was quiet.

"Taylor. Take one of the lab technicians with you and get to the filming location. Bring a couple extra agents with you to talk to everyone on the set, crew, and catering company who didn't get sick," Nick said.

"I'm going to have Earl send you a picture of a suspect. Show it around. See if you get any hits," Bradley said as he texted Earl.

"This guy can't die on us, Bradley," Nick said.

"I know, Nick. But we did everything we could," Bradley said.

"No. I mean, we need him," Nick emphasized.

Bradley thought Nick had the look of a lion about to pounce on a wild hog.

"What is it?"

"Come into the office."

Bradley followed Nick.

"Hazel, two cups of coffee, please," Nick said.

Once inside, Nick stood at the window, the one with the best view of the Charles River and the one where Derek stood when ideas formed or thoughts needed clarity.

"Remember you questioned me about staying at the office again, not going home?" Nick asked, then shook his head, "Jesus, that was only this morning, wasn't it?"

"Yes," Bradley replied, confused. Hazel came in and handed them each a cup of steaming coffee.

"Thank you, Hazel," they both said.

Nick continued, "I told you I stayed so I could review all the files to make sure we didn't have any evidence that Derek was the target of the bomb."

"Right."

"You know I'm a thorough investigator, right?"

"Yes. Come on, Nick. Get to it," Bradley urged.

"I had finished going through all the closed and current cases when I realized I hadn't looked at any of the cold case files. So, I examined all the unsolved cases that this office has investigated.

"Twenty years ago, there was an armored car heist in Dorchester. The suspects rammed their car into the front of a Baystate Security armored vehicle, got out of their car with guns drawn, and approached the driver and passenger. Would you care to guess what he said to the driver?"

Bradley lifted his eyebrows and said, "If you don't want to meet your maker, get out now!" Bradley felt an urge to jump to his feet but could only pound his hand on the arm of his chair.

Nick smiled and nodded. "The report also states that the Baystate Security guard who drove the armored car said he thought the two assailants had worn helmets when they rammed the vehicle."

"His stories are real?" Bradley said.

There was a knock at the door.

"Bring them in," Nick yelled.

The door opened, and a man in a work jumpsuit pushed a dolly with file boxes into the room.

"Where do you want them?" the man asked.

"Over by the couch," Nick replied. "Thanks, Stan."

Stan dropped the stack of files by the couch and left the room.

"Nick, the name of the book is *Meet Your Maker*," Bradley said. "The main character is based on one guy who pulls off some plausible heists."

"That's why I had Stan bring the cold case files."

Bradley thought for a moment, then said, "Can I use your computer?"

"Yeah."

Nick looked over his shoulder as Bradley sat at the desk and typed into the keyboard for several minutes. Then, with a wide grin, he slapped the desktop.

"What? What is it? I don't see what you see," Nick said.

"About ten years ago, when I was an intern, Derek had us go through all the cold cases and categorize them with keywords, phrases, and methods so we could search the records easier. That way if we got a case, we could see if it connected with any of the unsolved cases." Bradley pointed to a series of case file numbers. "I put the phrase *meet your maker* into the system, and it came up with three case file numbers."

Nick reached for a pad and pen. "What are the numbers?"

Bradley rattled off the three file numbers while Nick recorded them. Then they found the files amid the boxes sitting next to the couch.

Nick picked one of the files and handed it to Bradley. "This is the Baystate Security armored car report. You read the book, right?"

"Well, I scanned it quickly," Bradley said as he took a moment to review the pages. "This report reads like the novel."

"Where is the book?" Nick asked.

"Probably still in Interrogation Room A," Bradley said.

Nick buzzed Hazel over the intercom. "Hazel, could you go to Interrogation Room A. There should be a paperback book sitting on the table. Could you bring that in, please?"

"Yes, sir," she replied.

A minute later, Hazel came through the door holding the novel.

"This is a fun book, a lot of action," she said as she handed it to Nick.

"You've read it?" Bradley asked.

"Yes. It's very popular, you know."

"Thank you, Hazel," Nick said.

Bradley couldn't help but notice how much Nick's manners had improved by having Hazel at his side.

"Okay, the next file number is a theft from the Federal Reserve counting room. This one is very interesting because we have yet to figure out how they got through five sets of locked doors without being detected. Anyway, only one person spoke, and he said . . ."

Bradley flipped through the pages of the book scanning for the section he had skimmed earlier about the Federal Reserve robbery. "Sit tight or meet your maker?"

"Exactly, word for word. Jesus, Bradley. This is big."

"Wait, quiet. Give me a minute." Bradley read the passage about the robbery.

Nick watched as Bradley's face morphed to delight.

"It's genius, pure genius," Bradley stated.

"What is?"

"How they bypassed the five locked doors," Bradley said.

"What??? It's in the book?" Nick yelled.

"They removed locksets during the day and replaced them with their own. Then they had keys made for the original locksets before putting them back in their original door. They dressed as maintenance workers and did this during the day. No one questioned what they did because the locks were changed on a regular basis to, ironically, prevent theft." Bradley released a sardonic chuckle.

"Next," Nick asserted like a kid on Christmas morning. "The last file is the art theft. Remember that one? Christ, if we could solve that, we would go down in history. How many years ago was that? Thirty?"

"Older than both of us. Let me find it in here." Bradley flipped through the pages. "Here it is. What does the file say?"

Nick read from the report. "Only one of the two guards heard him say anything. The one guard remembers him asking, *'You want to meet your maker?'*"

"Yup. Just what it says in the book."

"What else does it say about the robbery?" Nick asked.

Bradley read further. "It says it was an inside job. The second guard was in on it."

"I knew it!" Nick bellowed. "I always thought that."

Bradley sat silent, deep in thought, while Nick rambled on about cracking the biggest cases in history.

"Bradley," Nick asked, "what's the matter? Why aren't you excited? You realize how big this is?"

"Could be big, Nick. Could be very big. We don't have any proof that these stories aren't just a figment of Micah's imagination. Or his ghostwriter, Ryan Danforth. Maybe they researched these crimes and had access to the reports. Let's not get ahead of ourselves."

"He had a ghostwriter?"

"Yeah, I finally got him to admit it just after you left the room. We need to talk to Danforth as soon as possible."

Nick pressed his intercom buzzer. "Hazel, could you send Agent Thompkins and Morrison in here, please?"

"Yes, sir."

"Nick, stop and think about this. If these stories are accurate, and that's a big if, the person who perpetrated them would not want the information out there, especially on a movie screen," Bradley said.

"But why wouldn't he have stopped it earlier? Why not stop the book?" Nick asked.

"How many hardened criminals do you know who read novels for fun?" Bradley asked. "It's probable he didn't know anything about the book until it became a big deal with a movie contract. Once he found out, he threatened the production company, he sabotaged the equipment and makeup trailer, and he blew up a limousine. And they still wouldn't stop filming. Now, he's poisoned everyone. He's getting more desperate."

Nick sat on the couch and placed his head in his hands. "Yeah. But who is he?"

"If these stories pan out, like we both think they will, if we can find the actual Denny Duke, we'll have our guy."

Mara knocked on the door.

"Yeah, come in," Nick called. Mara entered alone. "Where's Morrison?"

"He's not in the office right now. He's out working the limousine company leads."

"Call him in, now," Nick said, excitedly. "We're dropping the limo and Henry Case investigations."

Not surprised, Mara dialed Morrison's cell phone and told him to get back to the office right away.

"What's going on?" Mara asked.

Nick and Bradley told Mara everything they had discovered.

"Find out where this Ryan Danforth is," Nick said to Mara. Mara left the room.

Bradley moved to the far side of the office and dialed Holly's cell phone to ask her if she knew anything about Micah's ghostwriter. She told Bradley Micah swore he wrote the manuscript on his own. He even signed a contract stating that fact.

"I'm going to go help Mara," Bradley said.

Mara eyed Bradley as he approached. "We have three Ryan Danforths in the immediate area. One is an eighty-six-year-old retired carpenter, one is a fifty-two-year-old English teacher, and the other is a forty-seven-year-old advertising executive."

"You call the English teacher and carpenter, and I'll call the ad exec," Bradley said as she handed him a piece of paper with the information she had found.

Fifteen minutes later, Bradley and Mara were in Bradley's truck and driving to Dorchester to speak with Ryan Danforth, an ad executive with a lifelong desire to be a novelist.

"How did Micah come to find you, Mr. Danforth?" Bradley asked as they took a seat at his kitchen table.

"We grew up together. He knew I wanted to be a writer back then. I wanted to write novels, but that never panned out. Then, one day about six years ago, he showed up at my door. I hadn't seen him since we were kids. He told me about his idea for a manuscript, told me some of the stories, and it sounded exciting. Then he asked me to help him write the book."

"Like a co-writer?" Mara asked.

"Yes."

"I'm curious. Why did you decide to ghostwrite the book instead of negotiating with him to be co-writer?" Bradley asked.

Ryan fidgeted in his chair. His wife, Eve, sat across from him. He glanced at her before he spoke.

"My wife and I talked about it—a lot. She didn't want me to write the book at all. She didn't trust Micah. So, we compromised. I wrote the manuscript but wouldn't put my name on it. Micah and I would split any of the money it made."

"Mrs. Danforth, why didn't you trust Micah?" Mara asked.

"I could tell he was trouble. Just by the way he carried himself. Then when I asked him where the stories came from, he had to think about his answer before he told us he made them up. I didn't believe him."

"Why not?" Bradley asked.

She thought about her answer before asking, "Other than I don't think he has a brain in his head?"

Bradley held back a grin and nodded.

"He admired them too much."

Ryan rushed to add, "Look, Micah has a good imagination. He told me lots of his story ideas. I just picked the ones I thought would make a good book."

Mara and Bradley looked at each other.

"There were more stories that aren't in the book?" Bradley asked.

"Sure, he had lots of them. I got pages and pages of notes." Ryan said.

"We're going to need those notes, Mr. Danforth," Bradley stated. "Tell me, did he pay you? Did he follow through and give you your profits?"

"Yeah. Forty percent, like we agreed. Like clockwork." Ryan's eyes opened wide. "I paid my taxes on it!"

"I'm sure you did, Mr. Danforth," Bradley smiled. "What about the movie? Did you get money from that?"

"Yes. We're using it for our kid's college tuition," Ryan answered. "I didn't do anything wrong, did I?"

"No, sir. Of course not." Bradley paused, thinking how best to ask his next question. "Do you think the stories could be true?"

Eve dropped her eyes to the floor. "That was my fear," she said quietly.

"And you, Mr. Danforth? Was there some small part of you that thought the stories could be true? Is that why you accepted the role of ghostwriter—so that your name wouldn't appear on the book and no one except Micah or maybe his publisher would associate you with it? Were you afraid of retribution?"

Ryan Danforth hung his head and closed his eyes. "It's the best thing I've ever written. But I couldn't take the chance that whoever did these things might come after my family."

"Did he tell you where he got the stories, Ryan?" Mara asked softly.

"He tried to make some up—you know, change the details. But his accounts were terrible. It wasn't until he told me the real stories that I knew we had something," he sighed. "He didn't tell me specifically who he got them from, but I'm pretty sure they all came from inmates at Walpole."

"We'll take those notes now, Mr. Danforth," Bradley said. Bradley's phone rang. He didn't recognize the number, so he let it go to voicemail.

Once in the truck Bradley checked his messages.

"Bradley, it's Derek. Call me and tell me what the hell is going on. They tell me my cell phone is destroyed so you'll have to call me at this number. They wouldn't give me a goddamn phone all day. Call me."

"Shit. I have to call Derek. He sounds like he's losing it," Bradley told Mara.

He hit the call button on his phone. "Yeah!" Derek barked.

"It's Bradley. I just got your message."

"Where are you? What's happening with the investigation?"

"Derek, things are moving quick. We're closing in on this guy, and we need to move fast. I promise I will come see you and explain everything as soon as I can, tonight. As soon as I can."

"Wait, don't hang . . ."

Bradley hung up the phone. He knew Derek would make him pay for that. He called Nick.

"We need a list of everyone in Micah Wistoff's cell block while he was in prison," Bradley said.

"I already have someone working on it. I figured it was a likely place to start," Nick said. "You on your way back?"

"Yeah. But, Nick?"

"What?"

"You may get an angry call from Derek. I just hung up on him."

"You what?"

"I know, but I'm in a hurry. We need to see the arrest records of every one of those inmates. We have a lot more crimes to sort through than those in this book. Have someone start pulling the records together. Start with the people closest to him—cellmates, work partners, you know."

"Okay. What do you want me to tell Derek if he calls?"

"Oh, he'll call. Tell him I'm sorry. Then tell him to leave us alone and let us do our job."

"No. I don't think I'll do that," Nick replied. "Come see me when you get back."

Had they known what they were walking into, Doug and Lynn may never have stopped in to see Derek.

"What the hell is wrong with that kid of yours?" Derek yelled.

Both Doug and Lynn halted, stunned by the reception Derek gave them as they came through his door. Doug stood in front of Lynn much like a shield to fend off Derek's remark.

"What?" Doug asked.

"The bastard just hung up on me," Derek yelled.

Doug turned to Lynn. "Honey, could you go wait in the hallway, please?"

Lynn hesitated before she turned and walked out the door.

"I think you should relax, Derek. And you should think very carefully before you speak again," Doug said in a stern and forceful tone.

"Goddamn it, Doug, the son-of-a-bitch hung up on me!" Derek shouted.

Doug turned and shut the door to Derek's private room, then stood next to the bed, towering over Derek.

"Derek, do you remember what happened the last time you really pissed me off?" Doug asked.

Derek unconsciously touched his hand to his nose. "Jesus, Doug, I . . ."

"No, Derek. Now you're going to listen to me. I know you feel helpless right now, and everything is out of your control. But I won't stand for you talking about my son that way. The man who hasn't slept more than ten hours or stopped to eat a decent meal since that bomb went off. The man who won't take a minute to talk on the phone with his best friend because he has a job to do and he doesn't want to let him down. So, tell me what Bradley said to you before he hung up the phone, Derek."

Derek placed his palms over his eyes, then slowly slid his hands down his face.

"He said things were moving fast and he would come see me, tonight, as soon as he could," Derek said somberly.

"Look, Derek, I'm no doctor. But I know what you're going through. I've experienced it. Hell, Bradley's experienced it. You're lashing out at the people closest to you because you're angry, and scared." Doug pulled up a chair and sat. "It's a normal reaction."

Derek choked up. Doug could see him swallowing hard to keep the tears at bay.

"I can't lose her, Doug. I can't. There are too many things I promised her we would do."

"And you will, Derek. You have to believe that. Cate will come back to you-—to us." Doug put his hand on Derek's shoulder.

They sat in silence.

Then Derek said, "I'm sorry I scared Lynn."

"Oh, you didn't scare her. I sent her away because she was about to punch you in the nose."

"I probably deserved it . . . again." Derek made his best attempt at a smile.

Doug patted his shoulder.

The horse she rode was painted blue with a red saddle and white mane. It rocked her violently before throwing her into a high-walled fence. Her head hit first, then she slumped to the ground. She could smell the newly cut grass and fresh manure. Or was it charcoal and a thick-cut steak? Yes, that's what she smelled.

Cate opened her eyes slowly. The smoke from the charcoal fire made her eyes sting. *The sun is bright*, she thought.

"Where did I leave my sunglasses?" she asked, softly.

"Cate? Can you hear me?" someone asked.

"Yes. Can you hear me?"

"Yes, Cate, I can hear you."

Dr. Frost sent the nurse out of the room to fetch Dr. Weaver.

"Where is my horse?" Cate asked.

"He's safe. He's in the corral," Dr. Frost replied.

"She. It's a she."

"Oh, yes. I can see that now," Dr. Frost said. "Would you like a sip of water, Cate?"

"Yes," she smiled.

Dr. Frost held Cate's bandaged head up slightly and put the straw to her mouth. He was pleased to see Cate take a sip without any prompting.

"Cate, can you squeeze my hand?" Dr. Frost asked.

"Did you wash the manure off first?" Cate asked, sleepily.

Dr. Frost smiled. "Yes, I washed my hands."

Dr. Frost felt a slight squeeze from Cate's left hand.

"I bet you held on to the horse harder than that. Can you show me how hard you held on to the horse, Cate?"

Dr. Frost's fingers bunched together as Cate squeezed the imaginary reins.

"Very good, Cate."

Laney came into the room and stood just inside the door. She looked to Dr. Frost, and he nodded his head to indicate a positive response from Cate. She knew she needed to stay quiet and let Dr. Frost take the lead. They did not wish to confuse her.

"Which horse is yours?" Cate asked.

"I don't have a horse," Dr. Frost replied.

"Why don't you ride the purple one?" her voice trailed.

Cate's hand softened and fell slack.

"Cate? Can you hear me?" Dr. Frost asked.

Cate did not respond.

Dr. Frost checked the monitors. Her vital signs looked good.

"She's out again," he said to Laney.

"But she spoke," Laney smiled.

"She understood my questions, she asked me questions, she squeezed my hand, and she took a sip of water. These are all great signs. Of course, she is confused. She is living in some kind of dream."

"What happens now?" Laney asked.

"We wait."

There was a knock on the door. "Come in," Derek called.

Doug and Derek looked up when Dr. Frost, Laney Weaver, and Lynn entered the room.

"Derek, Cate woke up," Laney said.

Lynn put her hands to her face and gasped.

"Only for a few minutes, but she woke up," Laney recounted. "Dr. Frost was with her and will answer your questions. This is very good news, Derek."

Derek's eyes teared as Dr. Frost relayed what transpired. He explained the significance of Cate's understanding, her ability to squeeze his hand and to drink from a straw.

"I don't want to mislead you. It is possible that she may not wake again for some time, or at all. It has happened. But I am optimistic, and you should be too," Dr. Frost said.

"Derek, it seems she is living in a kind of dream world. She may not know who she is or where she is. But that is not unusual at all. Amnesia, after a coma, is to be expected. And many patients do wake thinking that their dreams are reality. We have a long way to go, but this is a great start," Laney smiled.

Derek couldn't speak. He covered his face with his hands, and his body shook from the sobs. Lynn stood by his side, her hand rested on his shoulder, and her happy tears splashed at her feet.

Doug reached for Laney and hugged her hard. "Thank God," he whispered. "Will you call Bradley, or should I?"

"I have to get back to the emergency room. All hell is breaking loose again. You call Bradley. He'll explain. Tell him I love him."

Laney gave Derek a hug before running back to the emergency room. Dr. Frost told Derek he would keep him informed and left the room.

"She's coming back to you, Derek." Doug flashed him a big smile then dialed Bradley's number.

Bradley, Nick, Mara, and Tony sat in Interrogation Room A, the table covered with computer printouts of convicts' records from the ten years Micah made Walpole his home.

Hazel appeared at the open door. "Excuse me, Agent Gaston. You have a call."

"I'll be right back," Nick said. When he returned twenty minutes later, his grayed face looked drawn and defeated.

"Micah Wistoff is dead along with two others from the movie set. I called another of the producers, and they refuse to stop filming. They said it would bankrupt them if they did."

"Jesus. This guy isn't going to stop. Can we at least get a few days?" Bradley asked.

"I tried. He said no. The best I could get is them allowing us to put our people undercover."

"But what about the actors and actresses that got sick? They can't work," Mara asked.

"The only food he contaminated was for the crew and extras, and I was told they could be replaced. Apparently, the stars of the film eat much better than the rest."

"We better find this guy fast, then," Bradley said.

The only cellmate Micah Wistoff had while incarcerated in Walpole was Vincent Vega. Vega had a long rap sheet, beginning as a boy with his last arrest landing him at Walpole for fifteen years, ten of them spent with Micah Wistoff. Three other convicts fit the criteria of inmates who regularly interacted with Micah Wistoff: Billy Handish, Elijah Herrara, and Hector Elizondo. They would concentrate on those four.

They checked each against Bradley's original profile of the suspect, including whether or not either possessed a hunting license. Billy Handish, at the age of thirty-eight, never had a hunting license and did not fit certain aspects of the original profile, but he spent much time with Micah, and he had the reputation of being socially awkward and mad at the world. Elijah Herrara and Hector Elizondo both hunted and were known for their cruelty when doing so.

Ryan Danforth's notes referred to an additional eight crimes not depicted in the novel. None of the unpublished stories included the *Meet Your Maker* comment so Bradley and the others assumed these misdeeds were performed by other offenders.

"Let's start with Vincent Vega. Where are his records?" Bradley asked.

"I've got them here," Nick said.

"What landed him in jail this last time?"

Nick read through the file folder. "A Cambridge bank robbery gone bad. It was just dumb luck. A group of four off-duty police officers happened to be in the bank at the time withdrawing money to go on a weekend bachelor party excursion. When two armed and masked men burst in and one of them started shouting, the off-duty cops outnumbered them and shot the accomplice in the gut. He died later at the hospital. Vega wisely dropped his weapon. The third guy, the driver, was picked up later."

"What did he shout?" Bradley asked.

Nick scoured the report. "It doesn't say."

"Well, that's disappointing. I guess it would have been too easy," Bradley scowled. "But the end of the book does describe a botched bank robbery where the main character says, "If you don't want to meet your maker, then get on the floor now," then gets arrested and goes to jail. There's no mention of off-duty police officers though."

"Alright, who's next?" Nick asked.

They combed the records of the three other inmates who might be complicit but could not easily connect them to the *Meet Your Maker* narratives.

"Hang on," Nick said as he perused a file. "This case sounds familiar." He read quietly while Bradley, Mara, and Tony waited impatiently. "Elijah Herrara was arrested for a jewelry store theft in Somerville. The report says he carried a pickaxe with an eight-inch handle. The yellow fiberglass handle was wrapped with silver duct tape."

"Okay. What does that have to do with the book?" Tony asked.

"Nothing. Nothing at all," Nick replied, then turned to Bradley. "Bradley, can you do your thing with the computer and look up a cold case? Two cases, actually, involving rape of a minor. Search for pickaxe."

Bradley found the two cases Nick had previously reviewed. Each was an unsolved home invasion with horrific details of an assailant using a pickaxe to subdue his victims. In both cases, the report describes the pickaxe handle as having been wrapped in duct tape. And each victim had focused so well on the weapon, they noticed the yellow handle showing through tears in the tape.

"Whose case was that?" Nick asked.

"One in Lowell, one in Nashua, New Hampshire. He crossed state lines, so it became a bureau case. The case belonged to Derek and his partner, Rob May."

"Mara, see if you can find Agent Rob May. If he hasn't retired, tell him we need to talk. Hell, even if he has retired. He's going to want to hear about this." Nick glanced at Bradley. "Should we tell Derek?"

Bradley thought about it. "Not yet. It's too much," Bradley said as his phone rang. It was his father.

"Cate woke up, Bradley. Only for a few minutes, but she woke up and spoke," he heard his dad say.

Bradley's eyes shut tight, and he threw his head back. He desperately tried to keep his emotions in check. He could feel his throat closing, making it difficult for him to swallow. When he felt calm enough to speak, he asked, "Could she feel her legs?"

"They don't know, Bradley. Laney said she's in kind of a dream world, but that's common. Dr. Frost said she spoke, she understood him and even took a sip of water and squeezed his hand. This is all great news."

"Yeah. Yeah, it is. How is Derek?"

"Emotional. Look, I know you're busy, but he could use you right now. If there's any way you can come, I think you should."

"Alright. Let me see what I can work out. Thanks for the call, Dad."

Bradley hung up and waited for his throat to recover.

"Cate woke up," he announced. "Only for a couple minutes, but it is great news. I need to go see Derek."

"Go ahead. We got this. I'll keep you posted with any developments," Nick urged. "Tell him . . . tell him . . ."

"Tell him we love him, and we are praying for both him and Cate," Mara interrupted.

Nick and Tony nodded.

"Okay. But Nick, this is our pool of suspects. I can feel it. We're close. We just need to dig."

"You don't need to convince me, Bradley. I agree. We are on the same page. Now go."

Bradley again managed to hit peak commuting time between five and seven o'clock on weekday evenings. It had been a long day, and his truck's digital clock displayed only 6:12. *How could that be?* He wondered.

Thirty-five minutes later, he wheeled into Derek's new private room.

"You hung up on me," Derek stated.

"I did."

"Cate woke up."

"I heard."

"You look like shit."

"I know."

Derek winced and placed his hand on his hip as he used the hospital bed remote to raise himself to an upright position.

"Well?"

"It's possible we'll know who our guy is by tomorrow. My gut tells me I'm right about who it is. We just need the evidence."

"Run it by me."

Bradley started from the beginning. He recounted the connection to the movie, then the book, the ghostwriter, and the distinctive accounts of the crimes. Then he detailed the contents of the threatening letters, equipment theft, arson, bombing, and, most recently, poisoning.

"His actions are intensifying. We can't get the production company to stop filming, so we could be looking at another escalation."

"Which one do you think it is?" Derek asked.

"I think the only one smart enough to successfully execute these crimes, assuming they are true, is Vincent Vega."

"What's your plan?"

"We're still working on it."

"Dammit, I wish I could get out of this bed. I feel useless." Derek showed his frustration by pounding his fist into the mattress.

"Actually, there is something you could do to help." Bradley handed Derek a new copy of *Meet Your Maker*. "You could read this and see what else is in there that could help. I only had time to scan it.

"Oh, and here." he reached in his chair pocket and handed him a yellow highlighter. "Use this."

"How's Derek?" Nick asked.

"Much better. I put him to work," Bradley spoke into the phone. "What's happening there?"

"We're leaning toward Vega. I've got the Cambridge Police Department digging out the file on the Vega robbery that put him away. I should have it in the morning. Listen, I'm putting Mara and Morrison, along with five other agents, on the filming set tomorrow. I need you with me. I know you'd rather be there, but I need you here."

"Yeah, no problem, Nick. I'm good with that. Hey, go home. Don't sleep there tonight. I'm heading home now."

"Yeah, me, too. Soon."

Several vehicles sat in front of Bradley's home. He recognized his parents' and the Richard's car but not the third, which looked like a rental.

Bradley had never met David's parents. They had arrived early that morning after multiple flights originating in Bora Bora.

Wendell stood medium height, trim body, thinning gray hair with a black and gray mustache and goatee. His well-tanned arms showed the wrinkles of time.

"Bradley, I'd like you to meet David's parents, Rhea and Wendell Carson."

Rhea Carson could have easily just stepped off the stage of the Mrs. America Pageant, minus the fancy gown. Her impeccable appearance came easy to her, and her smile needed no prompt. She had an instantly likeable quality about her, and it became obvious to Bradley that her husband adored her.

"It's very nice to meet you both. How are David and Sheila doing tonight? I haven't seen them since this morning," Bradley asked.

"Oh, I think you would notice a marked improvement. They were both quite high this morning when we arrived. David because of his shoulder surgery, Sheila for her burns. The doctors have discontinued the strong painkillers. By the end of the day, David was more himself," Rhea answered.

"And Sheila?" Bradley asked, concerned.

"She was quiet most of the day until she heard about Cate. Then she perked up. We all did."

"I saved a plate of food for you, Bradley," Lynn said. "It's in the oven."

"Well, Bradley, is there anything you can tell us?" Ron Richards asked.

"Just that the case is proceeding, Ron. I just left Derek. I filled him in on our developments. If he wants to tell you what's happening, that's up to him," Bradley said.

"Well played, Bradley. Derek taught you well, didn't he?"

Bradley just smiled and dug into his plate of pot roast. Rusty came and lay down by his chair. By the time he had finished eating, Rhea and Wendell made their apologies and, citing exhaustion, left for their hotel. Ron and Marci Richards were wrapping up conversation, and Bradley knew they would leave soon. He trundled over to the sliding glass doors, flipped the exterior light on, and he and Rusty went outside. Rusty immediately ran down the sandpit ledge to visit those down below. Bradley hoped Rusty would bring Zayt back with him.

He heard the slider open and shut behind him. Doug pulled up a chair and sat to his right.

"Nice night," Doug said.

"Yeah."

"You must be tired."

"I am."

"Too wound up though, right?"

"Yeah," Bradley exhaled.

"This guy is getting bold," Doug said.

Bradley snapped his head around.

"We watch the news, son. It's not hard to figure out. Three people died today."

"Do they know?" Bradley bobbed his head to indicate the Richards and Carsons.

"I'm sure Ron must be putting things together. We don't talk about it. David's parents haven't been here long enough to know what's going on. How was Derek when you saw him?"

"Better."

"Good. I don't want to have to send your mother in there to punch his lights out," Doug snickered.

"What?" Bradley asked.

"Nothing. Never mind."

Rusty came running from the neighboring property, the way he always comes home when accompanied by Zayt. Doug saw Zayt walking toward them.

"I'll go help your mother," Doug said. "Hey, Zayt."

"Hey, Doug." Zayt waved as Doug got up and went back into the house.

Zayt sat in Doug's chair.

"How are you holding up, dude?" Zayt asked.

"By a thread, man. Maybe a shoelace," Bradley snorted. "And you?"

"Shoelace sounds about right."

"How's Eddy doing?"

"He's gone. He left this afternoon."

"Aw, man, I'm sorry."

"Yeah, me, too."

Doug came out of the house with a couple of beers and handed them to Bradley and Zayt.

"Thanks, Dad." Bradley gladly accepted.

Doug smiled and walked back through the sliders.

"How's the case going?" Zayt asked.

"We'll have him . . . soon." Bradley seemed confident.

"Glad to hear it."

They sat quiet, drinking their beer. Then Rusty nudged against Bradley.

"I guess he misses you. He's not used to you being gone all day."

Bradley reached for Rusty and petted him. "I miss you too, buddy."

"You heard about Cate?" Bradley asked.

"Yeah. Your folks called me. I know I've said this before, but you're lucky to have them."

"Yeah, I know." Bradley turned his chair to face Zayt. "So, what are you going to do about Eddy?"

"I don't know. I haven't figured that out yet. How are you going to catch your suspect?"

"Haven't figured it out yet."

LONG TAKE

Bradley and Rusty sat at his computer at five the next morning. His parents still slept on the pullout sofa by the fireplace. Bradley hadn't even made coffee yet, not wanting to disturb them.

He had not slept well. The worst of his nightmares showed Cate stumbling and about to fall from a cliff. Bradley stood nearby with both feet stuck in cement. Struggling to break free, he reached for her. He stretched and reached as she in slow motion began to hurtle over the rocky edge.

Then he woke, in a pool of sweat.

Bradley logged into the National Crime Information Center, also known as NCIC, and searched for Vincent Vega. He was born in Mattapan, a Boston neighborhood, but his last known address was in Roxbury. The report lists him as fifty-three years old. Bradley brought up his last arrest, the robbery in Cambridge. He jotted down the names of witnesses and employees interviewed. He read through the statements and paid close attention to the four off-duty police officers who foiled the robbery. Witnesses mentioned that Vega warned them, but, Bradley surmised, they were either too scared to remember his exact words, gave conflicting accounts, or just not recorded in the report.

Bradley willed the clock to move forward so he could call the people on his list to ask them what, exactly, the suspect yelled out.

He texted Nick to suggest he give other agents a picture of Vincent Vega to keep with them while they worked undercover at the filming later that morning.

good idea, came back almost immediately.

jesus, don't you ever sleep, Bradley texted back.

i could ask you the same

see you in a bit

Sometimes Bradley thought he and Nick were kindred spirits.

Lynn began to stir, and Rusty ran to her. Rusty seemed to enjoy having Lynn and Doug stay with them. Of course, why wouldn't he, since Lynn doted on Rusty. And Doug, even though he tried to hide it, snuck him food from his dinner plate.

"Good morning, Rusty. You are up early." Lynn looked and saw Bradley at his computer. "Bradley, honey, you aren't getting enough rest. What are you doing working already?"

Doug stirred. "Who's working?"

"Bradley is. Honey, you have to take better care of yourself."

"I'm fine, Mom. And look who's talking. You two have been going nonstop. I should be scolding you. Are you helping Zayt again this morning?"

"Yes, but . . ."

"And are you packing lunches for the families?"

"Yes, but . . ."

"And are you making dinner for everyone?"

"No." Lynn smiled.

"What?"

"No, we're not making dinner.

"Oh? Why not?" Bradley asked.

"Because Ron and Marci are taking us all out to dinner tonight. We don't know where yet."

"That's great. I hope you have a nice time."

"You're invited, too, Bradley. With Laney," Lynn said, startled he didn't realize that.

"We'll see how the day goes." Bradley hoped it would be the day they captured the man who almost killed his best friends.

By six o'clock, Bradley sat comfortably at his office desk with a fresh cup of coffee. Nick had beaten him there by a few minutes.

Bradley said, "I made a list of people to call today, all witnesses in the Cambridge bank robbery. We need to find out what Vincent Vega yelled when he burst into that bank. If we can link him to the statement written in the book, we may have enough to get a warrant and bring him in.

"Agreed. By the way, last night, I talked to Rob May, Derek's old partner. He's working out of the satellite office in Springfield. He moved there when he got married. Anyway, I told him about Elijah Herrara. Because there's no statute of limitations on sex crimes involving minors, he's going to go after him. They have DNA evidence, so it shouldn't be too hard to prove their case. I told him that he needs to share credit with Derek if he's successful."

"Let's hope he can. Nice job," Bradley smiled.

"Back at you."

"So, Derek is reading the book. I'd like to give it a good read myself, but we don't have time. But who better to analyze it than Derek? And it keeps him busy. Speaking of busy, are we short-handed today?"

"Yeah, I thought it best to put Mara and Tony undercover. They know what to look for," Nick said.

"Isn't this Mara's first undercover assignment?" Bradley asked.

"Shit. I didn't think about that. Maybe I shouldn't have sent her."

"No, Nick. That's not what I'm saying. She's ready. She knows her job. I'm happy for her, that's all."

"Yeah? Well, now I'm nervous," Nick said.

"Alright, I'm getting back into the files. We're going to need more than a catch phrase to nail this bastard."

Bradley compared the timeline of each heist to the whereabouts of Vincent Vega. He needed to make sure Vega was not incarcerated at the time of the armored car, Federal Reserve, or art thefts. Although Bradley could not know where Vega was at the time of those robberies, he confirmed Vega was not in jail. Bradley pulled every bit of information he could find including family members, known acquaintances, and his limited work history. He also pulled a copy of Vega's hunting license.

Because Vega was a convicted felon, the only firearm he could legally own or hunt with was a black powder rifle, otherwise known as a muzzleloader. However, even though Vega was allowed to hunt with a black powder rifle, he was not able to purchase black powder. Massachusetts requires a license to carry to purchase ammunition, including black powder and the projectiles used in the muzzleloader, and the state does not issue LTCs to felons.

Vincent Vega would need someone else to purchase his black powder. Vega had a son and two daughters. The son, Antonio, was thirty-four years old and had three children of his own. His daughters, both married, had seven children between them. All ten of Vincent's grandchildren lived in the suburbs of Boston.

Antonio did not have any felony convictions. An architect with no criminal history, he held a license to carry permit. Vega's daughters had never been arrested, but one of his sons-in-law had a conviction for drug possession from when he was in his twenties. Both daughters had a license to carry permit.

Bradley got the feeling that Vincent made sure his children did not follow in his felony footsteps. And, it seems, he succeeded. *Unless one of them purchased black powder for their father,* Bradley thought, *which is a felony.*

The office had begun to fill with agents. Mara appeared wearing torn jeans, sandals, and a concert t-shirt from a band Bradley had never heard of. She swung by Bradley's desk.

"How do I look?" She twirled.

"Like you're ready for Woodstock."

"For what?"

"Wow! Never mind. I should remember to not use references dating before the 1990s. You look great. Congratulations on your first undercover assignment. What area are you covering?"

"I'm just kidding. I know about Woodstock. I'll be hanging around the director, carrying a clipboard and looking unimportant."

"Stay focused. It's easy to get caught up in the activity around you. Think of yourself as the Secret Service, always on alert."

"Okay. Today, the director of *Meet Your Maker* is the president of the United States," she laughed. "Thanks for the advice."

"Alright," Nick hollered as he came into the noisy room, "Where's my film detail?"

"See you later," Mara smiled, excitedly.

Mara, Tony, and three other agents gathered around Nick. He handed each of them photographs. "These are photos of our prime suspect. His name is Vincent Vega. The mugshot is old. He's fifty-three now. The other pictures are recent but don't show his face clearly. The wide-brimmed fedora seems to be a favorite of his, but it doesn't mean he always wears it.

Vega is only one suspect. He may not be our guy. Watch for anything unusual. You'll be spread out. Check in with each other on a regular basis. Keep us posted and don't get starstruck. Be vigilant and be careful. Good luck. There are two SUVs downstairs waiting to take you to Dewey Square."

Nick walked back to his office.

"Wait, Dewey Square?" Bradley called across the room.

"Yeah. They're filming the Federal Reserve scenes today," Nick answered. "Alright, get out of here," Nick said to the agents.

They left in a group. The remaining agents and interns returned to business.

Bradley followed Nick down the hall. When Nick noticed him, he stopped.

"What is it?"

"How long has this been scheduled?" Bradley asked.

"Since they made the schedule. They'll be there for two days."

"The schedule just said Summer Street. I didn't know they meant Dewey Square. I don't like this, Nick. South Station is right next door. It's the second largest transportation station in New England. And it's got a built-in getaway service. Vega has his choice of multiple subway, train, or bus services, not to mention the seventy-five thousand passengers who pass through there every day. You've got to get them to stop the filming. I don't have a good feeling about this."

"What do you think I've been trying to do, Bradley? They won't suspend filming."

"Vega knows every inch of that place, Nick. He's been there many times before. It wouldn't take much planning for him to put together some catastrophic plan, especially since the actors will be mimicking something he's already done. Then he pops into South Station and disappears. At least contact MBTA and have them put more security in there."

"Alright, I'll call them and voice our concerns. It wouldn't be so bad to have extra security around there anyway. Roads are going to be blocked and traffic is going to be a nightmare," Nick said.

A thought jolted Bradley.

"Shit. A perfect storm."

"What?"

"If people know they won't be able to drive to work, they'll use public transportation. We could easily assume a bump in the number of passengers moving through South Station."

"Well, yeah, it's better than a traffic jam."

"Nick, put yourself in his shoes. If you tried everything you could think of to stop them from filming and it didn't work, what would you try next? Who would you threaten next?"

"The actors?"

Bradley shook his head. "The city, Nick. The city of Boston issues the permits. Look, I don't want to be an alarmist, but I have a pit in my stomach that has South Station written all over it. What if he gives up on targeting the film production and goes straight for the city? He's killed four people already. What reason does he have to stop now?"

"That's one hell of a leap, Bradley."

"Yes, it is. But the hair on my arms is standing up. Something Jim said keeps coming back to me. He said the person who placed the pipe bomb in the limousine most likely was not trying to kill anyone. The Boston PD explosive expert told us the same thing; it could have been worse. Well, it's gotten worse, and now he's got nothing to lose."

Bradley's phone rang. He recognized the number as Derek's hospital room phone.

"It's Derek. Can we go into your office?" Bradley asked.

He waited until the door closed before answering the call.

"Good morning, Derek. I've got Nick here. You're on speaker."

"Hey." He sounded tired. "Good morning."

"You stayed up all night reading, didn't you?" Bradley asked.

"Yes. There's a lot of detail in this book. Did you read about the art theft? Changing the locksets?"

"Yeah, a master stroke. Crazy enough to be true, right?" Nick said.

"Yeah. Bradley, come see me. And bring the files."

"We're short-handed here, Derek. And I have calls to make," Bradley said.

"Go," Nick said. "I'll pull some people in to make those calls. Run your theory by him while you're there."

"What theory?" Derek asked.

"Take a nap, Derek. I'll wake you when I get there," Bradley said.

An hour later, Bradley rolled into Derek's room. He found him asleep with the book lying open on his chest and the yellow highlighter in his hand. Bradley placed his briefcase at the foot of the bed.

He sat quiet for a moment, watching Derek sleep, and realized how difficult it must be for him confined in that bed with his wife in a coma and haunting visions in his head. Bradley knew something about that feeling. He hoped he would be able to help Derek cope.

"Derek," Bradley whispered. "Hey."

Derek's eyes flew open, as if he were a deer frozen in the middle of the street with a vehicle powering toward him. He blinked rapidly, then turned his eyes toward Bradley.

"Sorry. I was . . ." Derek's voice trailed off.

"The dreams are the worst. Sometimes they feel so real."

"Yeah."

Derek reached for the remote and raised himself to a comfortable sitting position.

"How's the hip doing?"

"Fine. The physical therapist is coming soon. They want me up and walking before they discharge me later today."

"They're sending you home?"

"They think they are. I'm not going anywhere. I'll stay in Cate's room. Let them try getting rid of me. Did you bring the files?"

Bradley didn't challenge Derek's plan, although he knew it would probably not play out the way Derek wanted it to.

"Yeah. Where do you want to start?"

The first major robbery written about in the novel involved the Baystate Security armored car theft. Besides the act of ramming the vehicle and the *meet your maker* statement, there were a couple other details about the robbery in the police reports and foreshadowed in the book. One of the instances spoke to actions after the thieves got the security guards to open the back of the truck and remove the money. The thieves also forced the guards to open two locked boxes inside the truck that contained treasury bills. But rather than take the treasury bills, the thieves took the locks with the keys instead. The book version of the story had one of the thieves admiring the locks. The police report called it an *absurd fixation*.

Another similarity pertained to the perpetrator shooting the tires of the armored car even after they secured the guards in the back of the truck. The novel described the shooter as having an *irrepressible urge to flatten the fuckers*.

"What about this one?" Derek asked. "The book says that Denny Duke slipped five one-hundred-dollar bills into the pants pocket of each of the security guards. He told them he had nothing against a man earning an honest living."

"There's nothing in the police report about that," Bradley said.

"What if the guards never told anyone about that? Is there anything in that report that says the security guards were subjected to a search after the heist?"

Bradley searched the report. "No."

"You may want to follow up on that. Find those guards."

"Is there anything else unusual from the armored car theft?"

Derek flipped the page. "He went into detail about the car they used. It was a 1997 Cadillac DeVille d'Elegance in light driftwood metallic. They stole it from the Beacon Hill area."

"Right here," Bradley got excited. "The report says it was a tan Cadillac DeVille. No wonder Ryan Danforth didn't want his name on this thing. It's reads like a fingerprint."

Derek had found more examples of novel details matching police reports. The most interesting, one from the brazen art theft, included a Carlton Fisk-signed baseball from the desk of one of the security officers. The Red Sox catcher, affectionately known as Pudge, was a Red Sox first-round draft pick and a 1970s fan favorite for the eight seasons he played in Boston.

The book suggests the thief knew about the baseball before entering the building. The police report surmised it to be a spontaneous crime of opportunity. So then it became important to find out if the information in the police report was public knowledge. Usually, in an investigation, a few details are held from the press and known only to the investigating agencies and the perpetrators. Derek and Bradley hoped that some of the similarities were among the unpublished.

"Tell me about it," Derek said.

"About what?"

"The theory that Nick mentioned. You're uneasy, Bradley. I can tell. You have that brain-running-in-circles look."

"Is that really a thing?" Bradley questioned.

"Spill it."

"Our guy has tried threatening letters, vandalism, arson, a pipe bomb, and poisoning. Each incident has been an escalation in damage and casualties. Four people are dead. He's in it now."

"Yeah, I get it. So?" Derek asked.

"The production company is filming at the Federal Reserve Bank today and tomorrow. I think this is where he might make his next move."

Derek turned his head and looked out the window, as if he could see the Federal Reserve building in the distance. "That's two high-profile targets side-by-side, one of which is extremely vulnerable and busy."

"Am I crazy, Derek? Am I being an alarmist?"

"South Station has long been a concern, as is any transportation hub. No, I don't think you are an alarmist. Have you talked to David about this?"

"No. He wasn't in any shape to talk about much last I saw him."

"Go see him. Now. See if he can talk them into giving us a few days to nail this guy."

"Alright. I'll be back."

Bradley found David and Sheila resting in their room. David spotted him first and put his index finger up to his mouth suggesting Bradley tread quietly.

"How is she?" Bradley whispered.

"Uncomfortable. They're weaning her off the medications and she hasn't slept much. I'd rather not wake her if possible."

"I'll be brief."

"They're sending us home later today. Well, not home. Sheila won't leave Boston until she knows Cate is going to be alright."

"Where will you stay?"

"My parents have a hotel suite. We can stay there."

"Listen, David. I need your help." Bradley grew somber. "I don't know if anyone has told you this yet, but the bombing of the limousine was a direct attack on the movie production." Bradley stopped for a moment to let that sink in.

David closed his eyes and took a deep breath. "I was a little out of it when I saw you yesterday. Later, when the drugs wore off, I tried to remember what we talked about. All I knew was I had a bad feeling about the conversation." David turned toward Sheila, then back to Bradley. "I'm responsible for this," he whimpered.

"No, David, you are not responsible. The person responsible is still out there, and I need your help to get him."

"What the hell can I do? I can barely move."

"David, we have a potentially catastrophic situation with the filming at the Federal Reserve building. South Station is right next door with tens of thousands of people in and out during the course of the day. Now I don't know how much you've heard, and I hate to spring it on you like this, but this guy is getting bold. Four people are dead so far, and he won't stop until the filming stops."

"You want us to stop filming."

"Yes. I know it's asking a lot. But we are close to catching this guy, and I don't want to give him a reason to hurt anyone else."

"There are five other executive producers besides me. Have you talked to them?"

"Yes. They won't stop. They won't even delay it. They say it will bankrupt them."

"Bradley, if it were up to me, I'd send everyone home right now. But I'm only one of six."

"David," Bradley whispered, "all I'm asking is that you try. Today. Now," he urged.

"Yes, of course, I will. I'll start making calls. Bradley, how dangerous is this situation?"

"The bomb he put in the limousine was meant as a warning. This is what he thinks a warning should look like," Bradley pointed to Sheila. "Imagine what he'll do if he thinks it's his last chance."

David's eyes went wide. He picked up his cell phone.

"Text me when you know something," Bradley said as he quietly left the room.

"Well?" Derek asked when Bradley returned.

"He's calling the other producers now. We need a plan in case this doesn't work. My guess is we are alright for today. He wouldn't have known that his poisoning plan had been unsuccessful until they showed up for work this morning. Tomorrow is another story. We need to find Vincent Vega and detain him today."

"On what grounds? Because he shared a cell with a successful author?" Derek said sarcastically.

"I know. But I'd rather get written up for harassment than see South Station blown to bits."

"If you do anything that isn't strictly by the book, Davis will have your ass out the door before you can say *check please.*' And, you can't let that happen. The bureau's going to need you."

"What do you mean, the bureau's going to need me?"

Derek squirmed in his hospital bed and averted his gaze from Bradley. "Nothing. Just that I'm stuck in here, and they need you out there." He thrust his hand toward the only window in the room.

"Derek. What the . . ." Bradley's phone rang, and the screen displayed David's name.

"Bradley, I'm sorry. I tried. But these are the last two days of filming. They're not willing to give it up. Not even for a day. I'm sorry."

"Thanks for trying, David. Give Sheila a hug for me, alright?"

"Sure thing."

Bradley felt panic rising in his gut.

"He couldn't stop it. Tomorrow is the final day of location filming. This is Vega's last chance."

"Then you better get back to work," Derek said.

"I'm sorry about Eddy," Doug said.

"Yeah, me too," Zayt replied.

"I guess it's up to him now."

"He's just not thinking clearly. He's got all this guilt that he won't let go."

"You've done everything you can right now. Give him a few days. He knows you're here for him if he needs you. That's important. But he needs to take that next step on his own."

"Yeah, I know. I just don't like to lose people," Zayt said.

"I know," Doug responded.

Doug and Lynn packed up the leftover breakfast food before they left for the day. Their morning had been quite successful. Three residents of the REACH community had joined them in the kitchen to learn the process. Two already had some experience in food service, while the third expressed an interest in learning the job skill. Doug and Lynn were quite sure all three would do well in their new positions with Shea and Rosie to guide them.

"I'm going to miss working there," Lynn said as they drove away.

"We need to go home sometime," Doug replied.

"I know. I just wish we weren't so far away."

"It's only an hour, Lynn. It's not like we need to traverse the country to get here."

"Doug, you know what I mean," Lynn sniped.

"I do. And I understand. But we both agreed a long time ago that Bradley needs his space. This whole thing has been horrible, and I'm happy we could help in our own little way, but we need to think about getting back home. There's not much more we can do here."

Doug turned the car down a side street in the opposite direction of Bradley's home.

"Where are you going?" Lynn asked.

"I just have to make a quick stop."

The area they drove through became rundown and strewn with tents and boxes acting as shelters. Doug pulled up to a three-sided structure made from cardboard, corrugated tin, and duct tape with a clear, plastic tarp stretched over the top.

"Stay here. I'll be right back," Doug said.

He got out, rounded the back of the SUV, and lifted the hatch. He took a large box from inside. Lynn watched as he approached the provisional home. She could tell he spoke to someone inside but couldn't see who. He left the box and returned to the car.

"What was that all about?" Lynn asked, sounding concerned.

"It's Eddy. I saw him there last night when I went to the store. Zayt said I could take the leftovers from this morning and give them to him so he could disperse them."

"We didn't have that much in leftovers. And this alley is nowhere near the grocery store," Lynn observed.

Doug sighed before glancing at Lynn like a child whose hand got caught in the cookie jar.

"Zayt called me yesterday when Eddy left. So, before I went to the grocery store, I took a little time to drive around to see if I could find him."

"And the food?" Lynn asked with a tilt of her head.

"I bought a few extra items while I was at the store and left them in the back of the car. Are you happy now, Inspector Whitman?"

"Yes. Very." She smiled broadly. "You are a sweet man, Douglas. Why you insist on trying to hide that fact, I'll never know."

Doug chuckled as he shifted the car into drive.

Nick met up with Bradley as he swiveled behind his desk and said, "We've made the connection between Vincent Vega and *Meet Your Maker*. Two of the off-duty police officers from the Cambridge bank robbery heard Vega say, 'If you don't want to meet your maker, get on the floor.' That ties Vega to the phrase. We're getting a unit ready to pick him up. I only hope he's still at the Roxbury address. It's the only address his parole officer has."

"I want to go. I need to see where he lives," Bradley replied.

"I'll tell you what. We'll send the unit in. If it proves to be his place, I won't let anyone touch it until you get there. Until then, we need to make a case. What did Derek come up with?"

"Let me put it this way. If the stuff in this book is true, it's almost as good as DNA. What bothers me is, why would he tell Wistoff his business? What made him trust the guy?"

"Maybe we can get more out of Danforth, the ghostwriter," Nick said.

"I've been thinking about him. He seemed a little skittish speaking in front of his wife. Let's bring him in here, alone. Have you got someone we can send to pick him up? Make it more official?" Bradley smirked.

"Yeah. When do you want him?"

"How soon before you go to the Roxbury address?"

"A couple hours."

"Let's get Danforth in here within the hour," Bradley said. "In the meantime, I have a couple of security guards I need to track down. Who's available to call the officers and agents who wrote these reports? We need to find out what information was held back from the press. Then we need to search and make sure none of it ever leaked to the press. It could be time consuming."

"I'll get Carter's team on it right away. By the way, that kid Earl has been waiting for you to get back. He's in the conference room."

"Okay. Any news from the filming detail?"

"Everything is fine so far. No sign of Vega or anyone suspicious. And the film crew is eating bag lunches today."

"Have you updated Director Davis yet?"

Nick sighed heavily. "Not yet. I've got a call scheduled in fifteen minutes. I've got to get the search and arrest warrants in place."

"Cheer up! It could be worse."

"How could it be worse?" Nick grunted.

"You might have ended up in this job for good."

"Look! If I'm going to walk, I'm going to see my wife," Derek said.

"But Mr. Richards, that's a long way. I am just going to take you down the hall and back," the physical therapist explained. "Your wife is still downstairs in the ICU."

"I know. Let's go." Derek began to swing himself off the bed.

"Wait. Slow down." The therapist pulled the walker away from the bed. "I want you to ease yourself onto the floor with your leg stretched out straight. You will feel some discomfort in your hip, groin, and thigh as you put weight on it. This is normal because there will have been a slight change in the length of your leg. Your first step will be with the operated leg, your left leg. Take small steps and try to put even weight on both legs as you walk. Are you ready?"

"Yes, I got it. Let's go."

The therapist moved the walker up to the bed. Derek did as instructed. He stretched his left leg out straight and rested it on the floor. Using his arms and his right leg, he lifted himself to a standing position. A sharp sensation ran through his knee and into his hip. His grip tightened on the walker as pain splashed across his face. A bead of sweat formed on his brow. He stepped forward with his left leg, first with light weight testing the dependability of its use then more substantial weight as he stepped forward with his right leg.

"That was the hard one," the therapist said. "Let's try another."

Derek headed out of his room and to the elevators. Holding onto a belt wrapped around Derek's waist, the therapist went beside and slightly behind him. Pushing an empty wheelchair, an orderly walked with them.

If the therapist thought Derek would be dissuaded from the long walk to the elevator, he was wrong. Derek pressed the elevator button.

"Mr. Richards, this is not a good idea. If you overdo it, the swelling will inhibit your recovery."

Derek glared at the young man. "Trade places for a minute. If that were your wife lying in the ICU, would I be able to stop you from going to see her?"

The therapist contemplated for a moment.

"Get in the chair, Mr. Richards."

Once on the ICU floor, Derek rolled himself into Cate's room, leaving the therapist and orderly in the hall. He sidled up to the bed and reached for Cate's hand. She looked peaceful, almost smiling in her deep sleep.

He felt a tender squeeze of his hand. Derek's eyes flew wide open. "Cate? Can you hear me? Cate?"

Cate's eyelids fluttered. Slowly, like the sunrise cresting the horizon, her lids raised. Her emerald-green eyes radiated to him a thousand hues of infinite beauty. What Derek had been viewing in black and white, he saw in fanciful color.

"Hi," Cate said.

"Hi." Derek's smile exceeded its boundaries.

"I didn't think you would be back so soon," Cate said.

Derek remembered the doctors explaining Cate's dreamlike state.

"I couldn't wait to be back with you," he said.

A nurse rushed into the room.

"Did you get the muffins? They're Derek's favorite."

Derek swallowed hard, and a tear rolled down his cheek.

"Pineapple-macadamia. Just like you said," Derek choked out.

Dr. Frost entered the room and stood on the other side of the bed beside Cate. He looked at Derek and shifted his eyes toward the door. Derek took it as being asked to move away discreetly to let the doctor examine Cate. He distanced himself without leaving the room.

"Hello, Cate," Dr. Frost said. "How are you feeling?"

"Thirsty," she said as she swallowed.

The nurse raised the bed slowly to move Cate to an upright position, then handed the doctor a cup of water with a straw.

"Here, Cate. Could you take a small sip of water?" Dr. Frost held the cup in front of Cate's mouth.

Cate reached for the straw with her right hand, missing it twice before grasping it and taking a sip of water. Her arm then dropped to the bed as if it had no more strength.

The doctor reached for that hand and held it. "Cate, could you squeeze my hand?"

Cate smiled. "I like to hold hands." She squeezed.

"Can you squeeze a little harder, Cate?"

She squeezed again. The doctor's fingers barely moved.

"How about the other hand, Cate." The doctor held her other hand and asked her to squeeze. That time, his fingers scrunched together.

"Very good, Cate."

"Can I have my Margarita now?" Cate asked.

Derek smiled as he worked to hold back tears.

"Here you go, Cate." The doctor placed the straw up to Cate's mouth. She reached for the straw and placed it in her mouth. "Mmm. It's good," she whispered.

"Don't drink too much, now. You'll have to go easy," Dr. Frost said.

"I'll be good. Derek's picking me up later. We're going to the moon."

"Then you better get some rest."

"Alright." Cate closed her eyes.

Concerned, Derek looked at the doctor. Dr. Frost waved him into the hallway.

"She's just sleeping. These are very good signs, Derek. She is speaking clearly, her motor skills have shown quick improvement, and the strength in her left hand is good."

"She's confused. I don't think she knew who I was," Derek said.

"That's quite common. As I explained before, we believe she has created a world she can live in while she heals. Some of that world is from memories, some is fantasy. And even though she is awake now, she will exhibit confusion and maybe uncertainty. You should prepare yourself for that."

"Okay, I understand. But what does it mean that she didn't have any strength in her right arm?" Derek asked.

"Most likely the cause is spinal stenosis from swelling in her spinal column. Nerves run down the middle of your spinal column, and if the column narrows and puts pressure on the nerves, loss of function can occur. The hope is that her right side will return to normal once the swelling is reduced. Now that she is awake, we will put her back in the neck brace to prevent any further damage."

"What about her lower body, Doctor. Is she . . . will she . . ."

"It's too early to tell, Derek. Even if the damage is minimal, it could be several days or even weeks before we know the answer to that."

"Okay. But she's awake now, right?"

"Yes, she is. We will monitor her very closely. Her responses are hopeful. But we will have to be delicate with her, Derek. I understand your need to be with her, and you will. But I think it's best if I, or Dr. Weaver, are with you when you see her. Patients sometimes become agitated, and we would like to avoid that if we can."

The nurse approached Derek. "Your therapist needed to attend to someone, so he asked me to bring you back to your room."

"Thank you," Derek said as he looked over his shoulder at Cate.

Bradley met Earl in the conference room.

"What have you got?" Bradley asked.

"We might have him on camera walking to and from the makeup trailer an hour before the fire started. If the lab can enhance the video, we could have a good profile of him."

Earl ran the video for Bradley. The subject wore the wide-brimmed fedora and carried a duffel bag. The video showed only black and white images, so they could not identify the color of the bag. The subject walked from the southeast corner of the park to the trailer. Several minutes passed before he came back into view, empty-handed, and walked back the same way he came.

"Send it to me. Great work, everybody," Bradley said as he turned and sped out of the room.

Bradley forwarded the video as high priority to the lab for enhancement. He hoped to get an updated picture of Vincent Vega. He heard a phone ring, and it took him several seconds to realize it was his desk phone. Not used to anyone calling him on that phone, he answered it guardedly.

"Agent Whitman, this is Hazel. Agent Gaston would like you to meet him in Interrogation Room B, please."

"Thank you, Hazel."

Nick sat at the table with a file folder and papers spread before him.

"Ryan Danforth is on his way up," Nick said.

"How are we going to treat this guy? Are we looking to burn him?" Bradley asked.

"Not unless he decides not to cooperate. If we get what we want, I don't feel the need to pursue him."

"You don't *feel the need to pursue him*? Three days in the big office, and you sound like Joe Friday."

"Who the hell is Joe Friday?" Nick whined.

"*Dragnet?* In the fifties? One of the most famous police shows of all time?"

"Why do you even know that?" Nick asked.

"I studied everything about law enforcement since I was twelve years old. I couldn't get enough."

"Here he is," Nick said, looking through the glass wall. An agent escorted Ryan Danforth to the door. "Come in, Mr. Danforth. Sit down."

Danforth moved to an open chair without looking Nick or Bradley in the eye.

"Would you like some coffee or water, Mr. Danforth?" Nick asked.

That's when Bradley knew he was expected to play the hard ass.

"Water, please," Danforth responded.

Nick poured water into a cup from the pitcher in the middle of the table, then handed it to Danforth.

"Alright! Everyone comfy now? Can we get started?" Bradley snapped.

Danforth's eyes involuntarily peered into Bradley's. He saw what Bradley wanted him to see—impatience.

Nick pretended to be annoyed by Bradley's rudeness. "Mr. Danforth, I am acting Supervisory Special Agent Nick Gaston." He enunciated his title and name while glaring at Bradley, as if he were reminding Bradley who was in charge. "We need to follow up on a few things from Agents Whitman and Thompkins's initial visit with you."

"What things?" Ryan Danforth looked to Nick.

"Your lies, Mr. Danforth," Bradley spit. "All that crap about not knowing whose stories they are."

"For chrissake, Whitman, I told you to keep your conspiracy theory out of this. Now, just sit there and be quiet," Nick scorned.

Bradley sighed and conjured up a proper angry pout.

"I'm sorry, Mr. Danforth. Agent Whitman seems to think you were the guiding force behind the novel, *Meet Your Maker*, not Micah Wistoff. He's suggested that you knew Mr. Wistoff shared the company of a certain inmate and you encouraged him to befriend that inmate to get his story. That way, if there was any backlash, it would all fall on Wistoff. Now, I know that's crazy, but because my colleague has written a report about it and sent it to my boss," Nick glared at Bradley again and spoke in an unpleasant tone, "I need to follow up and ask you some questions."

"That's . . . that's crazy," Danforth stuttered.

"I know, and again, I apologize for the inconvenience. Could you walk me through the process? How did Mr. Wistoff contact you? Explain the writing process, publishing process, and why your name is not on the book, please."

Danforth relayed the same story he told Bradley and Mara. Micah showed up on his doorstep one day with an idea for a book. He told crime stories that he made up, but Ryan told him they weren't good. When Micah told Ryan actual crime stories, Ryan became interested and said he didn't know who the stories were about.

"And your wife didn't want you to write the book, is that correct, Mr. Danforth?" Nick asked.

"Yes," Danforth replied.

Bradley shouted. "That's because she knew if you did, you would end up dead, just like Wistoff did." Danforth squirmed and backed his chair away from Bradley. "And you knew it, too. That's why you arranged with Wistoff to ghostwrite the book instead of co-write it. You didn't want your name associated with it because you knew the stories were about . . ."

"Whitman!!! Enough. Get out," Nick yelled. "Now."

Bradley slammed his hand on the table, turned his chair, and left the room. He gave Danforth one more angry look through the glass. Once out of sight, he broke into a smile.

Back at his desk, he was finally able to call the first of the Baystate Security armored car company guards, Dennis Frakes.

"Mr. Frakes, this is Agent Bradley Whitman of the Federal Bureau of Investigation. I am looking into a cold case involving the robbery of the armored car that victimized you and your partner. First, let me start by saying that the statute of limitations has expired in this case. There is no legal recourse for how you answer my next question, so I suggest you just tell me the truth and we'll be done with it."

"Okay," Frakes said wearily.

"Did one of the suspects give you anything after he tied you and your partner up in the back of the truck?"

"Shit!"

"Can I take that as a *yes*, Mr. Frakes?"

"You said there is no legal action that can be taken?"

"That's right. I am investigating a different crime where this information is relevant. I am not going to send anyone to your door."

"He shoved five one-hundred-dollar bills in each of our pockets and said something about not having anything against a man making a living."

"Tell me about the locks."

"Yeah, that was strange. The guy went nuts over the locks. When he made us unlock the boxes, we both thought he would take the treasury bills, but he didn't want them—just the locks with the keys, maybe for a souvenir. They both had *Property of Baystate Security* written on them."

"Thank you, Mr. Frakes. I may be back in touch with you."

The only other agent in the room was Jim. Bradley went to him and asked that he tell Nick he had news.

Bradley met Nick in the hall out of sight of the interrogation room.

"It's him, Nick. No doubt now. The armored car security guard just confirmed that the suspect put five hundred dollars in the guard's pockets during the robbery. That information was not in the police report or in the press. The guard never told anyone. Yet, it was in the book. Now we know Wistoff got his accurate information direct from the perpetrator, Vega. How's it going in there?"

"He's scared shitless of you. I'm almost there."

"See what you can find out about the baseball stolen from the security desk at the art museum. Maybe he'll remember something that's not in the book. That robbery is the only one without a statute of limitations. That's where we need to focus."

"Right." Nick looked at his watch. "The SWAT team should be here in about twenty minutes. If I'm out, start briefing them." Nick went back to interrogation.

Bradley input Vega's last known address into a map program on his computer and found what he was looking for. Constructed of red brick and built in the 1950s, the single-family ranch house would have been considered upper-middle class in its day. The most current photos showed overgrown bushes and moss clinging to its base. The house paled in comparison to its neighbors.

Bradley used the internet to examine a street view of the property, its surroundings, and potential escape routes. He printed photos and maps to familiarize himself with the area before the special weapons and tactics team arrived. He had gotten halfway through the briefing when Nick emerged from the interrogation room and pulled him aside.

"Another connection confirmed. Danforth says that Wistoff told him the Carlton Fisk-signed baseball was a big deal for our suspect. He claimed it to be the homerun ball Fisk hit out of Fenway Park in the twelfth inning of Game 6 of the 1975 World Series. He said that Wistoff didn't believe our suspect. Danforth decided not to use that part of the story in the manuscript."

"And the police report didn't have anything about the baseball being stolen, right?"

"Right."

"Have we talked to the security guard who owned the ball?"

"I just did. He still lives in Boston. He confirmed that he told the police the baseball had also been stolen, but they weren't concerned enough about it to put it in the report."

"Does he agree it could have been an inside job? That the other guard was in on it?"

"He wouldn't say for sure, but he's always wondered how the suspects managed to get into the building," Nick said. "Let's finish the briefing."

"Nick, we've got a problem. I don't think I'm going to be able to get into Vega's house. There's no access for me short of building a ramp, and we don't have that kind of time. And even then, we don't know how accessible it is inside. It's an old house."

"Shit, I hadn't thought about that. Well, once we have Vega in custody and SWAT secures the property, we'll take pictures of everything," Nick said.

"I think you need to go in and take Mara with you. You know what we're looking for, and Mara has a keen awareness for details. I think you and Mara are our best bet."

"Alright, unless we find a way to get you in there," Nick said. "I'll send someone to pick Mara up and meet me at Vega's place. We'll go in as soon as it's secure."

"How sure are we Vega still lives there?" Bradley asked.

"Pretty sure. The electric and phone companies both have records of Vincent Vega paying those bills. And his vehicle registration shows it as his address."

"I wish Derek could be there when you pick him up."

"Me, too. Let's finish this briefing and go grab this guy," Nick said.

Bradley called Derek to tell him SWAT was on their way to Vega's address. Both felt displaced and anxious, wishing they could be on the scene.

"I'll stay on the line with my desk phone. Nick is going to patch me in live from the scene on my cell. You can listen in on the operation."

Derek stayed quiet for a moment, then spoke.

"I talked to Cate, Bradley. She woke up while I was in the room with her."

"Wow, that's great news. She must have sensed you were there, right?"

"I don't know. She didn't know it was me. She talked about me like I wasn't in the room," Derek said sadly. "But Dr. Frost says that's normal. It's just . . . hard."

Bradley paused, not knowing how to respond.

"I'm sorry, Bradley, I didn't mean to bring this up."

"Derek, you never need to apologize for worrying about Cate. You know that. But I know one thing. Cate is one of the strongest people I know. She's not going to let a little thing like a coma keep her away from you. She woke up for you, didn't she?"

Bradley's cell phone rang. "It's Nick."

Nick's face appeared on Bradley's phone screen.

"We're on the street a few houses down from Vega's. Mara is here with me. SWAT should be pulling in any minute," Nick said.

"Nick, I have Derek on the other line. He's listening in."

"Okay, good. Vega's car is parked out front, an old Cadillac DeVille. Wait, here they come. They're moving fast . . . they're out of the vehicle . . . up on the porch and around the house . . . yelling for him to open . . . now they're using the battering ram . . . they're inside."

Over the telephones for the next several minutes, Bradley and Derek heard heavy breathing in anticipation of Vega's capture.

"Someone's coming out . . . it's the SWAT leader. Mara, drive up to the house."

Bradley watched the view on his screen move into the distance as the car made its way forward. He heard the electric window open in the car.

"He's not inside, Agent Gaston. I'll come get you as soon as we deem it safe to come in."

"Dammit! Thank you, commander," Bradley heard Nick say.

"I guess we do this the hard way," said Bradley.

Derek replied, "He won't be coming back now. You'll need to get as much information out of that house as possible. Impound his car and secure any outbuildings. He's officially on the run."

"I'll let you know what we find inside," Nick said. "Derek, I'm sorry I let you down."

"Bullshit. You didn't let anyone down, Nick. You've got him on the defensive. Now go finish it," Derek said.

"Yes, sir." Nick disconnected.

"I'm sorry, Derek. I thought we had a good chance," Bradley said.

"Hey, I know you're going to get this guy, Bradley. I appreciate you calling and letting me listen in. Now stop apologizing and go do your job." Derek hung up the phone.

Bradley's frustration mounted. It angered him whenever his wheelchair kept him from doing his job the way he preferred to do it, which is exactly the emotion that tended to get him into trouble when he overstepped his bounds. But he couldn't afford to let that happen this time. He had to be patient and let the information come to him.

While he waited, he arranged for three teams of agents to surveille the homes of Vincent Vega's children after running the idea through Nick.

"Yeah, do it," Nick said. "Get them there as soon as possible. We're going in now. I'll call you if we find anything."

Next, Bradley studied the Dewey Square area of Boston. Atlantic Avenue runs along the front side of South Station and the Federal Reserve Bank building and intersects with Summer Street, which runs between the two buildings. Summer Street from Dewey Square to the opposite side of South Station was closed to traffic for several blocks during the filming.

South Station houses multiple modes of transportation and serves as hub for more than twenty-five eateries, shops, and banking venues. Because Massachusetts Bay Transit Authority police take charge of security within the station, Bradley not only contacted the Boston Police Department chief but also the MBTA chief's office to arrange for a meeting later that day. He knew Nick would need to update them on the day's events and develop a security plan for the next day.

The transportation hub's design works efficiently for travelers but presents a challenge for security. Not only can an individual enter using one of many street-level doors, but buses and trains arrive frequently from above and below the main floor, making it tricky to keep track of who goes where.

Bradley sat back in his chair and closed his eyes. He cleared his mind of everything except for Vincent Vega. *What is he thinking? What method would he use to carry out his final attempt? Where would he attack?*

Bradley surmised that Vega committed fully to his cause of derailing production of the film. He had already demonstrated his willingness to kill for it. He imagined Vega felt it a personal afront that Micah Wistoff usurped his deeds for his own gain. But Bradley did not believe Vega knew about Ryan Danforth's part in the arrangement. They would need to keep it that way.

As for the method Vega would use to wreak havoc on the film production, Bradley thought Vega already showed his hand. But he would need a substantially larger bomb to achieve the destruction he most likely craved—and a detonator. He would want to make sure the bomb exploded where and when he wished.

So where could he place a bomb big enough to do massive damage and inflict carnage? Bradley concluded he wouldn't be able to get close enough to the Federal Reserve building. There would be too many people around, especially with substantially increased security. Vega would know that. A bomb detonating anywhere in South Station would be catastrophic. But a large bomb on the Summer Street side of the station could not only do massive damage inside the station but also to production units staged on Summer Street and possibly to the bank building. If he wanted to make a statement, he would want to get as close to the filming site as possible.

The other alternative to South Station would be a bomb inside a vehicle. Vega could use a personal vehicle or delivery truck to park near the site. Legal parking in the area is minimal, but there are spaces reserved along Atlantic Avenue for taxis and deliveries. Bradley did not think that would be ideal for Vega, but he still imagined a potential threat.

He wasn't sure how much time had passed by the time Nick called, but to him it felt like hours.

"I'm sending you pictures now," Nick said. "He's our guy, and he's got a plan. We're searching for anything that might tell us what it is. Something spooked him to pack up and leave, and he obviously didn't want to use his own vehicle."

"I'll check the cab companies to see if anyone had a pickup at his address," Bradley said. "Have you found any bomb materials?"

"Yeah, it's in the pictures. And it's not pretty."

"I'll look at the photos and get back to you. I set up an appointment with BPD and MBTA in your office at five o'clock."

"Good. Morrison says everything is going smoothly at the film site. I told him our guy is on the run and may be heading toward them. Jesus, Bradley, if he hits today, we're not ready."

"I'll call BPD and have them send as many people as they can to the area. If he's planning anything for today, maybe we can slow him down by flooding Dewey Square with police."

"Okay. I'll finish up here, then head back to the office."

Bradley spoke with the Boston police chief and pressed the importance of police presence around the filming site for the rest of the day. Then he delegated the job of calling all the area taxicab companies to Earl and the rest of the interns.

He examined the pictures Nick and Mara sent. The first photo showed a mantle over a brick fireplace with a close-up of a Carlton Fisk-signed baseball. The next three pictures consisted of twelve empty one-pound bottles of FFG black powder, wire clippings, and metal piping. One of the photos showed an empty, clear bottle without a label. *It could be an accelerant,* Bradley thought. Another picture revealed an old wooden Winchester box filled with padlocks. Two brass-colored locks with keys, each printed in black marker with the words Property of Baystate Security, lay on top of the pile.

The rest of the photos displayed a long table holding live ammunition and rifle-, handgun-, and shotgun-reloading equipment. Reloading components including bullets, brass casings, and primers sat piled across the back of the bench table. Lined on a shelf above the table stood various bottles of powder, each specific to a reloading need.

"Well," Bradley said into his phone, "at least we know for sure it's him."

Nick replied, "Now we just need to find him. Any luck with the cab companies?"

"Not yet. We've still got a few to call. Have you found any address books, maps, or anything suggesting where he may have gone?"

"Mara's going through his desk and personal things now."

"I'll see if there's been any activity on his credit cards. Maybe we'll get lucky and he's staying in a motel nearby," Bradley said.

"Okay, good. I've got to go. The explosives team just got here. I'm going to head back to the office once I get them squared away. Mara can handle things here."

He hadn't stayed at that motel in more than twenty years, although nothing had changed. The furniture, short-nap carpeting, and television seemed original. Only three other rooms looked occupied, and those, he thought, probably only for the hour. It was a cash motel, and people there kept to themselves.

He felt it had been the right move even though he didn't sense the authorities had exposed him. Vincent Vega made one last trip to the box truck to remove a large rectangular package. He carefully placed it on the floor away from the room heater. He laid out his brown uniform to keep it from wrinkling and set the uniform hat on the table.

He was angry the film company made him go to all the trouble. He thought the bomb in the limousine would be all he needed. After all, they were Hollywood people. It was just bad luck an FBI agent and his wife had been riding in the limousine. Otherwise, he wouldn't feel the need to stay in the mangy motel, but he didn't want to take any chance the FBI might make some connections.

But he hadn't taken the Hollywood money into consideration. They weren't about to let a few nuisances keep them from making millions. That part he understood, and maybe he could even sympathize. Really, it wasn't the moviemakers' fault. They knew a great story when they heard it. His life was worth writing about.

Vega was at the top of his field. The art museum theft proved it. *But Wistoff had no business doing the writing,* especially since Vega could go to jail for the art heist referenced in *Meet Your Maker.*

I never should have trusted him. That fleabag of a cellmate won't be telling any more tales. Vega snickered at the thought. *And tomorrow, a lot more people are going to meet their maker.*

Vega smiled as he turned on the television.

Derek couldn't stay in that hospital room one more minute. The world spiraled around him, and he felt as if it sucked him into its vortex, rendering him motionless in the middle of the chaos. The time had come to leave the safety of the eye of the storm and swirl into action.

With the help of a nurse, Derek commandeered a wheelchair and rolled himself to David and Sheila's room. He hadn't seen them in three days since he had sat across from them in the limousine, but Bradley had kept him updated on their condition.

Both were awake and sitting up in their beds. Sheila saw him round the corner. Derek thought she was about to speak, but she could say nothing. She reached her arms toward him, and he could see tears develop in her unbandaged eye. He went to her side, and they hugged as best they could, Sheila wincing from the pain of stretching her blistered body, Derek from the discomfort of his incision . . . and his heart.

Once Sheila found her voice, she asked, "Have you seen Cate? How is she?"

Derek held her hand. "I spoke with her," he smiled. "She woke while I was with her. She's confused, but she is talking, and her strength is good. She's resting right now."

"Thank God," Sheila raised her eyes to the ceiling. "And you, Derek. How are you?"

"I'm fine. The new hip will take some getting used to, but I'll manage. What about you, Sheila? Are you doing alright?" he asked, his concern apparent.

The sound of metal trays hitting the hall floor made Sheila jump. David got out of his bed and sat beside her.

"It's alright, honey. I'm right here," David said.

"I guess I'm still a little jumpy," Sheila told Derek.

"We all are," Derek replied, then thought it best to detour attention away from Sheila. "And you, David? How are you doing?" Derek asked.

"I'm fine. I'm looking forward to getting out of here today."

"When are you flying home?"

"What, David? I told you I'm not leaving," Sheila insisted.

"Easy, honey, I know." David brushed Sheila's hair from her face, then turned to Derek. "We're not going home. We're going to stay in the hotel with my parents until we're sure Cate is alright."

"Hotel? No, you're staying at our house. Sheila, your parents checked out of their hotel today and moved to our house. You and David should stay in the other guest room. You know there's plenty of room. Besides, Cate would crucify me if she knew you were staying in a hotel. Have your things brought to the house."

"Derek, are you sure?" Sheila asked.

"Of course I am. There's plenty of room. And you should be with your parents. And David, your parents are welcome to stay also. We have another guest room downstairs."

"Thank you, Derek, but my parents are quite comfortable living in hotel rooms. They enjoy it." David shrugged his shoulders.

"Is that alright with you, David? Would you mind?" Sheila asked.

David smiled at Sheila. "That sounds great."

"David, can you and I talk business?" Derek asked.

David lowered his head. "I tried, Derek. They won't stop the filming. I'm sorry."

"No, I know. It's about something else."

Stumped by what Derek might wish to talk about, David replied, "Of course."

❧

"Zayt, you got a phone call on the main line," one of the REACH residents called to him.

Zayt made his way to the sales office where Shea sat at her desk.

"It's Sergeant Doyle," she said as she handed him the telephone.

"What happened?" Zayt asked.

"How do you know anything happened? This could be a social call. You always assume the worst, don't you, Gaines."

"How do I know? Because you've never made a social call and you always use my real name when the news isn't good."

"Well, . . . Zayt, . . . it's not all bad news. I've got Eddy and a friend of his here at the station. One of my guys picked them up for assault and battery. It seems Eddy was seen hitting a couple

207

of young men with a piece of wooden fence post while they lay on the ground and his friend kicked them."

"Shit."

"There's more. Eddy has learned to talk since you two got together. In fact, he won't shut up! He says the two men attacked his friend, Jake. Eddy came to his aid, with an improvised weapon, and then a few more people jumped in to help. When the patrolmen came by, the others fled. Eddy and Jake stayed to get a few more licks in before my officer cuffed them."

"Sounds like self-defense to me," Zayt said.

"Yeah, well, that wasn't my call. But here's the kicker," Doyle laughed, "no pun intended. Eddy says these are the same two guys that jumped him. He didn't know it at first, but now he's positive."

"Are they alright? Eddy and Jake, I mean. I don't give a damn about the attackers."

"Jake's got some contusions and bruising but refuses to go to the hospital. Do you want to hear the best part?"

"There's more?"

"Eddy asked me to call you," Doyle said. Zayt could tell Doyle smiled as he spoke, and Zayt found himself choked up.

"What do I need to do?"

"I talked to the officer. He hasn't filed his report yet, so I convinced him to see this as self-defense. The two attackers are in the emergency room, nothing serious, just precautionary. We will officially arrest them once they are released from the hospital. But Eddy and Jake could use a place to stay tonight."

"I'll send the REACH van to pick them up."

"I haven't told Eddy yet. He still thinks he's going to jail. Do you want to handle this or should I?"

"Let me. Maybe I can do better this time," Zayt said.

Zayt pulled the van into the Revere Police Department parking lot. Nervousness prevented him from displaying his usual swagger. Doyle met him at the front desk with a light smirk.

"You look like you're about to jump from a hundred-foot cliff. What's the problem?" Doyle asked, then met Zayt's eyes and saw fear of failure swimming in them. "You can only do what you can do," he told Zayt.

Zayt nodded.

In the cell, an agitated older man in dirty torn jeans and shirt stood in contrast with Eddy, who wore Bradley's Cambridge-style clothing.

"You must be Jake. I'm Zayt. Hey, Eddy, are you okay?"

"They never had a chance to touch me. This time Jake took the brunt of it," Eddy said. He looked ashamed.

"I tried to get them to come after me," Eddy continued, "but they wouldn't leave Jake alone. Now the cops want to throw us in jail for protecting ourselves. What the fuck?"

"The cops brought you in because they saw you beating two men on the ground with a fencepost while this guy—," Zayt pointed to Jake, "—kicked the shit out of them. What would you think?" Zayt asked before considering his remark. "But Sergeant Doyle explained the situation to the officer, and you won't be charged, so you won't be going to jail."

"Then what are you doing here?" Eddy asked.

"You called me, Eddy. You tell me what I'm doing here."

"Yeah, right," Eddy said. "Jake needs a place to stay. I thought you might be able to help him out."

"Sure, if you come with him," Zayt said.

"Zayt, I told you. I can't."

"I'm afraid you don't have much of a choice this time, Eddy. Doyle and I agreed that you and Jake stay at the REACH community for at least a week."

"Not going to happen," Eddy replied.

Zayt had anticipated Eddy's response, so for their own safety Zayt felt he had no choice but to out-and-out lie to Eddy. "Doyle said you're looking at up to two years in jail if you refuse. Both of you."

Zayt saw the panic in Jake's eyes and knew Eddy would never let that happen.

"Doyle can't do that," Eddy said.

Feeling a twinge of guilt, Zayt replied, "Don't be stupid, Eddy. Of course he can."

"Eddy, I can't be locked up. I'll die this time," Jake said as he walked in circles. "I can't, I can't . . . ," Jake continued to mumble.

"It's okay, Jake. We're getting out of here. Right Zayt? We're getting out of here now," Eddy said.

"I'll go get Doyle," Zayt said and walked to the front desk.

"Well, did you convince them to go back to REACH with you?" Doyle asked.

"Yeah, you could say that," Zayt smirked.

Doyle unlocked the cell to let Eddy and Jake out. Once they reached the lobby, Eddy turned to Doyle, who smiled.

"This isn't right. You can't tell me what to do or where to go. You can't threaten me. I'm a US citizen with rights. If you weren't a friend of Zayt's I'd have *you* arrested," Eddy hissed.

Not knowing that Zayt had painted him as the bad guy, Doyle's mouth dropped open, and his eyelids lifted into his brows.

Eddy rolled out the door with Jake behind him. Zayt looked at Doyle, smiled, and shrugged his shoulders before he walked out the door.

❧

"I know we agreed that Bradley needs his space, but it doesn't feel like this is the right time to leave him," Lynn said as she packed items into her suitcase.

Doug smiled. "Is it not the right time for him or for you?"

"Both. Either. I don't know. Something doesn't feel right."

"Derek, Sheila, and David are getting discharged today. Holly, John, and Mike are already trying to get back to normal in Amherst. And Cate . . . well it's still going to be some time before she is ready to go home, but she is making improvement."

"But this thing isn't over, Doug. Bradley hasn't been taking care of himself and you know it. He's obsessed with this case."

Doug understood Lynn's concerns. Bradley had, in the past, used any means possible to apprehend dangerous suspects even if it meant putting himself in danger. Doug stopped his packing and went to Lynn. He wrapped her in his arms and held her.

"We have to trust him, and we need to show him that trust. He's worked hard to confront his feelings of physical inadequacy. He's got to believe in himself as much as we believe in him."

"I know you're right. And I do believe in him. But he almost lost seven people he loves. This is too much." Lynn's misty eyes filled with tears as she placed her hand on her stomach. "I've felt this crater inside me since the explosion, and I feel like Bradley has positioned himself on the edge of that crater. I just think if we are here, he will feel more grounded."

"Okay, we'll stay," Doug smiled. "We'll stay until Bradley kicks us out." He chuckled as he wiped tears away from her cheeks. "Far be it from me to question the intuition of motherhood."

"Thank you." Lynn relaxed. "I'm probably being silly."

"No," Doug grinned, "but you are going to be late for dinner if we don't start getting ready."

"Oh, my lord, what time is it?" She glanced at the clock. "Five o'clock? We need to be at the restaurant in an hour."

Boston Police Chief Dale Hanson sat in front of Nick's desk next to MBTA Chief Sean O'Reilly. Bradley had positioned himself to the side with Nick seated behind the desk.

"We don't feel this is a potential threat. We believe it is an imminent threat," Nick said. "Tomorrow is Vincent Vega's final chance to complete his mission, which is to stop production of this movie. Why he is determined to do this is not important right now. But we believe we know how he plans to achieve it.

"Bradley?" Nick nodded for Bradley to take control of the narrative.

"Vincent Vega perceives that he has been and continues to be personally violated," Bradley said. "A man of his character sees that as the ultimate form of disrespect. He first attempted to derail the project by using intimidation, annoyances, and minor criminal activity." Bradley cited the threatening letters, stolen equipment, and pulling the fire alarm at the hotel.

"Those attempts failed to persuade the production company to quit," Bradley continued, "so he escalated his efforts by using enough force to get his message across but not so much as to kill anyone—first the fire, then the purposely mild pipe bomb. Unfortunately, when the limousine driver died, Vega found himself unintentionally fully invested in his mission. As we know, his efforts escalated from there to murder by use of poison."

"On the phone, you said you might know what he has planned. Did you find something at his residence?" BPD Chief Hanson asked.

"We did," Bradley replied. "We found empty black powder containers, detonator wire, and an empty, unlabeled bottle which is at the lab right now. It most likely contained an accelerant of some kind."

Bradley continued to explain his thoughts on how Vega may have planned to execute his next strike. He theorized Vega would plant the bomb inside South Station on the Summer Street side of the building, close to where the film crew would be.

"If I were him, that's what I would do," Bradley said. "But, as we all know, there are many other areas inside the station that are vulnerable. This is our greatest challenge."

"Okay. So, we put security at every entry point and beef up police presence on the Summer Street side of the station," MBTA Chief O'Reilly said confidently.

"No," Bradley said as he cast a glance toward Nick. "We don't."

Both chief's positioned themselves on the edge of their chairs. "What? What do you mean, no?" Chief Hanson asked.

Bradley took a deep breath. He knew what he was about to propose could be the last thing he ever did.

"We put just a few extra MBTA security personnel inside South Station just to make it look like we are taking that threat seriously. However, we keep the guards away from the Summer Street side of the building. We use the Boston police officers to flood the Federal Reserve Bank filming area, including the

Rose Kennedy Greenway where the spectators gather across Atlantic Avenue."

"But if what you think is true, my officers will be useless at the Fed building," Chief Hanson stated.

"Not at all," Bradley replied. "Vega will expect added security. If we can get him to believe we are safeguarding the Hollywood production more than his primary target, he will be bold and go for the gold, so to speak. If we flood the station, especially on the Summer Street side of the building, he could plant the bomb anywhere and we may not find it in time."

"How the hell are we supposed to find the bomb if we're not even in the building?" Hanson asked, frustrated.

"The FBI will have agents in the station—undercover, concentrated on the Summer Street side. We'll use the MBTA at various egress points. We need to show enough presence to make it believable but not so much that it deters Vega from his plan."

"Okay, let's assume for a moment the plan works and Vega plants the bomb where you think he will. What then?"

Bradley and Nick spent the next seventy-five minutes explaining their plan. The police chiefs listened intently, asking questions and making suggestions. Then they sat back in their chairs contemplating the discussion.

Boston Police Chief Hanson said, "It's risky, but it could work."

MBTA Chief O'Reilly countered, "This could be a disaster. But, I think you're right— it's our best option."

"Alright, let's put things in motion," Nick said as he stood. "And I want to thank you both for your input and your support. It's going to take all of us to keep this city safe tomorrow."

MASTER SHOT

"Bill and Janet won't be joining us for dinner tonight. They decided to stay at the house with Sheila, David, and Derek to help them get settled in," Ron Richards said. "Derek is furious the hospital staff wouldn't let him stay with Cate. I don't know if I've ever seen him that angry. I don't envy any of them having to spend the night with Derek in the state he's in."

"Bradley and Laney won't be able to make it either," Lynn said. "Bradley is still working, and Laney was finally able to leave the hospital, so she is going home to get some much needed rest."

"Has Bradley said anything? I couldn't get any information out of Derek," Ron said.

"Nothing," Doug said. "But I think they're getting close."

"What makes you think that?" Ron asked as the waiter filled their water glasses.

"Bradley has a tell," Doug said.

"A tell? What's that?" Rhea Carson asked.

"It's a poker term, honey," Wendell Carson explained. "It means that he does something unconsciously to tip his hand."

"What kind of thing?" Marci Richards asked.

"Well, in Bradley's case, his tone changes. His voice deepens barely enough to notice. When I talked to him earlier, he used that tone," Doug said.

"What in the world are you talking about?" Lynn asked. "Why haven't you told me this before?"

"I don't know. I guess I assumed you noticed it, too." Doug explained.

"Does Bradley know he does this?" Lynn asked.

"I don't think so," Doug said. "I never mentioned it."

"Is there anything else you know about our son that I don't?" Lynn gaped at Doug.

"Uh, I don't think so," Doug grinned.

"I wish Derek had a tell," Ron said. "I never know what he's thinking."

"He wears a blue shirt when he's nervous about something," Marci said.

"What?" Ron asked.

"He usually wears a white shirt unless he's nervous or expecting trouble," Marci replied.

"How on earth do you know that?" Ron asked.

"He's been doing that since high school, Ron. Any day he had a test, he wore a blue shirt. When he came home from college for the weekend, I could tell what kind of week he had by his dirty laundry. Remember the day he was going to find out if he got the job at the FBI? A blue shirt day."

A silence fell over the table until Rhea Carson began to giggle, then Lynn, then Marci. The husbands followed suit with snickering of their own. Then the waiter arrived with a bottle of wine.

"We set up an old canvas Federal Emergency Management Agency tent with cots for you and Jake. We keep them around for additional housing. There should be some sandwiches in the kitchen, but there's no food allowed in the tent. We don't want to attract any rodents. Why don't you show Jake around the place. I've got some things to take care of."

"Zayt, I'm only here for Jake."

"You're here to stay out of jail, Eddy."

"Yeah, about that. I don't believe Doyle made any kind of stipulation about us staying here for a week. I think you made that up."

"I guess there's really only one way to find out, isn't there? You can take a chance and leave and see if Doyle comes after you. Or you and Jake can relax here for a week, let his wounds heal, eat decent food, sleep without getting beat up, and maybe help a few other people."

"Help other people how?" Eddy asked.

"I don't know, Eddy. We all need help with something."

"What do you need help with, Zayt?"

Zayt thought long and hard before he responded. He knew if he evaded the question, he might lose Eddy forever. How could he ask Eddy to confront his survival guilt if he didn't confront his own demon?

"Fear," Zayt said before he turned and walked away.

"How did it go?" Derek asked.

"BPD and MBTA are on board," Nick answered through the speaker phone.

"They're right, though. This is risky. Timing will be crucial," Bradley said.

Derek responded, "Have the dogs go through South Station and the Federal Reserve Bank tonight. Let's make sure he hasn't already placed the bomb somewhere. After all, we still could be wrong about his intentions. I'd feel much better if we could grab Vega beforehand. Was there anything in the house to tell us where he might be?"

"Nothing obvious. Mara is on her way in now. I'll get a full report when she gets here. We have people at his children's houses, and we haven't found any friends or acquaintances where he might take refuge," Nick said.

"We didn't get any hits on his credit cards. He must be using cash. Vega is a real pro. He's not about to make that mistake. We're checking local hotels and motels, but we're running out of time," Bradley said. Then he went quiet and considered a thought.

"Hang on Derek. Bradley has that look on his face," Nick said.

"Good. We need something."

"We should have checked this sooner. He didn't take his car," Bradley said.

"Right. So, he either got a ride from someone, used public transportation, or . . ." The idea hit Nick. "Rental."

"If he's hauling a bomb around, he's not using public transportation. Let's start calling all the rental car companies in the area. He would still use cash, but he would need to show his license. Unless he has fake identification. It's worth a shot."

"Text me a list. I can make calls from here," Derek said. "Let me know what you hear from Mara." Derek hung up the phone.

"Who's left in the office?" Nick asked.

"I think a few of the interns are still here. What about the agents from the filming detail? They should have wrapped up by now."

"Call Morrison. Find out what's happening."

Mara appeared at the open door of Nick's office. "I just talked to Tony. They're on their way in. They did a sweep of the area before they left. Everything outside is clear."

"Did you find anything that can tell us where Vega is tonight?" Nick asked.

"Nothing so far. But he doesn't exactly have a filing system. We do have more than enough evidence to convict him for these crimes, though."

"Mara, did you find the wide-brimmed fedora there?" Bradley inquired.

"No. I went through the house and his car. I didn't run across the hat. He must have it with him, or he got rid of it."

"Doubtful he got rid of it. He had no reason to suspect we were on to him until we got into his house. With any luck, he still doesn't know we were there. If he took it with him, he'll wear it," Bradley concluded.

"Mara, you continue with Vega's things. Bradley, let's get started on calling the rental car companies. Pull in anyone who is available. And you better send some names to Derek, but let's not overburden him, alright?"

Bradley smiled. "Alright."

Bradley pulled a current list of area rental car companies from the internet. He found Earl and two other interns in the office. He explained what information they needed to ask for and expressed the urgency to gain it. Then he texted Derek a list of three companies to call.

That's it? Derek texted back.

Yes. We have plenty of people here, Bradley texted him.

Bradley knew Derek would stew over them pampering him. That coupled with the fact that the hospital wouldn't let him stay with Cate would make an unpleasant night for anyone around him. If they didn't keep Derek busy, it was likely just a matter of time before he fired back.

Much like Bradley, Derek could not stand idleness. Until Derek met Cate, his life consisted only of his work, a few casual relationships, and no friends. Cate changed everything. If Derek had been concerned that a strong relationship would soften him, the worry proved contrary. From the minute they met, Derek put himself in protection mode not only for Cate but for the rest of them as well. Derek believed it was his job to protect his family and his friends, and when something kept him from performing his duty, he lashed out with a ferocity few have seen.

Bradley spoke with Mara and made a plan to help them dodge Derek's verbal bullets. He texted Derek again. *We need help wading through Vega's papers. Mara can come to your house. Are you up to it?*

YES!!! Derek replied.

Nick agreed with the idea. "Let's keep him as busy as possible tomorrow, too. I don't want him showing up in Dewey Square."

Under normal circumstances, Bradley would worry about that. But he knew Derek wouldn't go anywhere near Dewey Square the next day. There'd be only one place he would be, and that place would be by Cate's side.

"Let's just get him through tonight without blowing up his blood pressure," Bradley said.

Bradley's text tone sounded. *Have you eaten?* The text came from his mother.

Not yet.

Are you at the office?

Yes.

How many are there with you? We will bring food.

You don't need to.

How many!!!

Six.

See you soon.

Bradley alerted the security officer in the lobby to expect his parents' delivery. Forty-five minutes later they arrived with two large brown bags and the sweet smell of Italian food. The conference room table soon filled with chicken alfredo, spaghetti and meatballs, a large antipasto salad, and a loaf of garlic bread. The restaurant had packed paper plates and plastic silverware with plenty of napkins. Nick was the only one not drawn to the table by the tantalizing aromas. Bradley texted him to come to the conference room.

"Mr. and Mrs. Whitman, you are lifesavers. Thank you," Nick said. Their mouths already full, the interns could only nod in agreement.

"Nick, I think we can get past the Mr. and Mrs. phase, don't you? It's Doug and Lynn," Lynn said.

"Well, thank you, Lynn. If you don't mind, I'll take this back to the office. I'm in the middle of something."

"Of course, we don't want to interrupt you," Doug said.

"How was your dinner with everyone?" Bradley asked.

"Very nice. Cate and Sheila's parents didn't come. They are all staying at Derek's—Sheila, David, Janet, and Bill."

"Oh, Derek didn't say anything about that," Bradley said.

"Ron said Derek's not in the best of moods," Doug said.

"Yeah, I could tell."

"They were heading over to the house with the Carsons after dinner," Lynn said.

"That's going to be a full house." Bradley chuckled thinking of Mara surrounded by Derek's extended family.

"Are you going to be here much longer?" Lynn asked.

Bradley's tone dropped slightly. "I'm not sure. Probably a couple more hours at least, maybe more. I'll call you if I'm going to be very late. Do you mind taking care of Rusty for me?"

Lynn noticed the change in his voice. "Of course, we will." She glanced at Doug. He grinned.

"We'll let you get back to work, and we'll see you at home," Doug said.

"Thanks for dinner."

Derek led Mara into his study without introducing her to the horde of people now in his home. He had reported back to Nick and Bradley that he struck out with his three phone calls, although Derek used colorful language to express his frustration at the limited sized of his list.

"I've been wondering why Vega chose to leave his house," Derek said. "If he didn't know we were on to him, which is evidenced by everything you found in his house, why wouldn't he just stay there?"

"Maybe he didn't want to take a chance that the bomb would destroy his house," Mara suggested.

"If it did, it would take him with it, so it doesn't make sense he would worry about that."

"Good point," Mara said.

"He's a meticulous man when it comes to planning. Could it be part of his routine or just an abundance of caution?"

"Maybe he's superstitious."

"You were in his house. Does he seem like a creature of habit?"

"Well, I can tell you he's not meticulous about keeping his living space in order. But his basement, where we found the reloading equipment and ammunition, was laid out methodically and well organized. So, he has priorities."

"What about his car?"

"Very neat and clean."

"Priorities," Derek mumbled. "Maybe habitual? What have you got in the boxes?"

"This one is from his kitchen table. He had it piled high with junk mail and papers, receipts, and bills. I haven't had a chance to look through any of it yet."

"What's in the other box?"

"Stuff I found in his bedroom closet. I figured it must be worth something if he kept it."

"I'll take the table. You take the closet," Derek said.

Derek sorted first by category—junk, receipt, bill, and so on, then by date. He went through the receipts looking for similarities. Vega frequented a local Chinese restaurant and a diner, eating at least a couple times a week at one of those establishments. Receipts from a convenience store also dominated the pile, yet he didn't have any grocery store receipts.

His bills were typical—electricity, water and sewer, and credit cards. He didn't carry a balance on his cards, and he did not have a mortgage on his house. Financially, Vega lived comfortably for someone who recently spent fifteen years in prison.

Ninety minutes passed before Marci Richards knocked on Derek's study door.

"Come in," Derek called.

"Derek. You have to eat something. I'm not leaving this room without you. And you, young lady? My son has not seen fit to introduce us so I will. My name is Marci," she crossed the room to greet Mara.

Mara stood and shook Marci's hand. "Hello. It's nice to meet you. I'm Mara."

"Mom, really. We are busy," Derek protested.

"Mara, have you eaten anything today?" Marci asked.

"Actually, no. I haven't," she replied.

"I could tell. You look drawn and undernourished. Come with me." Marci reached for Mara's hand. Mara looked back at Derek, uncertain, but saw he moved to follow them.

The transition from delving into a murderer's life to a living room of family banter felt to Mara like jumping into a pool of ice water after a long soak in a hot tub. The result? A stimulating jolt.

In the kitchen with a plate of chicken cacciatore in front of her, Mara faced Derek. "How is Cate? I didn't have a chance to ask before."

Derek's face softened as it usually did when he thought about Cate. "I'm sorry. I jumped us right into the work. She's doing better. She's awake but still confused. They wouldn't let me stay with her tonight." He finished with an edge to his voice.

"That must be hard for you. I'm sorry," she said softly.

The lump in Derek's throat, much like a sneeze that sneaks up on a person, returned. He cleared his airway but remained silent.

"Nick has been a surprise," Mara spoke in an upbeat tone. "He has been organized and unusually polite, two characteristics I never thought I would use to describe him," she smiled.

Derek chuckled. "Nothing like being thrown into the fire." He paused and put his head down. "Jesus, I can't believe I just said that. Thank God Sheila wasn't in here."

They finished their dinner without conversation.

"I'm sorry, Mara. It's just things that used to be normal or easy aren't anymore. Even the use of a metaphor," Derek said.

"No apologies. I understand."

"Why don't you head home. I think we've done everything we can tonight. Tomorrow will be a long, hard day."

Bradley dressed in street clothes—jeans, t-shirt, light jacket, and sneakers. By four-thirty, more than an hour before sunrise, he was out the door and headed to South Station. He managed all of it without waking his parents. Rusty, on the other hand, grew quite discontent when Bradley left again without him.

Without much traffic at that hour, he managed the trip in only twenty minutes. The plan had been to meet Nick, Mara, and Tony at five o'clock in the parking lot of the investment business on the corner of Summer Street and Dorchester Avenue. Jim would stay in the office. Bradley arrived early.

Bradley felt somewhat confident Vega wouldn't try anything until the movie filming started. The production crews' start time wasn't until eight in the morning, but Nick and Bradley weren't about to take any chances. They wanted surveillance to begin early.

Nick pulled up beside Bradley's truck five minutes later, then Mara, then Tony.

"Communication will be critical," Nick said as he handed out the radios and earpieces. "Don't change the station. Everyone involved will tune to this frequency. Keep the chatter to a minimum just in case he's got his own radio and happens upon us."

Derek struggled to put his newly pressed khaki slacks, part of the ensemble Marci had ironed the afternoon before in hopes of expending her nervous energy. Then he slipped on a blue shirt. He used the rented wheelchair to allow himself to bring coffee into his study.

At four-thirty in the morning, he did not expect anyone to wake for hours. He pushed the chair away from his desk and moved his wheelchair in its place. The piles from Vega's kitchen table still sat there. They had found nothing from the receipts or bills to give them a clue as to his whereabouts.

Without much thought, he began rifling through the junk mail, the only pile he didn't examine the previous night. He took a sip of coffee as he picked up a postcard advertisement and perused it while looking over the top of his coffee cup.

The blue card boasted a bright red business name, Blue Collar Truck Rental. Derek put his coffee cup on his desk and looked at the address label. The recipient's name did not read Current Resident as most advertisements do. Printed in black ink, it read Vincent Vega followed by his current address.

Derek booted his computer, scolding it as it slowly came to life. Once it did, he searched Blue Collar Truck Rentals. The website displayed a telephone number, which Derek promptly called. He reached an answering machine. Frustrated, he looked for the owner's name without success.

He clicked on the Services tab and noted that the business typically opened for daily pickups at five o'clock in the morning, allowing construction companies and other businesses to start their day early. He called Nick and told him what he had found.

"Have you got someone you can send over there?" Derek asked.

"Yeah, I'll send Tony. Text me the address," Nick said.

"Tony, call me as soon as you know anything," Nick said before Tony drove away.

"Could we get that lucky?" Bradley asked.

"Even if we find out what he's driving, we still have to find him," Nick said.

"Yes, but it's much easier if we know what he's driving," said Mara.

"For sure," Nick agreed. "I would give anything to be able to ditch this plan."

Bradley and Mara concurred.

The three left their vehicles in the business parking lot and headed to the Summer Street entrance of South Station. An MBTA transit officer stood at the entryway and eyeballed them as they entered. Understanding that all law enforcement officers would benefit from knowing each other's affiliations, Nick unobtrusively showed him his badge.

"When will they move the K-9 units to the train and subway terminals?" Nick asked the officer.

The officer checked his watch. "In ten minutes."

Nick nodded to the officer as he, Bradley, and Mara continued into the station. The building, originally constructed in 1899, had undergone many renovations but remained true to its neoclassical architecture. The interior resembled that of an airport with a food court, shops, and kiosks. Three banking institutions were represented as well as a major pharmacy, luggage repair, and bookstore. Chain restaurants supplied everything from coffee to pizza to crepes.

Bradley concentrated on the Summer Street side of the complex. Positioned just inside the main entrance at the corner of Atlantic Avenue and Summer Street, the three banks dominated the floor space on either side of the escalators which lead to the heavily traveled Red and Silver transit lines.

Straight ahead stood a small security kiosk. Following along the Summer Street wall, next came public restrooms, a likely spot for someone to plant a bomb. Past that was the information counter, the large and busy train ticket counter, and a bookstore.

Although they would move their positions throughout the morning, Bradley chose three suitable areas for himself to get the best vantage point. Mara would cover the Atlantic Avenue side of the building, and Nick and Tony would have the unenviable task of watching direct access from passengers disembarking from commuter trains.

MBTA security officers had the best photo of Vincent Vega that the FBI could provide and stood on alert tuned to a shared radio frequency.

Bradley watched as officers with bomb-sniffing canines vacated the main terminal.

Today is the day, the thought struck as he opened his eyes. His mouth curved into a smile. *Nobody messes with me. I should have just done this in the first place. Fuck that trying to send a message shit.*

He remembered the last time he woke in the same motel. His day hadn't gone as planned. But today, he would make up for that. He was proud of his ingenuity. The best plans are uncomplicated and, therefore, overlooked. *Maybe I will write my own book*, he mused, *and today will be the final chapter.*

His clock displayed half past six. He jumped out of bed with the energy of a man half his age, and a chortle escaped his lips as he walked into the tiny bathroom.

"It's a white box truck, license number KJC 889. He picked it up yesterday morning. They have his credit card information on file, but he paid cash for a two-day rental," Tony said into his phone as he exited the rental company.

"Thanks, Tony. Get back here as soon as you can," Nick said as he wrote down the information.

"I'll call Chief Hanson and ask him to send some units around to the motels again, this time looking for the truck. You call Chief O'Reilly. If we can't intercept him cleanly, at least we know what to look for once he gets here," Nick said to Bradley. "Mara, call Derek and tell him his information panned out. We may have a chance to contain this."

South Station officially entered its Thursday morning rush hour.

Bradley positioned himself next to a coffee kiosk where he could see the main and Summer Street entrances. Lines formed at the train ticket counter, and restrooms became popular. The plan called for several MBTA workers, male and female to frequent bathrooms to look for anything unusual, and Bradley kept his eye out for those going in with luggage and boxes. The banks had yet to open, but automated teller machines drew customers. An MBTA employee staffed the information booth, and Bradley noticed the bookstore getting ready to open.

The large clock hanging from the ceiling ticked to 6:35. Bradley had already watched intently as the magazine stand received two separate morning newspaper deliveries, but neither of the drivers looked the least bit like Vincent Vega. MBTA police had warned Nick and Bradley to expect a lot of deliveries throughout the day. Newspapers, magazines, food, coffee, clothing, and brochures represented only a few of the items restocked daily. By seven o'clock that morning, most shops, restaurants, and kiosks would be open for business and provisions.

⁕

"Tony better get back here quick," Nick spoke into his radio. "I can't keep my eyes on this many people. The trains must be at full capacity this morning."

"MBTA are watching, too," Bradley said. "But we could call someone in from the Federal Reserve detail across the street if the foot traffic gets to be too much."

"No, the film crew should be showing up shortly. We need to make sure he doesn't slip in among them. Now that we're here, I'm not sure our planned approach is the best."

Bradley spoke into his radio microphone, trying to ease Nick's apprehension. "You know, Nick, you ought to try a little optimism sometime. Maybe you wouldn't age so quickly if you did." Bradley flashed Nick a smile from across the concourse.

"Well, if we live through this day, I'll give it a try," Nick replied.

Bradley watched as a man entered through the front doors. He pushed a platform truck made of stainless steel. Four heavy-duty wheels rumbled across the tiled floor, the contents of the dolly piled high with plain brown boxes. Of average height, the man wore a brown baseball-style cap pulled down low over his face, and his brown delivery uniform looked crumpled.

"Alert," Bradley spoke quietly into the radio. "Delivery person from main entrance. Right height and approximate age. I can't see his features. He's pushing a platform dolly with multiple packages."

"I got him," Mara replied.

"I see him," an unfamiliar voice said.

The man didn't hesitate as he walked in a straight line toward the busiest area of the concourse where pedestrians emptied in and out of train platforms. He stopped next to the fresh-flower shop and spoke to the proprietor. She opened a box and retrieved a bouquet of flowers, nodded, put the bouquet back in the box, and signed something on his clipboard. The delivery man removed all the boxes from the dolly and stacked them neatly next to the cash register, then turned around and walked back out of the station the same way he came.

"MBTA. Get someone over to that flower shop and have them open the rest of those boxes. Don't alarm anyone. Say it's a random security protocol. Be casual about it," Nick said.

"Bradley, can you get eyes on his delivery truck?"

"I'm heading out the door now," Bradley said. Some seconds elapsed.

"It's an official company truck," Bradley told Nick. "I've got the license plate. He's packing the dolly up. Now he's rearranging packages in the back. He's not in a hurry."

"All the boxes contain flowers," came the same unfamiliar voice.

"We're clear. Everyone back to their posts," Nick commanded.

Ron pulled the car up to the main entrance of the hospital.

"Are you sure you won't let me help you up to her room?" Ron asked as the car idled.

"I'm fine, Dad. Go take Mom out for breakfast or something. Thanks for the ride. I really appreciate it. I'll see you later," Derek said as he closed the car door.

Using crutches, he ambled into the hospital. At only forty-seven years old, Derek felt like an old man. Even though the intellectual inside him voiced objection, he determined that if he were a younger man, the bomb would not have taken such a toll on him.

Derek didn't know it, but he exhibited some of the signs of post-traumatic stress disorder. He wasn't sleeping, and when he did, he woke angry. The inability to protect his family and friends dominated his nighttime dreams and his daytime thoughts. He found it difficult to concentrate for long in ordinary surroundings or to hold a routine conversation, yet thinking about catching their suspect gave him clarity.

Logistically, the day's entire FBI operation had already played out in his head. He saw it clearly as if watching on a movie screen. He reveled in the closing scene with the suspect captured, trying to escape, and shot through the head, Derek standing over him holding the gun.

But that's impossible, Derek thought. *That won't happen because I will be here, sitting next to my wife.*

"Hello, Derek."

"Hello, Cate."

He opened the back door of the truck, then returned to his room and lifted the box carefully. Watching his step, he placed the box in the back of the truck next to the hand dolly. His brown uniform showed hardly a wrinkle.

It's a good plan. Nobody notices these guys. They're all over the place.

He scanned the area just as a police cruiser drove by the motel. *Routine*, he thought. *he's gone already.*

He closed and locked the door before going back into his room. He had a little time to kill before he headed out.

The cruiser turned around at the next intersection and drove back to the motel. It parked across the divided roadway in a parking lot shared by a laundromat and liquor store. The officer used binoculars to check the truck's license plate.

"One of my patrolmen, Officer Raymond, located the white box truck at a motel in Watertown. He's sitting on it. I've sent backup and alerted our explosives team," Chief Hanson said through Nick's cell phone.

"Proceed with caution. This guy may not only have a bomb, but he is probably armed as well. Can you keep us posted on the radio?" Nick asked the chief.

"I'll have Officer Raymond tune to your frequency."

Nick informed those listening on the radio. "We could be putting this one to bed soon. One officer is on the scene. Others are on their way."

"This is Officer Raymond. I'm across the street from the Thunderbird Motel in Watertown. I'm looking at a white box truck, license plate number KJC 889. Twenty minutes ago the suspect loaded something into the back of the truck then returned to his room."

"Stay put, Raymond. The suspect is armed and dangerous. Help is on the way," Chief Hanson told his officer.

"Truck traffic is heavy. The trucks keep obscuring my view. I think I should move to the other side of the street, sir," the patrolman said.

"Negative, officer. Stay put."

"I can't see anything now. Traffic is stopped in front of me. Should I get out of my vehicle to get a visual?"

"Negative. Stay in your vehicle. Help should arrive any minute."

Bradley listened to the conversation and willed the officer to get out of his vehicle to keep an eye on the box truck. But the officer followed orders.

"Yes, sir."

Nick began fidgeting. He paced back and forth between a pizza shop and a luggage store.

"I hear the sirens approaching. Traffic is starting to move again, so they should be able to get through . . . Shit! He's gone."

"Repeat, Officer Raymond."

"He's gone. The fucking truck is gone. Godammit! He had to go east on Main Street unless he circled the building and went out on the other side. Dammit!"

"Find that truck," Chief Hanson bellowed.

Bradley sighed, then did a quick calculation and spoke into the radio. "Okay, so it's going to take anywhere from fifteen to thirty minutes for him to get to this area, depending on his route and if he decides to stop anywhere."

"What's happening on the filming site, Carter?" Nick asked.

"They've started filming. A crowd has already gathered on the Rose Kennedy Greenway to spectate. The police presence is massive. He'd be crazy to try to do anything here."

"Alright, be prepared," Nick said. "Is everyone in position?"

One by one each agent checked in. All were ready to perform their part.

He rushed to her side and caught a crutch on the wheel of her bed. The crutch fell to the floor, but he didn't stop for it. He didn't even notice pain shooting through his thigh. He leaned in to embrace her. They stayed clutched in each other's arms, their salty tears melding with sweet tenderness.

"Thank God," was all Derek could say.

"I'm sorry I worried you," Cate said, mirroring Derek's melancholy demeanor.

"I'm sorry I couldn't protect you," he replied.

"How could you? I didn't give you a chance." Cate's lips pursed.

"I don't understand," Derek said as he pulled back from the embrace.

"While I slept, I kept going back to that moment. It's the only thing I remember from that night—the moment I chose to sit in back of the limo with Sheila and Mike instead of sitting beside you. I never would have forgiven myself if one of us didn't survive," Cate sobbed.

"Oh, Cate. What a perfect pair we make. Well, you don't need to worry anymore, because I'm never leaving your side again."

"Derek, there's something I need to tell you."

Like water boiling over the top of a large pot, South Station bubbled, spilling passengers onto the concourse in rapid overflow. News coverage of the road blockages had apparently inspired a large portion of private commuters to favor public transportation that day.

While the bulk of people moved quickly through the station, many took time to enjoy the amenities, creating long lines at the restrooms, coffee shops, and food service establishments.

Navigating the concourse in his wheelchair, Bradley moved from the main doors to the Summer Street exit and back again. Most people stopped to allow him to pass, something they would never do if he were walking on two feet. He always found it ironic that one could be physically present yet nevertheless invisible to so many, as he had experienced many times in his life.

He checked the clock. It had been twenty minutes since the officer announced the truck had disappeared.

A familiar voice sounded in Bradley's earpiece. Agent Christine Woods from the White-Collar Crimes Unit relayed, "A white box truck is coming down Atlantic Avenue. License number ... KJC 889. This is our guy. He's looking for a place to park."

Silence.

"He's still in motion. He couldn't find a parking spot. He took a left at the Summer Street traffic lights," Woods said.

"This is it. Everyone needs to be in position now. He'll come back around for a second pass," Nick said.

Bradley sat himself at the coffee kiosk with an empty cup in his hand.

"A spot just opened up on Atlantic Avenue. If he gets there in time, he could park near the Atlantic Avenue doors," Woods said.

Everyone listening on the radio heard Nick whisper, "Come on, asshole."

"There he is. He's turning onto Atlantic from E Street ... he saw the spot ... he's pulling just in front of the taxi stand. Expect him through the Atlantic Avenue entrance."

More silence. Bradley held his breath.

"He's stepping out of the truck. He's wearing a brown delivery man's uniform, brown baseball-style hat, and sunglasses. He's going to the back of the truck ... wait. He turned around. He's getting back into the truck."

"Dammit," Nick whispered into the radio. "Everyone hold their positions."

"Okay, no, he's getting back out. He's holding a clipboard. Okay, he's walking to the back and ... opening the door. He's got one of those ... what do you call them? ... a dolly or hand truck."

Silence.

Silence.

"Here's the package. It's a plain brown box about two feet square, maybe a little bigger. No markings. He's shutting the door."

"Here we go," Nick said.

Mara stood in line at the pastry kiosk, a straight shot from the Atlantic Avenue entrance. "I've got him," she whispered. "No positive ID . . . I can't see his face. Repeat, no positive ID. He just passed me, heading your way, Bradley."

"I see him now. He looks like he's heading to either the ticketing area or . . . the bookstore." Bradley cursed himself for not anticipating the significance of the bookstore. "It will be the bookstore, I'm sure of it. CIRG team, move to the Summer Street entrance and hold there."

One of the many responsibilities of the Critical Incident Response Group, an FBI tactical unit, is disruption of hazardous devices. Although they knew Vega planned to plant a bomb, the type of detonation remained uncertain. He could plan a remote detonation, where he held a device to detonate the bomb some distance from himself. Or he could use a timer device, with a counting mechanism, such as a clock, in the bomb to detonate at a set time. Another, and most unlikely detonation method, would involve spontaneous combustion like he used in the makeup trailer fire and limousine bombings.

Until they knew his chosen method, they would need to take care about how they approached Vega once he placed the bomb. If he planned to detonate remotely, he would certainly have the device at his ready. They would have to incapacitate him quickly and efficiently.

"He's at the bookstore," Bradley spoke into the radio as he wheeled himself just twenty feet from Vega. "It looks like the manager wants to open the box before she signs for it."

"Get ready to move in," Nick said.

Bradley saw that Nick had placed himself diagonally across the concourse from where Bradley sat, and Mara had closed in as well. They had good position if something went wrong.

They watched as the bookstore manager opened the box before removing it from the dolly. Then she smiled, took the clipboard from Vega, signed it, and handed it back to him. Vega removed the box from his hand truck and pushed the package against the back wall of the store, the wall that abutted Summer Street.

Nick spoke again. "Hold. Everybody hold your position." Nick sent a questioning glance toward Bradley.

Vega turned with his dolly and walked back to the Atlantic Avenue exit.

"Suspect is leaving. Put all available eyes on the suspect. Do not apprehend. I repeat, do not apprehend," Nick said.

Bradley waited until Vega walked away before he went into the bookstore, showed the manager his badge, and moved toward the box. He opened the lid and saw a layer of books titled *Maker's Mark*. He lifted one from the box and saw another underneath. He lifted that one and saw cardboard.

"Is he out?" Bradley asked.

"He's just exiting now," Mara spoke.

"I need the CIRG team now!!!" Bradley spoke loud and clear. Then he moved people away from the area.

"Let's get these people out to the train platform. We can't have a mass exodus through the main, Atlantic Avenue, and Summer Street doorways," Nick said.

"Attention, please. For your safety, we are evacuating the concourse. Everyone please calmly head to the train platform through the exits on the back side of the building." MBTA and FBI agents herded the crowd outside onto the platforms.

They repeated the instructions as six members of the FBI Critical Incident Response Group, dressed in protective gear, burst through the Summer Street doors and met Bradley in the bookstore. They carefully removed the books from the box and pulled the false bottom piece of cardboard away.

"It's a timer. I repeat, it's a timer. We have eight minutes and fifteen seconds on my mark . . . mark," a CIRG team member said, then went to work to try to defuse the bomb.

"Sir, you have to leave now," one of the CIRG team said to Bradley.

"Yes. Is there enough time?" Bradley asked.

"I don't know," he replied.

Rolling his empty dolly and wearing a full smile, he walked out the door. He climbed into the back of the box truck and inched the doors closed, allowing a shard of light to show through. He changed out of the useful brown uniform into a pair of blue jeans and colorful Tommy Bahama button-down shirt. Then he ceremoniously placed his dark blue, wide-brimmed fedora on his head, donned his sunglasses, and climbed down from the truck.

He breathed deeply, satisfyingly, and confidently. *Now comes the fun part*, he thought. He abandoned the truck and crossed Atlantic Avenue on foot, glancing over his shoulder to take one last look at an intact South Station. He saw a man in a wheelchair exit through the front door and chuckled. *You're a lucky bastard, getting out while you can.*

Vega looked ahead to the Rose Kennedy Greenway where a crowd had amassed to watch filming of the fated movie. Because

Summer Street had been blocked to traffic only on the South Station side of the intersection, he had to wait at the traffic light for the crossing signal.

As he waited, he got a whiff of fresh steamed hot dogs. He spotted the food vendor on the other side of the street, glanced at his watch, and decided he probably had time. In any case, it was the perfect vantage point to watch his show. He was pleased to see filming activity on the Summer Street side of the Federal Reserve building. He thought there might be, considering that's where he had parked his getaway car when he actually did the robbery.

The walk light flashed. He strolled to the hot dog vendor, waiting only for one customer ahead of him, ordered two with the works, paid the man, and within the crowd found a sunny spot that enjoyed a clear view of the action. A glance at his watch told him he had roughly three minutes to wait.

"Clear the set," the director yelled through his bullhorn.

To Vega's dismay, most of the people who had been on Summer Street vacated, leaving only the camera operators on the opposite side of the road. That's when he noticed the 1998 black Cadillac DeVille parked on the street.

"That's a beauty," he murmured, "but I didn't use a Cadillac for this job."

A woman standing near him sent him a questioning glance. He scowled back at her and checked his watch. Two minutes.

"Two minutes. How are they doing?" Bradley asked, speaking into his radio.

"They're still working on it," Nick said, nervously. "What's happening out there?"

"He's watching the show." Bradley sat near the hot dog vendor. "Who's got the bullhorn in case we need these people to get down?"

"Tony has it. He's with the director now."

Bradley looked toward Vega, then scanned his surroundings. "We are as ready as we can be," Bradley said.

"Be careful, Bradley," Nick said.

Bradley smiled. "I'm touched that you're worried about me, Nick."

"Worried about you? No, I just don't want to fill out all that paperwork if you die, dude."

Bradley chuckled.

He shoved the last bit of hot dog in his mouth, spilling mustard on his shirt. Then he wiped his hands on his jeans and checked his watch. *Thirty seconds*. He scanned the crowd, giddy at the thought that, in less than half a minute, those people's lives would change forever. That's when he spotted him. A man stood barely twenty feet to his left, wearing casual clothes and an earpiece in his ear.

The explosion rattled the windows in the Federal Reserve building and sent massive amounts of debris into the air. An immense cloud of smoke and dust engulfed the closed section of Summer Street. Spectators screamed and ducked for cover or ran away from the scene. Vega stood still, hearing the sound of the building collapsing but not seeing it through the smoke.

He beamed as he squinted to see through the fog. Then he remembered the man with the earpiece. He turned and saw the man moving toward him. Vega spun around and headed back the way he came. He moved swiftly through the huddled bodies.

As he broke through the crowd, he saw a man close in from his left and a woman from his right. What he didn't take notice of was the man in the wheelchair who waited for the perfect time to emerge from behind the hot dog cart, ram him, and give the chair a quick turn so the footrests of the chair swiped Vega's legs out from under him.

Vega landed hard.

Mara and two other agents were on top of him before he could recover. Handcuffed with his cheek pressed against the ground, Vega looked up at Bradley and smiled.

"It doesn't matter. I did it. They can't finish this fucking movie now," he sputtered.

Suddenly, the sound of laughter and hooting exploded around them. One by one people jumped to their feet and clapped and shouted in celebration.

Bradley smiled back at Vega. "Lift him up," he said.

The two male agents each grabbed an arm and lifted Vega off the ground. The light wind had whisked away the bulk of the smoke and dust from the explosion. Vega couldn't believe what he saw.

South Station stood intact and unharmed. The movie's cleanup crew had already begun to sweep the debris away, including fake blocks of granite, building materials, and paper strewn about.

"What the fuck?" Vega turned toward Bradley.

"The magic of the movies," Bradley smiled.

MISE-EN-SCÈNE

"I can't feel my legs," Cate said.

Derek didn't flinch. He placed his hand on Cate's leg and looked her in the eye. "We'll take things one at a time, Cate. Side by side, you and me, one at a time," He leaned in and kissed her.

"What if I . . .?"

"Uh, uh. No. No what-ifs. From here on, it's only *what's next.*"

Cate began to cry.

"Hey, the doctor told me it could take weeks before we know if it's permanent. You're still healing, Cate. It's only been three and half days. We'll need to be patient." Derek pulled the only chair over to Cate's bed and sat. "And I'm going to be right here."

Cate allowed herself to think the best, then managed a small smile. "Okay, what's next?"

Derek informed Cate that Sheila, David, and her parents were staying at the house. He filled her in on everyone's status, including the fact that the FBI would hopefully soon capture the man who caused her pain.

"Why aren't you there, Derek? You should be there," she said, wide-eyed and worried.

"I'm where I belong, Cate. I'm right where I want to be." Derek spoke the truth. He felt no desire to take part in Vega's takedown. He felt no guilt about not being there, and he felt no obligation to the Federal Bureau of Investigation to be sitting at his desk instead of sitting next to his wife.

He had made his decision, and it felt right.

His text tone sounded. Bradley had sent him a message.
We got him.

Derek put his phone back in his pocket and placed his hand on Cate's cheek.

"A massive explosion took place this morning on Summer Street between South Station and the Federal Reserve Bank building," the television news anchor stated. "The controlled explosion was part of filming *Maker's Mark*, the latest Hollywood movie being shot here in Boston. Although spectators were taken by surprise, the Boston Police Department and movie producers have confirmed that the explosion scene had been planned months in advance.

And now for the weather . . . "

Director Davis switched off the television in Derek's office. "Well, I never thought I would see the FBI use an explosion to distract a suspect, but it seems to have worked. Tell me, how did you manage it?" he asked Nick.

"Derek worked it out with the movie producer David Carson, the one in the limousine with his wife, Derek, and the others Sunday night. His production company was more than happy to help and promised not to disclose the true nature of the operation. They thought it the least they could do for refusing to stop filming."

"What about logistics, the where and how of it all?" Davis asked.

"Well, that was Agent Whitman, sir. His profile of Vincent Vega proved to be on the money. He figured Vega would hit South Station. In fact, he pretty much pinpointed where Vega would place the bomb. He also knew Vega would want to wait around and watch the fireworks," Nick said as he motioned his arm toward Bradley.

"No, sir. It was a group effort. Nick had us working as a solid team. Everyone deserves credit for this one, sir. Including you, for picking the right man to lead us," Bradley said with a smile.

"Well, Agent Whitman, I'm very glad you feel that way," Director Davis said. "Because, as of right now, Agent Gaston is officially the new supervisory special agent of the Chelsea office of the Federal Bureau of Investigation, if you agree to take the job."

Nick and Bradley exchanged a confused glance.

"I don't understand, sir," Nick said.

"Last night, Derek Richards called to inform me that he would be retiring. He offered to stay on for the transition to go smoothly but with everything he's got to deal with, we decided it best if he concentrate on his and his wife's recovery."

Stunned, uncomfortable silence filled the room.

"But, sir, I'm not ready for this job. Bradley . . . Agent Whitman is much more qualified than I am," Nick said.

"Don't be stupid, Nick," Bradley said. "It was never going to be my job."

Davis shifted his eyes toward Bradley. He knew Bradley understood that, due to Bradley's past transgressions, he couldn't offer the position to him.

"You've proven you're up to the task. Take some time to think about it. Until then, you remain acting supervisory special agent."

"Is there any hope Agent Richards will change his mind?" Nick asked.

"I don't think so," Davis replied. "Good job today. Tell your team I said so. Agent Gaston, call me tomorrow, and we'll talk about the position."

"Yes, sir."

⌘

Bradley wasn't sure he wanted to disturb them. He found them holding hands and laughing almost as if nothing had changed. *But everything had changed*, he thought. He decided to turn around and just go home when Cate spotted him.

"Bradley!" she shouted.

Her smile radiated the room, and he realized how much he had missed seeing her sparkling emerald eyes. He pasted a worn smile to his face and went straight to her side. He glanced at Derek and could see relief.

"Thank God you're okay," Bradley said as he hugged her.

Cate turned serious. "Derek told me you got the man that did this to us."

"We did. We are processing him now," he said, then turned to Derek. "Your idea worked perfectly. Have you seen any news?"

"No," Derek replied. "And I don't care to." Derek searched Bradley's face to see what, if anything, he knew. He detected nothing but exhaustion. "You need sleep, Bradley. You look terrible."

"You look wonderful to me." Cate held out her other hand for Bradley's. "My two favorite men in the whole world. I can face anything as long as I have you."

Bradley questioned her comment with a glance.

Cate looked deep into Bradley's eyes, knowing it would be difficult for Bradley to hear.

"My neck injury . . . Bradley . . . I can't feel my legs," Cate said, her voice steady and strong.

His eyes welled as his chest seemed to compress under the weight of her words. He lowered his head to try to hide his tears and fear. A rush of feelings swept over him like a rogue wave. It grasped him and violently plummeted him into the depths before spitting him out, wet, scared, and beaten. Old scars tore open, and new scars ripped his heart leaving behind the frightened six-year-old boy in his backyard. He couldn't speak.

"Bradley!" he heard Derek say. "Are you okay?"

"Huh? Yeah, I'm sorry Cate. I'm so sorry." Bradley looked down at the floor. He couldn't let her see him like that. "It's still early, Cate. A lot can change in the next few weeks."

He backed away from the bed. "I've got to go." Never once lifting his head, he turned and left the room.

He managed to get halfway down the hall before the sick, dizzy feeling overwhelmed him, and a knife pierced his chest. Sweat formed on his brow and upper lip, and he became aware of his quick, deep gasps. He closed his eyes and tried to concentrate on slowing his breathing to a normal rate.

Back in her room, Cate pleaded, "Derek, you have to go talk to him. I shouldn't have blurted it out like that. Please, go make sure he is alright."

"He'll be fine. He just needs to process it."

"Please, go talk to him." Her green eyes conveyed worry.

Derek nodded, reached for his crutches, and slowly lowered himself to give Cate a kiss before he hobbled out the door.

Bradley opened his eyes and saw Derek standing over him, one hand holding his crutch, the other on Bradley's shoulder. When did he get here?

And a nurse had appeared. "Sir," she said. "just breathe easily. In, out, in, out . . . that's it. Good. That's it, nice easy breaths."

Bradley dug his palms into his eyes, and his fingers lay spread across his forehead. It took a moment for him to understand what had happened.

"I'm sorry," he said as he pulled his hands away from his face. "That hasn't happened in a long time."

The nurse placed a blood pressure band around his arm and pumped air into it. Bradley glanced up at her and said, "It was just a panic attack. My pressure's going to be a little high for about an hour. Then it will be back to normal." He gave her a faint smile.

"You're right," the nurse smiled, "it is high. You'll need to relax for a little while."

"Thank you, yes. I will." Bradley tried to return the smile before the nurse went back to her desk.

"Are you alright?" Derek asked.

"Why didn't you tell me?" Bradley asked.

"She just told me a few hours ago. I haven't talked to anyone but her since."

"I'm not talking about Cate, Derek."

Derek paused. "Ah." His head bowed, he peeked at Bradley without raising it. "You talked to Davis."

"No, but I was in the room when Davis offered Nick your job," Bradley said sternly. "Have you told Cate?"

Derek shook his head. "She's got enough to think about. I told her I took some time off."

"You didn't even think to mention it to me? Maybe talk about it?"

"Calm down, Bradley. You need to relax, or you're going to blow a gasket." Derek shuffled his way to the bench in the hallway and sat. "There's nothing to talk about. I've never been more sure about anything in my life," Derek said. "And Cate will understand."

"Don't you get it? Cate will blame herself, Derek. Forever. Talk to her. Before your decision becomes final, talk to her."

Bradley turned and rolled down the hallway toward the elevator. "Hey," he called back, "and don't worry about Cate. She's much stronger than I am."

Nick thought about the conversation he had with Bradley before he left. Each hoped Derek would change his mind. But Nick had to consider what he would do if Derek did retire. He was confident he could do the job, especially with the support of Bradley, Mara, and the rest of the eighth floor. He felt they made an exceptional team. But he wasn't quite sure he wanted the job.

"I'm no goddamn desk jockey," he would say over and over to anyone who would listen. And he wasn't. Even the past four days, he had skirted the line between boss and field agent.

He always assumed that Bradley would be heir to Derek's position, and he welcomed that. But knowing it would not happen made things much more complicated. If Nick didn't accept the job, Davis would bring someone in from outside the Chelsea family.

The thoughts running through his head made Nick restless, and he didn't get any work done. He told Hazel he would be out for a while and walked into the bullpen. Those at their desks were busy with paperwork, on the telephone, or deep into their computers. Mara peeked up from her computer when Nick came into view and approached her desk.

"What are you working on?" he asked.

"Just cleaning up my report from this morning," she replied.

"Would you like to join me for a walk?"

"Where to?"

"Nowhere in particular."

"You mean just take a walk?" she furrowed her brows.

"Yeah."

"Is everything alright?" she asked.

"Yes, Mara. Everything is fine. I just wanted to know if you would like to go for a walk with me," Nick huffed.

"Yes. I'd love to." She stood and smiled.

"Okay," Nick grinned.

They turned right onto Maple Street and then a left onto Beech. Halfway down Beech Street, Nick said, "If I ask you something, would you give me an honest answer?"

She stopped, looked dead into his eyes, and said, "Absolutely."

They continued to walk.

"This job, Derek's job I mean. Do you think I could ever be suited for it? I mean, I know I can do it, but would it ever suit me?"

Mara pondered Nick's question. "I think you are the only one who can answer that. But I will say this. I can't think of a time since I've known you that you've done better work than you have this week."

"Thank you." Nick felt a strange flutter inside. He didn't know what to make of it. He had never felt it before.

Beech Street dumped them onto Carter alongside Chelsea High School. They crossed the street and took a right toward Vietnam Veterans Memorial Swimming Pool where they found an open bench outside the fenced-in pool area. They sat quietly listening to the children laugh and splash in the water.

"It's been a long day," Nick said.

"Yes, it has. And it's only two o'clock," she smiled.

Nick slowly turned his hand over, palm up, and rested it on his leg. Mara placed her hand in his, and he felt the strange flutter yet again.

361 DAYS LATER

"Why don't we just go into the dining room?" Bradley asked as he moved his wheelchair toward the outdoor rooftop lounge.

"Because it's a beautiful night and I don't want to rush it. I want to make this night last," Lynn smiled as they exited the elevator on the top floor of the Envoy Hotel. "We have plenty of time before we have to meet the others for the movie premiere. And we're all dressed up anyway. Let's enjoy the night."

Once outside, Doug suggested they sit on the Fort Point Channel side of the building. "Less wind," he professed.

Bradley turned the corner and . . . "SURPRISE! HAPPY BIRTHDAY!"

There stood Zayt, Shea, Sheila, David, Holly, John, Mike, Laney, Nick, and Mara.

"What the hell is this?" Bradley yelled.

"It's your thirtieth birthday party on your thirty-first birthday," Sheila laughed. She looked stunning, Bradley thought. With the help of plastic surgery and make-up, her scars were barely visible and her slightly droopy eye the only sign she had almost lost her life.

David, Holly, John, and Mike's broken bones and scars had long since healed. Their emotional scars still lingered but did not control their lives.

Bradley made the rounds, beginning with Zayt and Shea. "Now I know where your loyalties lie. I saw both of you this morning and not a word. You could have at least warned me."

"Dude, you may carry a gun, but your mother carries the ammunition. I don't ever want to get on her bad side," Zayt said.

"Besides, they thought it would be the best way to put that whole Vincent Vega thing behind—for everybody," Shea said. "Have some champagne, Bradley. Loosen up."

Shea went to greet Lynn and Doug.

"So, what happened with Eddy? Did he show?" Bradley asked.

Zayt smiled. "Not only did he show, he brought her flowers. Her favorites, but I forget what they're called."

"So, how did it go?"

"I think they're going to be alright. I mean, it may take time, but I think Eddy is ready to be a husband again. And Debbie definitely wants to be his wife again."

"I'm proud of you, man. You did a great thing."

"Nah, not me. Eddy did all the work. I'm proud of him," Zayt said.

Bradley excused himself when he saw Nick standing alone. "Hey, boss. Hanging out with all your friends, I see."

"I was hanging with everyone on this deck who could match my wit until you showed up."

Mara joined them and placed her arm around Nick's waist. Nick leaned in to kiss her.

"I always thought you were a smart woman, Mara. I may have to re-evaluate your ability to profile people, based on your choice of companion."

Mara laughed. "Speaking of companions, your fiancé looks spectacular tonight, as do you, Agent Whitman."

"It's about time someone noticed my boyish good looks and star-like quality," Bradley grinned.

"And your humility is just astounding," Laney said, joining them.

Bradley and Laney continued on to say hello to Holly, who had broken away from her husband and father to greet them. "Hello, beautiful," Bradley said.

"My knight in shining armor," Holly said as she reached to give Bradley a kiss. "Happy Birthday."

"This must be an exciting night for you," Laney said. "Your publishing company will get credits, right?"

"Yes, it will, and it is exciting. But not because of the movie. Because we can all finally be together again like we planned last year."

"Are Cate and Derek coming?" Bradley asked.

"Sheila said they are going to meet us at the theatre," Laney replied.

"Let's all sit down so we can talk, shall we?" Lynn shouted above the individual conversations.

They settled in their reserved section where the firepit sat surrounded by couches on three sides.

Bradley noticed a particularly long hug between Mike and Sheila before they sat down.

"What's going on in your life, Mike?" Bradley asked.

"Nothing, really. Same old grind," he replied.

Holly started to laugh. "Oh, come on. Really? You're not planning on telling anyone?"

"What? What is it, Holly? Tell us," Lynn said.

Sheila smiled at Mike and watched him blush.

"David, help me out here," Mike said.

"Sorry, Mike. We're outnumbered," David quipped.

"About six months ago, Dad took a trip to Hollywood to visit Sheila and David." Holly said, then looked to Sheila.

Sheila said, "And, while he visited, he took morning walks in the neighborhood."

Then Holly took over. "And every morning, the walks would take longer and longer."

Sheila again. "And here I am thinking, good for him. He's being healthy and taking long walks."

Then Holly. "But he wasn't. On the first morning, he met one of their neighbors, a woman just three estates up the street."

Back to Sheila. "Who lost her husband six years ago in a plane crash," Sheila scowled. "Sorry. I didn't mean to sound excited about that part. Anyway, it turns out that she would purposely wait for him to walk by every morning that week."

"And invite him in for coffee and pastries," Holly interjected. "So much for being healthy."

She shot Mike a fake scowl.

"By the end of the week, his morning walks lasted into the afternoon," Sheila laughed.

"But then he had to come home," Holly said sadly. "And he was miserable."

"I was not miserable," Mike said.

"So, he made another trip. But this time he didn't tell anybody," Sheila said. "Until I saw him with Olivia at the local farmer's market."

"Busted," Holly laughed.

"Alright, alright. I'll tell the rest of the story," Mike said.

"You'd better. I'm on the edge of my seat," Lynn said.

"And don't leave out any of the juicy parts," Doug said.

Mike explained that he and Olivia found they had a lot in common and enjoyed each other's company. "She retired after her husband passed away and spent a few years in quiet but not total seclusion. She's an architect. And she's quite amazing."

"That's it? Amazing? That's all you're going to give us?" Doug chuckled.

"When will we get to meet her?" Lynn asked.

"She's coming tonight. She flew in late this afternoon and will meet us at the theatre. Maybe we could get together for dinner before she has to fly home?" Mike suggested to Doug and Lynn.

"Absolutely. We wouldn't miss it for the world. We're so happy for you, Mike," Lynn said.

Trying to shift attention away from himself, Mike said, "Happy Birthday, Bradley. A little late, but we finally made it."

"Cheers!" they said in unison.

"Cate and Derek wanted to be here, but Cate had an appointment. They're going to meet us at the theatre later," said Sheila.

"I don't mean to bring up bad memories, but I heard Vincent Vega filed an appeal today," David said.

"Yes, he did. But you don't need to worry about him. He'll never get out," Nick said.

"He's probably just looking for more material for his book," Holly said.

"His what?" Bradley asked.

"You didn't hear?" Holly laughed. "Vega is writing his own book. He wants me to publish it when it's done. He said as long as I already know some of his story, I should hear the rest."

"Who's writing it for him?" Sheila asked.

"Nobody. He said he's going to write it himself," Holly snickered. "I can't wait to see the manuscript."

"I've heard it all, now," Nick said.

With drinks and dinner behind them, they said goodbye to Zayt and Shea.

"I'm sorry I couldn't get more tickets for the premiere," David said to Zayt.

"No worries. It's not really my thing. Besides, I'm going to have a long day tomorrow. Thanks to your parents' generous donation, we are taking delivery of ten more tiny homes."

"They were happy to do it."

David pulled Zayt aside, out of earshot of the rest of the group. "I wanted to let you know. Tonight at the movie premiere, my production company is going to announce that a portion of profits from *Maker's Mark* will be donated to the REACH program. If this movie is as successful as we think it will be and you are as good at managing as I think you are, you should never have to worry about funding again."

Stunned, Zayt lowered his head in reverence. "Thank you, David. I know I should say more, but I'm speechless."

"No need, Zayt. Take care of yourself." David shook his hand and rejoined the group.

After saying her goodbyes, Shea stood by Zayt. "What's up with the goofy look on your face?"

Zayt just smiled.

The driver opened the limousine door in front of the large marquee overhanging the brass-framed glass doors. Listed on the National Register of Historic Places, the Wang Theatre qualifies as a crown-jewel Boston venue, completely at odds with the car crashing, explosive, action film about to debut. But the guest list was not at odds. City and state officials alongside

Hollywood's elite graced the red carpet splayed across the sidewalk and through the open doors.

In his truck, Bradley and Laney followed behind the limousine and parked in a nearby reserved parking space. The friends collected on the sidewalk to the right side of the red carpet.

"Should we wait here for the others so we can all go in together?" Lynn asked.

Sheila said, "David got a text. My parents, along with David's, are already seated inside. I'm not sure if Cate would want the fanfare. Maybe we should wait inside the doors."

David and Sheila led the parade, David looking impeccable in a tuxedo but Sheila stealing the attention of the journalists and spectators' cameras. She wore an ivory scooped-back gown with black floral embroidery dripping from her shoulders and fitted through the thighs where the fabric flared in folds incorporating black lace inlays. Her long blonde hair waved simply and elegantly across her shoulders.

Lynn and Doug next grasped the attention of the paparazzi as Lynn's small frame sported a stunning black satin halter gown featuring a full open back and its bodice embroidered with red, green, and gold mini roses. Her dirty-blonde hair piled high on her head, accentuating her long thin neck.

Holly wore a multi-pastel spaghetti-strapped A-line gown as she walked arm-in-arm with her father's date, Olivia, dressed as elegantly and simply as Holly had ever seen. The architect wore a curve-hugging, dark-gray-with-silver-glitter-knit dress, its cascading drape sleeves formed a dramatic drape in the back, and her tied-back black hair showed off her beautiful Mediterranean features. John and Mike could only follow in their almost identical conservative, single-breasted tuxedos, since the focus lay solely on the women.

Bradley chose a midnight-blue tuxedo with black lapel, and Laney complemented his choice with her light blue, blouse-sleeved gown with front slit to her knees and gathered front stitch up to the base of its v-neck. The addition of a black lace sarong completed her ensemble.

They waited in the lobby just inside the front doors for Derek and Cate. An electric charge seemed to fill the air. Excited guests and nervous producers poured in and headed to the hospitality booth for free champagne. Sheila could not relax. She worried about Cate.

Two months earlier, Cate had announced that she would not attend the premiere. She explained to Sheila that she didn't feel ready emotionally or physically to be out in public. As the premiere date approached, it had only become worse as the media repeatedly replayed that fateful day. The friends' painful story belonged to all of Boston and Hollywood. Then, ten days before, Cate called Sheila to ask if they still had two seats available for her and Derek. As much as it delighted Sheila, the idea also made her anxious. She couldn't help but feel responsible for what might happen.

The next limousine pulled up to the curb, and Sheila saw Derek step out.

"They're here," she said.

In his traditional black tuxedo, Derek turned and reached into the car. The ten of them watched as one white-sandaled foot emerged from the car, then the other. Cate sat perched on the edge of the limousine seat with her feet planted on the sidewalk.

A collective gasp nearly drowned nearby conversations as Derek outstretched both hands to take Cate's. She grasped them and stood.

"Oh, my God." Sheila put her hand to her mouth.

"Oh, Cate," Holly said in amazement.

"Thank the Lord," Lynn whispered as she squeezed Doug's hand.

"Did you know about this?" Bradley looked to Sheila.

She shook her head, and tears filled her eyes as Bradley sat motionless.

"Are you alright?" Laney asked him.

He could only nod his head.

They watched as Cate stood, looking radiant in an emerald-green satin gown, her brunette hair feathered and shortened to shoulder length. She placed her arm through Derek's and took her first step onto the red carpet, slowly and deliberately, her eyes straight ahead.

For those lining the red carpet, it started as whispers, then progressed into smiles, and before Cate took her fifth step, everyone watching began to clap and cheer. Derek's eyes swelled, and Cate lifted her chin to finish her journey among her family and closest friends.

Bradley rolled his chair to Cate as a single tear fell down his cheek. He reached for her hand and held it.

"Save me a dance?" he smiled.

Cate returned his smile. "Always."

TO READ AN EXCERPT FROM THE

MANUSCRIPT BY VINCENT VEGA

ENTITLED *MAKE YOUR MARK*

GO TO

CHRISTINENOYESAUTHOR.COM/VEGA

ACKNOWLEDGEMENTS:

I am thankful for the incredible support and encouragement I continue to receive from friends, family, devoted readers, and spirit guides. This story speaks of those bonds and is a continuous reminder that I/we should treasure every moment we have together.

Thank you, Richard Bruno, for agreeing to copy edit my manuscript. I appreciate you lending my story your expertise and thoughtfulness.

And to my editor, publisher, and very good friend, Marcia Gagliardi of Haley's Publishing—thank you for loving and nurturing my fictional family as much as I do.

ABOUT THE AUTHOR

Christine Noyes

photo by Paula Francis

You can't always plan where life will take you. That is certainly true for Christine Noyes. Growing up in Shrewsbury, Massachusetts, as a tomboy, she spent her youth building forts, playing sports, and enjoying the perceived innocence of the 1960s.

Not having a clear vision of what her life should be, she went where she was most comfortable, to the kitchen. Beginning her work life as a cook at her grandfather's restaurant at the age of eleven, she spent the next several decades re-inventing herself, becoming an accomplished chef, a sales representative, an entrepreneur, and now a writer and illustrator. She never chose her professions. They chose her.

She married her husband and soulmate, Al, in 1989. They moved to Orange, Massachusetts, where, after Al's passing, Chris remains today with thirty years of wonderful memories to keep her company.

When not at her keyboard, she can be found in her kitchen: back to her roots and love of cooking.

from the next Bradley Whitman novel

by Christine Noyes

THE PATHSIDE PREDATOR

PROLOGUE

Relishing the last bit of life leaking from her body as the crimson-coated knife slid from her throat, the killer faced a nagging question. Did I put the trash out this morning? Imagining the unusually warm autumn day might cause discarded red snapper from the previous night's dinner to steam in the plastic bag evoked a queasy reaction.

Turning attention back to the task at hand and careful not to damage the woman's areola, the butcher used the razor-sharp blade to remove her right nipple. Always at that point in the process, the euphoric mood deadened—much like the torn flesh from the defaced breast.

A SERIAL KILLER

Sergeant Donovan Doyle of the Revere Police Department held a red paisley handkerchief to his face. As sun beat down and burned the early morning dew, Doyle wiped fresh sweat from his brow.

"Well? What do you think?" Doyle asked the medical examiner.

Doctor Maria Reyes sent him an impatient glare.

"I'll let you know what I think as soon as I am done, Sergeant."

"Maria. Is it? Or isn't it?" Doyle asked, equally impatient.

Both turned their heads as tree branches snapped on

the hiking path to their right. Detective Reed approached, accompanied by two patrol officers. Like Doyle, not wanting to disturb the area surrounding the victim, they kept a distance.

"Hello, Detective Reed," Doctor Reyes said. "It looks like you have a victim of the Pathside Predator."

Doyle threw up his hands in frustration. "You couldn't tell me that?"

"Relax, Donovan. Not everything is about you," Reyes responded.

Detective Reed cast Doyle a questioning glance. Doyle shrugged his shoulders and shook his head in response.

"What do we have, Doctor?" Reed asked.

"Female, Caucasian, approximately thirty-five years old. She shows signs of sexual assault, although there's no semen. She has defense wounds on both arms and legs, and it looks like she was punched in the face at least twice. But the knife wound to her throat is what killed her. I'd put time of death somewhere between seven and ten o'clock last night."

"What about her breasts?" Detective Reed asked, knowing the killer's unique signature.

"The right one. A clean cut," Reyes responded.

Reed lowered his head and took a deep breath. He examined the victim from a distance. Her appearance showed similarities to those in photographs distributed to police departments around New England. The most recent reported kill took place in New Hampshire nine weeks prior. If the killer followed the pattern, law enforcement would find four more victims in Massachusetts before the murderer moved on to another state.

Reed turned to Doyle. "Call Gaston."

Federal Bureau of Investigation Supervisory Special Agent Nick Gaston picked up his ringing phone.

"Are you sitting down?" Doyle asked.

"Sergeant Doyle. It's been a long time. What can I do for you?" Nick asked.

"I hate to put a damper on this fine day, Agent Gaston, but we have a serial killer in our backyard."

Nick sat back in his chair. "Go on."

Doyle described the crime scene, relayed the coroner's findings, and reminded Nick Gaston of the pattern that the media-named Pathside Predator adhered to. "There will be four more unless we catch this bastard."

"I'm sending a team," Nick said.

"We could sure use Whitman on this, but I don't think there's an easy way to get him to the crime scene," Doyle replied.

"I'm calling him anyway."

Agent Bradley Whitman sat in his home-based office consisting of a large corner desk, top-of-the-line computer system, all-in-one printer, and three overhead monitors. File cabinets lined the wall to his right. Beyond the cabinets sat his bed and then bathroom, the bathroom the only room with walls in his home.

He had bought the abandoned industrial laundry-service building ten years before, just after taking the job with the FBI straight out of Massachusetts Institute of Technology. He shared his home with Rusty, a black-and-rust-colored Doberman Pinscher who had saved his life as Bradley worked on a case.

Many doubted Bradley's ability to land a job with the FBI, but none of those knew him well. As a boy, Bradley struggled with his physical limitations. An enterovirus struck him when he was six years old leaving both legs paralyzed. Instead of throwing himself into sports as he would have preferred, he threw himself into books, research, and problem-solving.

When he was twelve, Bradley's parents took him on a cruise. The trip, having become more of an adventure than anticipated, gave him his first opportunity for independence and furnished him with the confidence that he could make a difference in the world. His position as an analyst with the Chelsea, Massachusetts, division of the FBI, provided the perfect opportunity. His career has not always gone by the book, but he always strove to be the best and most reliable analyst in the bureau.

When he saw Nick's name pop up on his cellphone, Bradley answered.

"Bradley, I'm going to give you a chance to test that new wheelchair of yours."

"What have we got, Nick?"

"The Pathside Predator has made it to Massachusetts and struck in Revere last night," Nick sighed.

Silence.

"The cool-down period is getting much shorter. Send me the location," Bradley said and hung up.

Since the realization eight years prior that a serial killer roamed Connecticut, Bradley had followed the case. The murders seemed to stop after authorities found the fifth victim within the span of two years. Then, a year after the last Connecticut murder, another spree began in Rhode Island with five more victims in twenty-two months.

Once again, a year passed before a woman walking her dog found a body off the South Woods Trail in New Hampshire's Pisgah State Park, bringing the investigation in the purview of the Boston division of the FBI. After the coroner's examination and consideration of similar circumstances, police and FBI investigators concluded the murder connected to those in Connecticut and Rhode Island.

FBI officials assigned the New Hampshire cases to the Portsmouth, New Hampshire, field office with assistance from the Chelsea division.

Bradley remembered it being only nine weeks since the fifth body turned up in New Hampshire, indicating to him that the length of time had diminished for what investigators had called the one-year interstate cool-off period. If the idea of a standard cool-off period meant anything, apparently something or someone had made the killer move up their timeline.

Bradley hoped that, by rushing into another murder and changing their apparent modus operandus, the perpetrator made a mistake.

Bradley had received his new 4x4 all-terrain power chair three weeks before and had not yet tried many of its features. His new chair could climb stairs and slopes, ride on sand, and travel through snow, the perfect New England ride for an adventuresome paraplegic. With four oversized nubbed tires, he could use it on everyday floor surfaces and still take it through mud and negotiate bumpy roads. The chair came equipped with a smaller fifth wheel in back to use on flat surfaces. As the fifth wheel lowered to the floor, the two large back tires lifted off the ground, allowing the chair to run on three wheels to save battery power.

West of Massachusetts Bay, Broad Sound collects the Atlantic Ocean and snakes its bounty through the bogs of Revere. City-owned Sea Plane Basin boasts two-hundred-twenty-seven acres of marshland, split almost through the middle by Salem Turnpike running from Revere to Saugus. Overgrown in some sections, Sea Plane Basin Trail winds through the tranquil northern section of the picturesque parcel. Stopping only because the Revere coroner's vehicle and a police cruiser blocked him from going further, Bradley drove his custom truck along the area's gravel path.

Using his truck's mechanical lift system, he lowered himself in his chair to the gravel, then rode the path on four wheels toward the police officer who stood a hundred feet from the vehicles. Showing his credentials to the officer, he turned the chair off the path and up the slight slope to follow the patrol officer to the scene. Bradley could feel the gyro system in the chair adjust the angle of his seat as he moved through the tufted terrain. The soft sandy turf would have given him incalculable trouble in his old chair, but he moved smoothly and effortlessly despite the obstacles. The idea of such newfound freedom of travel exhilarated him.

The feeling soon waned as he spotted the blue tarp covering the victim's body. The forensic team continued their examination of the surrounding area as Doctor Reyes stood off to the side, alone, waiting for the go-ahead to remove the body. Bradley gave her a quick nod as he approached the scene.

"Sergeant Doyle. It's been a while," Bradley smiled.

"Nice rig you've got there. Has it got a Hemi?" Doyle snickered.

Bradley smiled. "Where's Detective Reed? Nick said he'd be here."

"You must have taken different paths. He just went back to the car. He wanted to radio the chief. Are you ready to see her?"

"Yeah, let's see what we've got."

She wore only her socks and running shoes. Her matted long brown hair splayed across the moss-covered soil. Her bruised right arm lay, outstretched, as if she reached for something and her left arm rested across her body, her hand covering the offended breast. Spurts of blood from her throat, stabbed not slashed, painted her pale skin as if an abstract piece of art—controlled chaos.

The position of her legs suggested extreme effort on the part of her attacker as they lay unusually wide open to show a small amount of blood that trickled down her inner thighs, evidence of penetration.

Bradley began to feel nauseated. Although he had seen many dead bodies, the woman's plight hit him hard, perhaps because she reminded him of his own fiancé, Doctor Laney Weaver, who shared physical likeness with the victim.

"Have we found any of her clothing or personal items?" Bradley asked Doyle.

"Nothing. Either everything got hauled out or nothing came in."

"What about footprints? One set, two?"

Doyle shrugged. "It looks like the area's been cleaned. We'll have to wait and see what they come up with."

"Doctor Reyes," Bradley called, "were her legs moved into position pre- or post-mortem?"

"My best guess is post-mortem. It's a strange detail. The way the blood dripped on her thighs suggests her legs were much closer together when she was sexually assaulted and judging by the light amount of blood, I'd say that also occurred post-mortem."

"It is a strange detail, and a new one," Bradley whispered.

Bradley noticed a sweeping mark in the dirt near the victim's legs. He recalled seeing the pattern when he was a child, before his own legs became useless. He lay down then in the snow, flapped his arms, and spread his legs wide open again and again, then stood up and looked back at the angel imprint he had left behind.

To the doctor he said, "What do you make of this?" as he pointed to the angel skirt scraped into the earth.

"Very good, Agent Whitman. I planned to include it in my report. Look at her right sneaker."

Bradley saw what looked like a shoeprint on the side of the woman's sneaker. He imagined how that might have happened. Then he noticed a large bruise the size of a grapefruit, on her left thigh.

"The killer placed a foot on her right shoe and pushed on her left thigh to spread them apart?" he questioned.

"As near as I can figure, yes," Doctor Reyes answered.

"But why?"

"That's not my area, agent. I only worry about when and how. It's up to you to discover the who and why."

"Thank you, Maria. Would you let me know when your full report is ready?"

"Of course, Bradley. I like the new chair," Doctor Reyes smiled then prepared to take the body to the morgue.

Bradley and Doyle moved out of her way and out of earshot.

"Of course, Bradley. I like the new chair." Doyle mimicked Maria's tone to Bradley.

"What's the matter with you?" Bradley asked, smirking.

"Ah," Doyle gruffed, "she won't give me the time of day. All because of a little misunderstanding."

"What kind of misunderstanding are we talking about?" Bradley's eyebrows raised.

"Just a wee bit of a mistake, a miscommunication, that's all." Doyle spat.

"I'm hearing a lot of misses here. What exactly happened Doyle?"

"I asked her out to a nice dinner at Fox and the Knife, you know, the Italian place on West Broadway."

"Yeah, I hear it's great."

"It is. So, we decided to meet there at seven o'clock," Doyle said.

"Okay, so what happened? Were you late?" Bradley asked, sorry he got himself involved in the conversation.

"Sort of. I thought the date was for last night, Thursday, but she said it was on Tuesday. She waited for me for over an hour before she realized I wasn't coming. Then she left a nasty message on my cellphone."

"Oh, that's bad, Doyle. That's really bad. You stood her up!" Bradley's mouth formed an involuntary grin.

"Not intentionally. I tried to explain, but she wouldn't listen to me."

"Do you blame her? Jesus, Doyle, you're a cop. Details should not elude you." Bradley started to chuckle.

"Dammit, Whitman. This isn't funny. She's really mad. What should I do?"

"Move to another county," Bradley laughed.

Doyle clenched his fists as blood rushed to his face and his pale cheeks turned the color of rosé wine.

"All right, calm down. You're going to have a coronary, and I don't think Maria would tend to you right now." Bradley paused. "Here's what you do. Tomorrow, send her flowers with a sincere apology letter. The day after, send her chocolates with another apology letter. The day after that, send her a fruit basket with yet another apology letter."

"Jesus, Whitman, I'm a cop. That's a week's salary for me," Doyle said.

"After the fruit basket, she will want it to stop. She'll call you. That's when you really lay it on thick. Tell her what an ass you are, and how badly you wanted to get to know her better. Tell her you know you don't deserve another chance but hope she will consider it."

"For chrissake, Whitman. You want me to get on my knees and beg, too?"

"If that's what it takes," Bradley said.

"I'm all done here, Agent Whitman," Maria Reyes called out.

"Thank you, Maria. I look forward to your report," Bradley called back. She flashed him a bright smile.

"Yes, thank you, Maria, ah, Doctor Reyes," Doyle stuttered.

The doctor shot him a steely-eyed glare.

Doyle dropped his head and stared at the ground.

"Jesus, I felt that from here," Bradley smirked.

"I'm glad my misfortune amuses you," Doyle growled as he walked down the hill.

COLOPHON

MVB Verdigris is a Garalde text family for the digital age. Inspired by work of sixteenth-century punchcutters Robert Granjon, Hendrik van den Keere, and Pierre Haultin, MVB Verdigris celebrates tradition but is not beholden to it. Created to deliver good typographic color as text, Mark van Bronkhorst's design meets the needs of today's designer using today's paper and press. A full-featured OpenType release with an added titling companion, it's optimized for the latest typesetting technologies, too.

Garalde: the word itself sounds antique and arcane to anyone who isn't fresh out of design school, but the sort of typeface it describes is actually quite familiar to all of us. Despite its age—born fairly early in printing's history—the style has fared well. Garaldes are the typefaces of choice for books and other long reading.

www.ingramcontent.com/pod-product-compliance
Lightning Source LLC
Chambersburg PA
CBHW050125030726
47505CB00007B/2048